Trail of Kisses

He took hold of the blanket and turned it back.

He was naked, and he was climbing into her bed. She lost her breath.

The man slid his cool, moist body down alongside her own hot one and rolled to face her. The moment had arrived...

The Jackson woman sighed softly. Passionately? She moved a hand to the back of his head, drew him closer while her other hand began tracing up and down his back until all logical thought and every honorable intention spilled away...

He began blazing a trail of kisses up to her cheek, then across to one eye, then the other. The tip of her nose. Each corner of her mouth. Carrie never dreamed any man could make love with such tender passion, much less a Comanchero...

Love So Wild

by the bestselling author of *Captive Angel*
and *River Temptress*

Praise for
Elaine Crawford's CAPTIVE ANGEL:

"Tempestuous... exciting... colorful... Ms. Crawford will provide readers with a pleasant evening's entertainment!"

—*Romantic Times*

*Titles by Elaine Crawford from
The Berkley Publishing Group*

**CAPTIVE ANGEL
RIVER TEMPTRESS**

Elaine Crawford

J
JOVE BOOKS, NEW YORK

If you purchased this book without a cover, you should be aware that this book is stolen property. It was reported as "unsold and destroyed" to the publisher, and neither the author nor the publisher has received any payment for this "stripped book."

LOVE SO WILD

A Jove Book / published by arrangement with
the author

PRINTING HISTORY
Jove edition / April 1994

All rights reserved.
Copyright © 1994 by Dianna Crawford.
This book may not be reproduced in whole
or in part, by mimeograph or any other means,
without permission. For information address:
The Berkley Publishing Group, 200 Madison Avenue,
New York, New York 10016.

ISBN: 0-515-11354-9

A JOVE BOOK®
Jove Books are published by The Berkley Publishing Group,
200 Madison Avenue, New York, New York 10016.
JOVE and the "J" design are trademarks belonging
to Jove Publications, Inc.

PRINTED IN THE UNITED STATES OF AMERICA

10 9 8 7 6 5 4 3 2 1

In Memory of Marilyn

*And my special thanks to Sally and Sue
for all the long-distance running.*

We have wept the blood
    of countless ages
as each of us raised high
    the lance of hate.
Now let us dry our tears
    and learn the dance
and chant of the life cycle.
Tomorrow dances behind the sun
    in sacred promise
of things to come for children
    not yet born . . .

from "Tomorrow"
by Peter Blue Cloud

1

May 1876

CARRIE JACKSON LATCHED the rough-hewn door behind her and clomped across the splintery porch planks in Charly's cast-off farm boots, the same old boots she'd worn for gardening these past nine years since her brother—the lucky one—had escaped. Pulling a pair of canvas gloves from her skirt pocket, she looked out across the predawn desert at the Mimbres and beyond them to the towering Black Mountains. She always enjoyed this mystical moment when the gentle brush of morning gave the lofty silhouettes the appearance of being close enough to touch. Lingering, she watched the sun's first rays trim the peaks with gold.

Oh, to be an eagle, she thought, her throat constricting with hopelessness. *To soar high. Away. To be free. Free as Charly.*

With a sigh, she worked her slender fingers into the bulky gloves and walked down the steps.

A gust of chill air caught a tendril of her wheat-colored hair and swept it across her eyes. While tucking it beneath her faded calico sunbonnet, she heard a faint rumbling. Tensing, she moved to the corner of the small adobe house and peered down the cutoff in the direction of the wagon road that flanked the Rio Grande. Blinded by the rising sun, she could see only a glittery cloud of dust moving toward her. But the sound was unmistakable. Several horses raced in her direction.

"Damn! Father said he'd be staying in town till tomorrow night. And it looks like he's bringing that wolf pack he calls his deputies with him, too."

Whirling around, she grabbed a hoe that stood propped against a nearby post and strode out to her vegetable patch on the other side of the square adobe, then stepped across the rows of sprouting corn to reach her peppers. With the sharp edge of the blade, she attacked the pesky weeds surrounding her leafy little plants.

"No doubt," she muttered to the wind, "he's coming for that blasted buffalo gun." What fool could possibly have been crazy enough to cross Wiley Jackson, the notorious lawman, this time?

In the eleven years since her father had left the army to become sheriff of La Mesilla, she couldn't remember a single runner—Mexican, Indian, or white—that he hadn't downed one way or another. And with that hellish Sharps rifle he treasured so much, he could kill at a thousand yards.

The hoofbeats drummed louder, closer.

Carrie turned her back. She didn't want to see the men's faces. She hated the wild glaze of blood lust that she knew would be in their eyes. And more, she despised the glances Deputy Fry always managed when her father wasn't looking—that knowing lift of his scraggly brows, that slack-mouthed grin as he tipped his hat brim. Most of all, she loathed the disgusting way his eyes roved her body.

Her hands froze around the handle of the hoe. There could be no doubt. The deputy knew all about that night. About the evil thing her father had done. Her shame. They all knew. But Fry took particular pleasure in reminding her of it with his every sly gesture. God, how she hated him. And her father. Hated them all.

Cringing at a foretaste of the sickening deputy's watery leer, she looked down and noticed how the worn cloth of her oversize work shirt clung to the tips of her breasts. She quickly loosened the fabric cinched at her waist by a length of twine, blousing it to conceal her curves. Then, reaching up, she pulled her sunbonnet farther down over her head till the wide brim shaded most of her face. The more unsightly she looked the better.

The galloping horses neared the house.

She busied herself, chopping weeds.

The riders didn't stop. Didn't even slow. Instead, they veered past the adobe and thundered into the middle of Carrie's garden. Their animals skidded to a halt, spewing clods in every direction.

In a rage, Carrie spun around.

Two men, already dismounted, were upon her.

She choked on a gasp as one, a hulking brute, snared her and swung her around. Encircling her from behind, he crushed her to him, trapping her hands in his, cutting off her air.

She kicked at his shins as her heart banged out of control. Who were they? What did they want? She tried to scream, but her effort died on a strangled croak as she struggled for breath.

A smelly little man knocked the hoe away and tied her hands with the speed of a calf roper, then yelled, "Get her up on the horse!"

The larger one released his rib-crushing hold and tossed her into the saddle of a nearby bay.

Escape her only thought, she slammed her boot heels into the animal's flanks.

It bolted, crashing past the two men.

"Get her!" shouted one.

The horse's head jerked abruptly to the side.

A dark man, still mounted, held its reins in a grip that gave evidence to his strength. From out of black foreboding eyes, he stared at her while his bare, bronzelike arm pulled her bay next to his own paint.

Flinching, she raised her bound hands to ward off an expected blow. She held her breath, waited.

The man's eyes held hers a moment longer, then he glanced away as the little man on the ground retrieved the long end of the rope binding her and yanked it down.

A moan escaped through her lips. On reflex, she clamped them together. She mustn't cry out. Mustn't beg. Talking would only make things worse. It always did with Father.

"Got a feisty one here," cried the man on the ground. "We'll take care of that. Swede, get her feet in the stirrups."

Defeated, she clutched at the saddle horn as the bulkier of the dismounted pair forced one of her boots into place while the other tied it down, then snaked the line under the horse's belly and secured her remaining foot within the second stirrup. Finished, they then ran to their horses and mounted.

As they did, Carrie couldn't accept the reality. Her thoughts swirled as if they were caught in a dust devil.

The dark one, who had the look of an Indian, brought Carrie's bay with him as he nudged his horse toward the skinny man's. "You wanted her, Bert, you haul her." He tossed the reins to the small one. "Now, let's get the hell out of here before Jackson and his bunch catch up to us."

Amid shouts and the slapping of leather, they were off again as swiftly as they'd arrived, ripping across what remained of the garden. Leaning low, they raced out across the desert, dragging Carrie behind.

Galloping at full stride over rough, uneven terrain, Carrie's muscles knotted with terror as she flew past clumps of cactus scattered among the rocks. Fiercely, she clung to the saddle horn. "Please, God," she mouthed, her gaze darting ahead to every rut, every lizard hole, "don't let him fall. Don't let him go down."

The bay stumbled.

Carrie plunged forward. The picture of the horse tumbling headfirst, rolling, mangling her, flashed before her.

But, thank God, the animal regained his footing.

Shoving herself upright again, she pressed her knees tighter against the lunging bay's sides.

To ease her panic, she tried to think of something else. Anything. Forcing her attention up from the ground she looked past her three captors to the ruffled sandstone buttes of Florida Mountain that outlined the southwestern horizon.

The renegades probably planned to lose her father in its deep gorges, then escape south into Old Mexico. But, quite obviously, they knew little of Sheriff Jackson. He'd simply circle around and be waiting for them when they emerged on the other side. No one ever eluded him. No one, that is, except her brother. But then, she recalled, a bitter taste mingling with the dust in her mouth, her father hadn't considered dear sweet Charly worth the chase. No, she thought, Charly hadn't measured up. Never could bring himself to bully the other boys, torture a stray cat.

Carrie's vision blurred. She swallowed hard and shook away the welling tears. *"Don't."* No time to cry over Charly now.

She tried to redirect her mind to the good years before the war, in Carolina, when life had been beautiful and green and folded in love. But the jolting ride constantly jerked her back to the harrowing present.

After what seemed an eternity, the lead rider raised a hand, then reined in his black-and-white paint. The other men did the same, slowing their mounts to a jarring trot, then to a walk as they guided the winded and lathered animals down into a dry wash.

Carrie's own panting breaths eased along with her fright at this gentler pace. Noting the depth of the cut they rode into, she looked behind her and saw that she and her captors were well below ground level, out of sight of the posse that surely followed close behind. These men had no doubt done something in her father's town. And, she had no doubt, *he was coming*.

Turning forward again, she watched the man who pulled her massage the shoulder that held her reins. He was the one they'd called Bert. The spindly no-account was lucky his arm hadn't been jerked out of its socket. Too bad it hadn't. Then on a drift of air she sniffed the acrid stench of his sweaty body. Her nostrils flared at the offense. Then she caught sight of his stringy, greasy hair.

As though he could feel the scorch of her gaze, the man turned and stared back at her.

At the first clear look at his face, horror gripped the back of Carrie's head in its icy fingers, and a chill shuddered down her length. His nose had no form. A scar pulled down one side of his mouth, another scratched raggedly across his brow, and a number of other nicks and jags pocked his face.

Her expression must have mirrored her alarm because the grotesque man smiled wide, displaying a jumble of yellowed teeth.

6 / Elaine Crawford

Quickly she averted her eyes and lowered her head, hiding beneath the drooping brim of her sunbonnet until he turned forward again.

Several minutes passed before she mustered the courage to look up again. Peering past the scarred one, she studied the much larger man riding on a heavy-boned dun. Hadn't he been called Swede? Swede and Bert. She mustn't forget their names.

Concentrating again on the big one, she noted that his fat-padded frame still heaved with labored wheezes from the hard ride. But unlike the skinny man, he seemed in good repair. His denim britches and plaid shirt appeared almost new, and beneath a brown felt hat, his sand-colored hair looked recently trimmed.

The creek bed curved around a bend, and the man turned his plodding horse into it, giving her a better look at him. Above a potbelly that rubbed against his saddle horn, his face was flushed and a bit puffy. But overall, it seemed rather pleasant, especially compared to the repulsiveness of the first one's.

At the thought, another shiver ran through Carrie. She looked over her shoulder, wondering how far behind her rescuers were. Close, she hoped . . . unless they hadn't split up, and the entire posse was circling the mountain. Unaccustomed to riding horseback, her bottom already ached from the jouncing. Turning forward again, she lifted her eyes skyward. In an hour or so, the sun would bear down relentlessly, heating up the desert floor like an old tin pan. And to complete her misery, the kindled air would roast her lungs.

The Swede unhooked his canteen and unscrewed the lid. Just as he raised it to his lips, the front man reined his strikingly marked pony about, and the bulky one quickly lowered the round container to his lap.

The leader, who would pass for a full-blooded Indian if his features had been a bit broader, his skin a shade darker, halted and faced the Swede. With his defiant chest garbed only in a rawhide vest, his sinewy arms looked menacingly lethal as he pointed toward the nearest Florida butte. "I'm going to ride up to the top of that mesa and take a look," he said, his voice sounding low, unhurried, like a storm's distant thunder. "Stay down here in the wash. It'll take you into a walled canyon. I'll be back before you get too far in." Then his eyes cut to the scarred one. "Did you hear what I said, Bert?"

"Yeah. But hurry it up, Chama." The dirty one's voice rang thin compared to the deep timbre of the other's. "I wanna know where that posse is."

The leader's eyes strayed to Carrie, and their onyx glint softened. Gentled?

Lured into their depths, she couldn't turn away. They held her as surely as the leather thong circling his neck entrapped a chunk of turquoise.

Then, in the next instant, he sent his pony into a sprint and rode off with such strength, such innate grace, it would be easy to believe he and his magnificent stallion were one.

She watched him go, watched the proud tilt of his chin, the way the sun reflected off his cropped black hair. Even after he disappeared around the next bend, her eyes remained fixed on him until the realization seeped in that soon all that strength and pride would be crushed.

She drew in a shaky breath and closed her eyes against the unholy evil her father would inflict. She would give anything not to have to watch the horror this time.

2

THE SUN HAD climbed halfway to the top of the empty blue sky by the time Carrie and the two men neared the first plateau. As they traveled up the wash in silence, the banks jutting up on either side began to heighten. Then, gradually, the steep inclines turned to smooth sandstone walls of pastel oranges, blemished only by slate-colored rain streaks. Within the narrow meandering gorge, every groan of saddle leather seemed amplified, and every clang of horseshoe against rock bounced through the canyon in eerie echoes. Carrie knew that if any of her father's posse ventured in, her captors could easily detect them.

"Hey, Shipstead!" the mangled one yelled, startling Carrie as he broke the long silence.

The Swede jumped, then swung around. *"What?"* Amber liquid trickled from a canteen poised at his mouth. "Dammit, Bert. Look what you made me go and do." He swiped at his chin, then brushed his shirt.

The scarred one reined his roan next to the big man's dun while pulling along Carrie's horse. "Thought you told Chama you wasn't gonna drink till the job was done. You know how sloppy you get."

"The job *is* done," came the other's gruff retort. "The bank went smooth as silk, an' we got that girl you had to have easy as spit."

Got that girl . . . you had to have? She'd been captured for the nasty one? Her insides curdled with revulsion.

"An'," the Swede continued, "I ain't seen hide nor hair of no one back there. So don't see as how a little somethin' to wash down the dust could hurt."

8

"You're right, Shipstead," the filthy one agreed with a quirk of his scummy head. "Sure as hell couldn't hurt to clear the throat. An' mine's plumb parched."

The Swede's grip tightened around the canvas-covered container, and he took a big gulp of the liquor before relinquishing it to Bert's eagerly grasping fingers.

The scarface guzzled down several swallows while the big man stared, mouth ajar. When Bert finally lowered the canteen, the other one wrenched it away and helped himself.

Distressed by the extra potential danger of drunk and unruly men, Carrie looked behind her, hoping against hope to see, or at least hear, pursuing horses.

"How about a little somethin' for the dust?" Bert called, a sneer in his whiny voice.

Swinging back to face him, she steeled herself for the worst.

But he wasn't looking at her. Instead, both he and the Swede watched as their leader rode into view from around the bend ahead quietly on his unshod pony.

Drawing closer, the half-breed's eyes narrowed in a dangerous-looking glare, and his face seemed carved in wood.

Carrie couldn't help sensing in him an assurance, a power, the other two lacked. She wondered if her father knew of this Chama. Perhaps by another name, an American one. He'd obviously spent many years in the white man's world, as he spoke without any trace of an accent.

The Swede, Shipstead, rapidly capped the canteen with fumbling fingers and looped it over his saddle horn. "Any sign of the posse?"

"Saw their dust heading south," the man said, his casual-sounding voice a contradiction to his glowering expression.

The Swede's weighty frame heaved with a sigh. "That's how you figured it. You said they might just head for the border, thinkin' to cut us off."

"Yep. Every last one of 'em went that way."

"Hot damn, Chama!" Bert hooted as he dragged Carrie alongside. "Looks like we're free as a bird."

Hope plummeting, she looked from man to man. They had predicted which way her father would go, and now that the entire party's direction was confirmed, they would surely use it to their advantage. It might be days before the posse caught up to them. Her heart froze . . . *and nights*.

"We still got a ways to go." The leader's features remained ungiving, his jaw rigid. "So keep your mouths shut. Someone might hear your voices echoing through these canyons and tell Jackson which way we went."

"You ain't got nothin' to worry about, *Brother* Chama," Bert sneered and flung wide his arm. "Why, we're bein' quiet as li'l ol' church mice. Ain't we, Karl?"

Shipstead grunted and looked from the half-breed to him.

Chama reined his paint off to the side. "I'm going back a ways to cover our tracks. When you come to the end of this cut, climb on up to the top of the ridge. From there you'll be able to see a branch runnin' north. Follow it downstream across the valley. I should catch up to you before you cross under the bridge to Lordsburg. But if I don't, make sure nobody sees you from the road."

"Yeah, yeah. We ain't stupid, you know." Bert kicked his mount into a walk.

As Carrie was led past the half-breed, the expression in his eyes softened as it had the last time he'd looked at her. But why? Any beauty she might possess was certainly hidden by the floppy sunbonnet concealing her lengthy mass of blond hair and most of her undoubtedly dust-streaked face. As she was taken away, she glanced down at the faded brown shirt and scratchy gray wool skirt that hung limply about her.

No, it had to be pity.

Her sense of hopelessness returned with force, constricting her breathing and causing her throat to burn. Lowering her lashes, she tried to concentrate on the swirling patterns of sand in the dry wash as the scarred one pulled her on up the deep trench.

Karl Shipstead rode past Carrie and caught up to Bert. "Wormely, you shouldn't have asked Chama if he wanted a drink."

"That's right," the other drawled, then in the blink of an eye, he snatched Shipstead's canteen strap from around the pommel. "Chama don't never drink when he's on a job." Unscrewing the cap, he downed a swig. "He don't smoke. Don't whore around. If a body didn't know better, they'd think heaven's own angels was gonna to fly down and just swoop him up. He's *so* righteous."

Carrie grimaced at the blasphemous, albeit encouraging, remark.

Laughing, Bert stretched his bony arms and flapped them up and down, the canteen swinging from the strap in his hand.

Karl wrenched the whiskey flask from him, and as he did, he also jerked the reins of Carrie's bay from Bert's grasp.

The leather straps dropped to the ground, and Bert stopped his horse to reach under her horse's chin to retrieve them. When he straightened, his squinty little eyes locked on to Carrie. Excruciating seconds passed before he nudged his animal ahead, catching up to the Swede.

After this second close exposure to his mangled features and another whiff of his reeking stench, she couldn't stop her benumbed gaze from trailing after him. She stared at the back of his shirt. It was unbelievably filthy—a dingy gray-brown. And his hair roped down his shoulders in about the same nasty color. Carrie's fingers recoiled inside her heavy gloves at the thought of its greasy feel. Sooner or later, she knew he'd want to stop, want to touch her. Want to ...

Suddenly desperate for air, she breathed deeply. How would she survive him? She couldn't. She'd rather die than let that hideous creature put his putrid hands on her.

Time dragged as they rode deeper into the mountain, and she watched the two men continue to take sips from the canteen of whiskey until they emptied it. Finally, as the sun, hot and pressing, reached its zenith, they neared the tree-lined bank of the shallow creek. At the sight of the precious sparkling water, joy surged through Carrie. Her throat had become so parched she could barely swallow.

The outlaws let out a whoop and let the eager horses run splashing into it. They jumped down and fell spread-eagled, soaking in the glorious cooling wetness with no regard for their holstered guns. They laughed and flopped around like dull-witted louts. A couple of minutes passed before they joined the animals in lapping their fill.

Still tied to the saddle, Carrie stared down at the crystalline liquid as it gently sliced past her mount's legs. The water beckoned. Her every inch yearned to be in it, to feel its soothing fingers flow over, caress her own sweltering body.

Looking up, she opened her mouth to ask the Swede to untie her, then quickly clamped it shut. Only a blathering fool would get down in a stream with besotted criminals.

I will sit here quietly, she vowed. *Sit in the shade of these river willows. Enjoy the cool breeze, the water bubbling over the rocks. I will not listen to my aching body. I am not thirsty. I'm just fine, just fine . . .*

After lolling for several minutes in the water, the Swede lumbered to his feet and waded to his horse. He unhooked his canteen and opened it. Holding it upside down above his head, he caught the last few drops of whiskey in his mouth, then stooped and filled it in the stream.

He straightened to his ponderous height and, still dripping wet, stumbled over to Carrie. "Suppose you're thirsty, too," he mumbled thickly and placed the canteen between her bound hands.

Closing her eyes, Carrie gave a fleeting prayer of thanks and lifted the flat round can he'd wedged in the fork of her hands—hands that had long since grown numb. Slowly, carefully, she tilted her arms upward, straining to keep the container balanced. If she dropped it, she didn't know if the big man would give it to her again. Trembling, she carefully maneuvered the rim to her dry lips and gingerly tipped it up.

Icy water filled her mouth faster than her swollen throat could swallow. Some overflowed and trickled down her neck and into her shirt.

Out of the corner of her eye, she saw the Swede's bloodshot eyes ogle the droplets sliding over her hot skin and into the dark warmth between her breasts.

She took a rushed last gulp and, though still thirsty, lowered the canteen, offering it back to him.

When she did, his attention rose to her face as he accepted the flask.

Diverting her own gaze, she gripped the saddle horn, hoping desperately that he wouldn't decide to act on what was certainly on his mind.

The seconds stretched unmercifully as he continued to stare up at her.

If he but reached out to touch her, she knew she wouldn't be able to stop the scream welling in her breast.

Suddenly he wheeled around and slashed through the current toward his horse. He mounted, then edged his dun close to hers.

She held her breath.

He grasped her bay's reins. Then his deepset gaze locked on to Bert, who still lay sprawled in the shallow water. "Wormely. Get your ass on your horse. Ain't got all day, you know." Slamming his heels into his mount, he startled it into a spry walk down the creek.

Towed in the Swede's wake, Carrie's panic subsided as a refreshing spray of water teased her sweltering body, cooling her but never quite enough while they covered the next several miles amid the clear sand-bottomed stream in silence.

As the hours dragged by the saddle rubbing against Carrie's inner thighs and calves began to feel like a sandstone. But no matter how painful it became, she would never have drawn attention to herself by telling them. Her silence was her only protection, as fragile as it might be.

Loud splashing sounded from behind.

Carrie's heart leapt. *Please, God,* she mouthed, *let it be the posse.*

Karl Shipstead and Bert Wormely wheeled their horses into the trees, then slid rifles from their scabbards. With shoulder muscles straining beneath their shirts, they aimed in the direction of the noise.

Her father, had he turned back? Come in time to save her?

14 / Elaine Crawford

Then, like puppets on strings, the two relaxed and lowered their weapons.

Carrie sagged, too, knowing without looking that it wasn't the posse. The half-breed had returned.

"You made pretty good time, considering," Chama said as his thick-chested paint pranced through the water toward them.

"Whatcha mean, *considerin'*?" Bert slurred.

"Considering you're both red-eyed drunk." His brows resembled ravens poised for flight as the intent gaze of his ebony eyes moved from one to the other.

Shipstead shifted in the saddle and looked away.

But Wormely stretched himself tall. "We're takin' care a things just fine. We ain't helpless, you know."

Chama studied him a moment. "No, that you aren't." Though his precisely carved features showed nothing, something in his tone told Carrie that he didn't trust the scarred one any more than she did.

But, then, why should he, she thought. *They're all nothing but a bunch of lawless marauders.*

"The creek's starting to curve west," Chama continued. "Climb out here and keep heading north. I'll catch up to you again by the time you reach the Mimbres Mountains."

"What the hell," the skinny one bawled. "The way you keep takin' off all the time, I'm beginnin' to think you're scared to take your chances with the rest of us."

"Look, Bert." A weariness marked the half-breed's tone. "Last night in Doña Ana I overheard a couple of prospectors. Seems a troop of soldiers from out of Fort Selden are up in the mountains looking for Geronimo. I'm gonna find out which way the bluecoats headed." He crooked a winged brow. "Unless you'd like to have 'em drop by for supper."

The Swede nudged his horse closer, his wide forehead scrunched. "How come you didn't tell us about them before?"

"Forget the damned soldiers," Bert spat. "I wanna know about Geronimo."

The half-breed's expression relaxed, and a lopsided grin dimpled one cheek. "Don't worry, he isn't within thirty miles of here."

Bert's beady gray eyes doubled in size. "That's *all*?"

"Yup." Chama's gaze drifted to Carrie. Something flickered in the depths of his dark eyes, then his smile faded. His glance shot back to Bert, then swung to Karl. He opened his mouth as if to speak, then hesitated. Finally, he said, "Be back by dark." Then, without looking her way again, he lunged his pony up the bank and disappeared.

A profound sense of loss deluged Carrie as she watched him leave. But it came from far more than the fact that Chama had left her with Bert again. The tenderness, the pity, she'd seen the other times he'd looked at her had vanished. Her eyes burned with disappointment, and she allowed herself to admit that she'd been hoping the half-breed might save her from the disgusting one. And she knew better than that. No gallant knight would be coming to save her. As usual, she was utterly on her own.

Bert's mewling voice broke into Carrie's misery. "Damn if I ever go on a job with him again. For all we know, he's got them savages out there just waitin' to jump us, so he can have all the money for hisself." Jerking on his reins, he spurred his roan up from the streambed.

Following behind, the Swede wagged his head. "Naw. You know better than that. Chama can be trusted. I'd stake my life on it. Long as you ain't a bluecoat, you got nothin' to worry about."

"Yeah, an' one of these days that harebrained thinkin's gonna cost you your scalp. Hell, man, the only reason he rides with us is to get money to buy rifles for his stinkin' redskins."

At Bert's last remark, Carrie cut a glance to him. Did these outlaws ride with renegade Apaches?

"All I know is," Karl said, his voice a gravelly rumble, "if I needed someone at my back, he's the one I'd want."

Looking north toward the Mimbres, Carrie spotted the half-breed ascending a small rise in the rumpled terrain. As the man disappeared over the crest, horrifying questions began to flap, one after another, like Monday morning's wash. Was she being taken to some hidden Chiricahua *rancheria* high up in the mountains? Or worse, what if her captors were Comancheros? The anguish of being handed over to the worst dregs of mankind, be they American, Indian, or Mexican, drained the blood from her face, blinding her for a moment. She'd heard the stories. The few captured women who survived the tortures of a Comanchero camp were then sold to brothels down in Old Mexico.

Carrie shook the ghastly tales from her head. Her father would come. No ragtag band of Indians would stop him. And even if these men rode, instead, with some depraved pack of misfits, he would still come. But, God help her, he'd have to go back to La Mesilla to get more men. He'd be too late. She cast a glance to Bert and shuddered. But no matter how long it took, or what became of her, she knew her father would relish the battle. The rankling thought caused her lips to twist into a bitter smile. He always enjoyed a good slaughter.

Her gaze rose to the rugged plateau of one of the Mimbres looming before her. It was hard to believe that this very morning she'd longed to escape to them.

As they inched across the miles of ovenlike desert, the sun seared a sluggish path across the sky. Carrie's entire left side burned from the western rays, and the glare from the sand branded her eyes. Her lips had now cracked in several places, and all the moisture had been sucked from her mouth by the hot air. Exhausted, her head became too heavy to hold upright. She nodded forward, dozing sporadically. She awakened only when Bert's tinny whine pierced her consciousness as he complained about the heat, or when her horse lurched, forcing her now-raw inner thighs to rub agonizingly against the shift of groaning leather.

At long last they reached the first rocky foothills sprinkled with stunted piñon trees and spiky yucca plants, their tall stalks loaded with the creamy blossoms of May. The sun now dipped low, its rays softening until the desert turned to pinks and beiges, bringing new life to the land. Climbing the rock-strewn slope, the smothering heat fell away from Carrie like drifting feathers. Her sense of imminent peril, too, lost its grip as a light-headed numbness released her from all pain, all care. She gave herself up to the peace of the downy cloud now embracing her. Weightless, she soared higher, higher . . . gliding on virgin wings.

3

A CALLUSED HAND scraped beneath Carrie's skirt. Scratched up her bare leg. Rubbing. Squeezing. Stinking.

She opened her mouth to scream, but nothing emerged except a strangled croak.

It was a horrible nightmare. She had to wake up. Wake up! If she could just raise her head. Sit up. But her body refused to obey. She remained slumped over.

The rough hand burrowed deeper, shoving toward her inner reaches.

Oh, God! She drew in a sharp tortured breath. *God, no!* her mind shrieked, but only a groan escaped.

"I said, get her down!" a deep voice boomed.

The hand halted.

"Now." The voice . . . belonged to the half-breed.

The hand . . . *Oh, my Lord. It was Bert's.*

A low wheezy growl came from the filth's throat, and he muttered something as his scratchy claws slipped away.

With the hateful hand removed, any small spark of energy drained from her body, leaving it a quivering mass. The saddle horn gouged into her, but no matter what, she couldn't muster the strength to rise up. She lay in a vulnerable heap, feeling every move of Bert's fingers as they unlashed the ropes from her legs.

Through a fuzzy haze, she heard footsteps crunching the gravelly ground all about her. Twigs broke. Leather creaked. Then a wavering light lured her eyes open, and she saw Karl nursing a campfire to life.

Bert moved within inches of her face, blocking the light. "Get down." His stale breath assaulted the sun-scorched tip of her nose.

She tried to sit up, but her lifeless hands and arms wouldn't respond.

"*Lady,* get off on your own, or I'm gonna drag you off."

She willed her stiff fingers to move, but crushed beneath the weight of her body, she felt only a small fluttering. Pains shot up her arms, and they began to burn and tingle.

"I ain't kiddin'. Get down!" He grabbed her around the waist and yanked her from the saddle. She spilled, dead weight, into his bony arms. He staggered and collapsed, crashing to the ground with her on top of him. He grunted, then yelped, "Hellfire!"

Carrie's heart leapt with panic. The monster had her! She shoved at Bert's chest with her bound hands.

"Ahhh. So missy wants to play hard to get." He pulled her against his grimy shirt. Throwing a leg over her, he rolled on top. His whiskery stubble scratched across her cheek. His odious lips sought hers.

She couldn't bear it. She writhed beneath him. Pushed. Whipped her head from side to side. She tried to move her legs, but they felt as limp as a willow switch.

His whiskey mouth zeroed in.

Gagging, she closed her lips tight to ward off his demanding tongue.

Undaunted, he also found a breast, squeezing, digging his nails into her tender flesh.

Suddenly his body, his grasping hands, were wrenched away. "Hey! What the hell?"

The half-breed had hauled him off, and now set him on his feet.

"Looked like you were having trouble getting up," Chama drawled.

"Did you hear me askin' for help?" Bert's voice rose to a high pitch as he angrily slapped dust from his britches.

"No." Chama's brows dipped. His eyes found Carrie sprawled at his feet.

She returned his stare, her breath coming in spurts to match her thudding chest.

"But the lady sure looks in need." The half-breed knelt down beside her and placed a hand to her cheek. "How long since you gave her any water?"

"Who gives a shit?" Bert spat.

Chama spun around on his haunches and stared up at the smaller man.

Bert took a backward step. "I—uh— Well?" He shrugged. His gaze twitched to Shipstead. "She never once asked fer a drink. Not once. Did she?"

Tossing some twigs on the campfire, Karl reared his head but didn't look their way. "I gave her a drink when we first got to the creek, 'bout noon."

Firelight emblazoned Chama's glare as it found Bert again. "Look at her. You said she wouldn't be any bother. Wouldn't hold us up. Hell, what's the use. Go finish bedding down the horses."

"All right. But, remember, *she belongs to me*."

"Yeah, sure," Chama muttered, then glanced back to the Swede. "Shipstead, bring my canteen and my serape."

Carrie saw the muscles in the half-breed's jaw relax and knew she was safe, for now, anyway. Her breathing eased. She started to thank him, but she hesitated to speak, to cross that precarious line. Instead, she closed her eyes with profound relief and gratitude.

After the half-breed pillowed her head on a rolled-up serape, he untied the rope at her wrists and let her drink until her parched insides were sated. He then cooled her face with a dampened kerchief, his gentle strokes lulling her. Sleep beckoned . . . until she felt him fumbling at her throat.

Her eyes sprang open as he untied her bonnet and tugged at it. His own eyes widened, and he paused. Then, slowly, he fingered a wave of her exposed hair.

She froze. She knew Indians prized long blond scalps. Knew how much they liked to dangle them from their lances.

Glancing from her, he looked around him. Then, with quick, deft movements, he stuffed the strand within her calico cap again and retied it. His gaze veered back to meet hers.

For a moment she saw something in his expression. A

promise? As her fear diminished, his attention drifted off into the darkness. He touched the turquoise stone at his throat and his fingers lingered a long moment. Then, returning to her again, he removed her gloves and began to massage the blood back into her hands. At first, she thought she felt a slight tremble in his touch. But then his moves became steady, sure, and she dismissed the silly notion. This self-assured man couldn't possibly be nervous.

Finishing with her hands, he scooted down to her feet. Taking one into his lap, he removed its boot. Then with both hands, he began to work it, rub it, his thumbs making circles on the ball, then splaying the toes.

In her half-conscious state, it felt so tantalizing, so sensuous, she heard herself sigh.

When she did, his hands stopped massaging for a moment before continuing the seduction of her foot, but for only a dozen or so seconds more before removing her other boot. Yet in that fragile moment, she had no doubt he would keep his unspoken vow. He would keep the ugly one from her. Hope spread through her, and she gave herself up to sleep, despite the clang of cook pots, the creaking groans of unsaddling, accompanied by the raspy sound of Bert's grumbled curses.

"Ma'am?"

Carrie was being shaken awake.

In the faint firelight, she recognized the clean planes of Chama's face.

He bent down to her. "Can you sit up? It's time to eat."

She nodded and made a feeble attempt as his hand slid behind her back. Propping her against a saddle, he adjusted a blanket about her—a scratchy army one that must have been draped over her while she slept.

"Karl, pour the lady some coffee, and bring her a plate."

"Sure thing." From the other side of the campfire, the big Swede stumbled up from the ground with surprising energy for someone who'd drunk half a canteen of whiskey. He heaped a plate and handed it to Chama, then filled a steaming cup from a pot resting on a flat rock beside the flames.

Karl offered the aromatic brew to Carrie, but her lethargic muscles didn't respond.

Chama took the tin cup and held it to her lips. After she took a few sips, the half-breed dropped down beside her and, to her amazement, picked up her spoon and began to feed her, first a spoonful of bland but filling beans, followed by tangy slices of canned peaches.

She slanted a fleeting glance up to his face.

Catching her looking, a smile tickled the corners of his mouth as he shoved in another spoonful.

With anxious eyes, Karl also hovered like a nervous bride—one who'd just cooked her first meal. "Is ever'thing all right? Does it taste good?"

She nodded and attempted a pleasant expression as he watched her chew. Her gaze gravitated past him to the glowing circle of firelight. It danced crazily up craggy walls on either side—walls of granite, not sandstone. A sure sign that she'd been taken well into the Mimbres. She wondered if, by now, her father knew he'd been tricked. If he'd started back from the border yet.

Remembering her meal, she turned to Chama and found him staring at her with unguarded candor, the empty spoon poised inches from her mouth. The intimacy of their closeness merely embarrassed her a little when it should have frightened her. Blaming her capricious state of emotions on her fatigue, she took the utensil with a shaky hand and scooped up another bite from the plate he held.

"Atta girl." The loathsome sound of Bert's voice startled her. She located him seated to the side of the fire. He wagged his own spoon at her and snickered around a mouthful of beans. "Fill up. Want you right as rain and ready for fun."

The maimed face looked even more grotesque in the flickering light, and she couldn't take her eyes from him.

Chama tugged on her hand.

She relinquished the utensil and looked back at him. Then she saw that a peach slice had slipped from her spoon to her lap.

"I'll help you finish, so you can get some rest," he said as he resumed feeding her. "Got a long ride tomorrow."

A clang resounded.

In a swift instant, Chama dropped the spoon and pulled a revolver from his holster as his head snapped to the source of the noise... a metal plate bouncing off the stone wall. Bert's.

The skinny man lunged to his feet and swerved around the fire, fists clenched. *"The woman is mine. I decide if and when she gets any sleep."*

Slowly holstering his gun, Chama unfurled to his full height. Muscles rippled across his shoulders and along his bare arms as he faced the smaller man.

Carrie tensed. Would he continue to champion her? Or would he decide she was too much trouble?

"I'm going to say this just once," Chama said in measured tones. "I didn't like the idea of taking the girl, but you wouldn't budge 'less we did. So, this morning after we robbed Jackson's bank, we stole his daughter. On top of that, we fooled him into riding for the border. By now, he's bound to be one fired-up son of a bitch." Bristling, Chama edged closer.

Bert stepped back.

"You insisted on taking her. Had to have her for protection. *Remember?* Now, alive and in one piece is the only way she's gonna do you any good."

Bert glanced down at Carrie, his loose-jointed body becoming pole-stiff. He jerked his attention back to Chama. "Who made you boss?"

The half-breed closed the space between them, every fiber in his body appearing coiled to strike.

Bert's eyes flicked wide, but he stood his ground as Chama leaned within inches of the ruined face.

"You *will* keep your hands off her tonight. *Comprende?*"

Fear scrunched Bert's features as he measured the threatening force. Wheeling around, he stomped away.

Chama continued to watch as the seething man disappeared into the darkness. Then, turning to Karl, he raised his brows.

The Swede smiled nervously and shrugged.

Pretending she hadn't been concerned by the frightening

confrontation, Carrie grabbed the handle of the coffee cup and took a sip. Though she sensed that Chama's gaze had shifted to her, she kept her face hidden beneath the bill of her bonnet, afraid to see if he was now having second thoughts.

"Looks like I dropped your spoon," he said in that soft rumble of a voice. He stopped to pick it up. "I'll go wash it off."

Carrie stayed his hand. She'd been too much bother already. Courage regathering, she looked up and shook her head.

He rose to his feet. "You sure?"

The gentleness in those two words told her what she wanted to know. He didn't think her too much trouble, he would keep the promise she'd seen in his eyes. Lying down again, Carrie huddled deep within the blanket. Though sleepy, her mind retraced the events of the day—of the times the half-breed had come and gone, and, thank God, returned again. This man with the imperious curve to his cheekbones and bleak slant to his mouth had fed her as if she were his own child. This same man who flaunted the sure eyes of a skilled hunter, whose brows flared like some poised bird of prey, had tenderly bathed her face and rubbed the numbness from her body.

Grogginess weighted her lashes, and they drooped. But she tried to shake it off. She needed to concentrate, to understand why this one who, because of his heritage, should have been the least concerned with her well-being instead had taken on the responsibility with uncommon gentleness.

Maybe, she thought, not daring to let her hope soar irretrievably, maybe he really was only protecting her so she could shield him later from her father. At the thought, she tried to picture Chama hiding behind her skirts, but couldn't. This man who moved with untamed arrogance appeared incapable of cowardice.

But perhaps he thought she'd bring a higher price at a renegade camp if she were in good condition. Her brows crimped at the vexing thought. No matter how he acted now, the man was, after all, half Indian. And she'd never heard anyone accuse a raiding savage of being even remotely merciful toward a captive.

But, no, he wasn't like that. She remembered that crystalline moment when he had spoken to her with those dark luminous eyes.

Brimming with a contrary mix of emotions, a shudder rippled through her. Fearing someone had seen it, she cautiously peered out from the blanket toward the three men, who once again sat around the campfire having a cup of coffee.

Her eyes met Chama's. Her mysterious guardian *had* noticed her movement, and as before, his midnight eyes conveyed the promise.

No phantoms remained. She felt the last remnants of tension unravel as blessed sleep claimed her.

"How much you think we got?" Wormely asked.

Chama saw the eager shine in Bert's eyes as the scrawny man turned to Shipstead.

Slouched over a cup of coffee, Karl looked hangdog tired. "I dunno. A lot, I guess."

"Looked like thousands to me." Bert set his tin cup on the ground beside him. "Let's get it out and count it."

"No, not tonight." Chama stretched out his long legs and crossed them. "If the wind comes up, we might lose some of the bank notes in the dark."

Bert's expression hardened. "There you go again. Goin' against ever'thing I wanna do."

"Chama's right," Karl mumbled. "A breeze is pickin' up. An' it's gettin' downright cold."

"Yeah," Chama said, easing up to his feet. "Think I'll go put on a shirt."

"That's another thing," Bert said, irritation still in his tone. "When the rest of us is tryin' to cover up for the robbery so no one'll recognize us, you strip down to that Injun vest of yours so's they can describe you down to the last goose bump."

Peering down at the squirrel of a man, Chama chuckled. "Well, I'll bet when the banker and his wife went to wake up the sheriff, all they said about me was that I was some wild-eyed savage. But you? I'm sure they gave one helluva description of you."

"They wouldna been able to if that addlepated female hadn't ripped off my bandanna."

Karl grinned, his expression lifting out of its weary sag. "Yeah, she took one look at Bert's face and keeled over in a dead faint. Sure got her husband out the door and down to the bank in a hurry, though. Gotta real prime weapon there, Bert. Open the safe or I'll show my face." Chortling at his own joke, the big man slapped himself on the thigh.

"That ain't funny." Bert rubbed at the scar distorting his mouth.

Chama glanced across the small blaze to see if the noisy talk had awakened the Jackson woman. She lay on her side, facing them, the blanket nearly covering her bonnet. He saw no movement save the slow rise and fall of her shoulder. Noticing his saddle gear lying a few inches from her head, he remembered the shirt and walked around the campfire to fetch it. Kneeling down, his gaze couldn't help following the blanket's curve over her hip while he fumbled with the leather thong that latched the flap of his saddlebag. He was all thumbs. He'd always prided himself in the sureness of his every move. But, as earlier, in the close presence of this woman, his fingers lost their certainty. No other woman had ever been able to steal his power. Not even Juanita. And he hadn't even gotten a good look at this one yet. But there was something about her. A quiet strength, a nobility . . . so like his mother.

He frowned as he lifted the pouch flap and rummaged for his shirt. He'd been a fool to let Wormely talk him into taking her. But he'd needed another gunhand, and it had been too early in the season for most of the regulars to reach the hidden valley. Besides Karl, Bert had been the only other white man around that he could even halfway trust. He'd had no choice since word was out. The gunrunners would be reaching the valley any day now. And without one last robbery, he wouldn't have had enough money for all the rifles and ammunition he wanted to buy.

The army had to be stopped. Each year they whittled away more and more of Indian country, stealing with it his people's freedom. Finding the shirt, he scrunched it in a choking grip as he thought of the bloodthirsty bluecoats. Pillaging, killing. Who would've thought the Comanche could be corralled, or his mother's people, the Kiowa. But last year, they, too, had been herded off to a reservation. And the Navajo had long since been "tamed." But after the siege at Canyon de Chelly . . . Chama sighed, remembering the winter of starvation back in '64. Now, the only free Indians left in the territory were a few bands of Apaches.

Then he recalled what he'd heard just the week before. Vittorio, mighty chief of the strongest band, had struck a bargain with the army to keep from going to San Carlos Reservation. Chama shook his head at his old friend's foolishness. Vittorio couldn't possibly think he could keep his people safe by agreeing to stay at Ojo Caliente under the soldiers' *protection*.

Chama ran a hand down the wide scar on his side, a permanent reminder of the last time he'd stayed in a camp *protected* by the bluecoats.

If the rumors were true, if the Sioux and Cheyenne were really gathering to make war on the army up in the Dakotas, now would be the best time to strike here. And hard. Run those ruthless bluecoat bastards out of these mountains for good. Give 'em a taste of their own blood. But to do it, cases of rifles were needed and bullets by the barrel. This year might be the last chance to make the leaders in Washington regret their greedy conquest.

Remembering the shirt, he pulled it out of the saddlebag and secured the leather flap.

A muffled groan came from Miss Jackson.

The sound tore at his gut, and his mind flicked to his mother. Remaining in a crouch, he waited for the woman to grow quiet again.

She shifted slightly, then her breathing eased into a steady rhythm.

Looking down at the shrouded form, he pictured her eyes, bluer than the stone at his throat. His hand absently went to the talisman that warded off evil, and he thumbed the leather-bound piece of turquoise. Earlier tonight, when her eyes had reflected the firelight, he could've sworn that something mystical in them had reached out to him. He could still feel the curious tickling sensation that had traveled down his spine. From the look on Karl's face, the Swede had been stirred, too. Maybe the power of turquoise was in the color, not the stone. If that were so, the magic in her eyes might be strong enough to protect her from the fate Bert had planned. No, not likely, he thought. No chant, no charm or power his mother ever invoked had saved her.

The gentleness of her Kiowan features floated before him, and the torment in her dark liquid eyes haunted as they always did. He dropped his hand from the talisman and wondered why he bothered to wear the damned thing in the first place. Every Apache he knew wore turquoise, and it hadn't kept them safe from that darker shade of soldier blue.

Lunging to his feet, he strode back to where the other men sat, then removed his vest and slipped chilled arms into the long sleeves of his gray-and-white striped shirt. While he buttoned it, Bert's thin voice broke the silence.

"Karl, you been around these parts for quite a spell, ain't you?"

"Yeah."

"Well, there's somethin' that's been puzzlin' me all day. That woman over there." Bert jerked his head in her direction. "You know how men get to talkin' and crowin' about when they done somethin' big, an' how they brag on how brave they was?"

"Yeah?" The Swede's jowls lifted into a strange grin.

"Well, ever'time some joker gets carried away with hisself, somebody always says, if you're so brave, how come you ain't sparkin' Sheriff Jackson's daughter? Well, I figured she must be one fine-lookin' woman. Only reason I took a chance on goin' into La Mesilla was 'cuz I been near chompin' at the bit just thinkin' about her."

Karl's smile widened. "I bet you was."

"That's right. But today, when I finally get my chance, what do I get? A woman dressed worse'n some ol' sodbuster's wife.

And did you get a look at them god-awful farm boots?"

Karl exploded with laughter.

Carrie woke with a start. What on earth, she thought at the sound of the Swede's loud guffawing. Her heart drummed. Had he started drinking again?

Bert kicked the big man's boot. "Shut up and tell me what you're laughin' about."

Peeking over the frayed edge of her blanket, she saw Chama glance her way. She quickly closed her eyes. When she opened them a couple of seconds later, he'd turned away.

Karl's jiggling girth settled as he finally managed to control himself. "Sorry. I'll try to keep it down."

"What's so damned funny?" Bert said, tossing the dregs of his cup into the cookfire. "I just wanted to know why ever'body's so interested in a woman that dresses like a field hand."

My God, he's talking about me. Carrie's nails dug into her palms almost unnoticed.

With a knowing grin splashed across his face, Karl looked up to Chama standing a few feet away. "You tell him. I don't think I can keep from laughing."

His head above the light, the half-breed's features were hidden in the darkness. "Tell him what?"

"You don't know, either? I'll be damned." Karl turned back to Bert. "Well, ol' boy, to answer your question, I don't think anyone much has even seen her. She's kept herself purty much hid out on that ranch the last seven or eight years . . . ever since it happened."

Oh, God, no. He's going to tell them. Stifling a cry, she shoved a fist into her mouth. *He's going to bare my shame in front of them. In front of Chama.*

4

"MOVE CLOSER," THE Swede said, his deep gravelly voice lowered to a conspiratorial hush. "Just as soon not wake the lady."

Unwilling to peek past her blanket, Carrie could only hear shuffling as the men scooted, but could imagine their expressions, especially a scar-twisted grin on Bert Wormely's face.

"Well, it's like this," the Swede continued in a whisper. "Seems the little lady had herself a gentleman caller sneakin' out to see her whenever her pa was gone. Some young miner from up Silver City way. An' all I can figure is the lad didn't know nothin' about the sheriff, or else he was just a senseless fool." He paused, and Carrie hoped against hope that he'd decided not to continue.

"*Go on.*" Impatience rang in Bert's shrill voice.

"The sheriff and one of his deputies," Karl rambled on, "caught 'em together." He paused. "They castrated the poor whippersnapper."

Bert gasped.

After that, the crackle of the campfire was the only sound breaking what seemed an endless silence while Carrie relived for the thousandth time the horrifying night and Michael's agonizing scream. It ripped through her brain as she felt again the pain in her own jaw where she'd been struck by her father and knocked across the room, too dazed to help stop it. And she would never forget the blood, the deputy's nervous snicker, or her father hoisting up Michael's agony-twisted form and tossing him out the door.

"I knew Jackson was one mean son of a bitch, but that's . . ." Bert's words faded into a croak. He cleared his throat. "That's plain butchery."

"And looks to me like you're next in line." After another silence, the big man started guffawing again. The echoing jeers careened off the canyon walls with almost as much force as they did inside Carrie's head.

"Shut up!" Bert squawked. "You want the whole territory to know where we are?"

When the Swede regained control of his laughter, Bert spoke again, this time sounding very calm and businesslike. "You know, men, I've been thinkin'. I've been actin' real selfish where the woman is concerned. No sense me hoggin' her all to myself."

"But, Bert, it was all your idea," Karl said, continuing to toy with his disgusting cohort. "You deserve every bit of the glory. I wouldn't think of stealin' away any of it. After all, when we tried to talk you out of it, you flat insisted on takin' her. Right then and there, I figured you had to be the bravest man alive. Fact is, ol' boy, my opinion of you rose plumb to the sky," he finished as his voice crumbled into snickers once more.

"It's been a long day," Chama broke in without a trace of discernible emotion. "And we'll be in the saddle all day again tomorrow. We should get as much shut-eye as we can."

They must've heeded the half-breed because as Carrie continued to feign sleep the rustle of their movements told her they were preparing for bed. But whether or not Chama was capable of controlling Bert made little difference anymore. Instead of compassion, there would be nothing but revulsion in Chama's eyes in the morning. All was lost. She prayed to God the sun would never rise again.

Carrie felt the soft cuddly warmth of her grandmother's lap. It seemed an eternity since she'd been rocked to sleep outside on the big veranda that shaded the plantation manse. A cool breeze brushed across her cheek, much cooler than usual for a balmy summer afternoon, but very refreshing.

"I see you already had a piece of her. Now it's my turn," came a voice from far away.

Someone was trying to interrupt her nap, but she didn't want to wake up just yet. She was far too cozy.

32 / Elaine Crawford

Grandmother Mary edged away from her.

She followed after, nuzzling deeper into the cushiony bosom. As Grandmother's comforting arms enfolded her again, she sighed and drifted off into nothingness.

Chama raised up on one arm in the predawn light and stared at Bert Wormely, who, in turn, glared with piercing narrowed eyes at him and the woman lying together on the ground. "One blanket wasn't enough for her after it turned cold," he said flatly.

"Yeah?" Bert said, clenching his fists. "And I'll bet you warmed her up real good, too. Get up. I want my turn at her."

A rush of anger surged through Chama—Wormely was nothing but miserable white trash. Chama had to take a calming breath before he could control his tone. "Have you started the coffee yet?"

"I ain't interested in coffee right now."

"Get interested," Chama rasped with intensity.

Wormely glared back. Several seconds passed before he finally averted his gaze and turned away.

Chama watched Bert's every move as the scrawny man jerkily, angrily, stoked up the fire and filled the pot from his canteen, then went to a saddlebag to fetch the bag of grounds. No doubt as long as he kept Bert off the woman, the wiry snake would be meaner than a bobcat.

Proving Chama right, on the way back to the campfire Bert gave a vicious kick to the rump of the still sleeping Shipstead and hissed, "Roll your fat, lazy butt out."

Someone shook Carrie's shoulder, pulling her out of her warm haven, urging her to awaken. Why wouldn't they leave her alone? With reluctance she raised her lashes . . . *to find a man lying next to her, staring at her.* Her eyes widened. Then in a rush, she recalled her situation and, mustering her every reserve, commanded herself to remain still.

The half-breed peered deeply into her eyes for a few seconds more before removing his hand from her shoulder. Oddly enough, the disdain she had anticipated was not evident. He tossed the blankets off the two of them and uncoiled to his full, lethally built height as he looked down again. "You have to get up now," he said in an exceedingly gentle tone. As impossible as it seemed, he was treating her with the same consideration as before.

Then, suddenly, Carrie became aware that a very virile man had just left her bed. Her heart skipped a beat at the thought of what might have happened during the night. She immediately dismissed the notion—surely she would've awakened if he'd attempted anything.

Covertly, from beneath the wide bill of her bonnet, Carrie watched the man as he gathered up her gloves and boots. The expression on his face still revealed nothing untoward as he placed her things beside her. She knew she should thank him but she couldn't bring herself to leave the safety of her silence even for him. Instead, she smiled slightly and nodded.

As he walked away, she labored to sit up, her body in stiff protest. Muffling a groan, she managed the considerable chore. Then, while hugging the blanket around her to ward off the chill, she noticed that instead of the one, there were two. She looked up to the half-breed again as he hoisted his saddle off the ground and sauntered to his pony. Chama had shared his second blanket with her. But had he done it for her sake or his?

The aroma of coffee drew her gaze to the campfire, and she saw the big Swede hunkered on a rock near a small blaze. He was trying to pour himself a cup with trembling hands. She smiled to herself and wondered what he would give about now for a shot of that whiskey he'd squandered yesterday, now that he needed it to take away his "shakes."

The scarred one was down on his knees, busy rolling and tying his blankets and tarp. The fact that his back was turned to her relieved her immensely. She didn't think she would ever be able to endure his mangled face without cringing, let alone his touch.

Realizing how vulnerable she was on the ground, Carrie

picked up one of her boots to put on. She certainly didn't want him to get the notion to come and help her out. As she drew her leg close, sharp pains shot in all directions throughout her body. My God, she was saddle sore. With a grimace, she shoved her foot into the boot, trying to ignore the pain of stretching and pulling. Even her fingers trembled as she tied the laces, but her desire to get up before he noticed her was sufficient incentive. The filthy creature would never touch her again. Never!

As she slid her hands up her legs to reach for the second boot, she felt something lumped beneath her skirt. After a quick glance to make certain Bert wasn't watching, she slipped her fingers under the material and discovered some strips of cloth wrapped around her knees and just above. Her face reddened at the thought of someone being so familiar with her. Rapidly smoothing down her skirt, she ignored her screaming muscles as she grabbed the second boot and wrenched it on.

Afterward, she reached up to check her hair and realized she still wore her ugly old sunbonnet. She must look absolutely awful. With a slept-in work shirt belted at the waist with twine, the drab wool skirt, and the clumsy farm boots, she must look awful enough to curdle milk. Good! She straightened the bonnet and tucked in a few stray strands of her wheat-colored hair, then inching beneath the calico covering, she felt around on the thick coil drooping at the base of her neck. Finding some of the pins holding it, she shoved them in tighter. Under the circumstances, that would have to do.

Now, the moment had come to attempt to rise. She took a deep breath, then stalled another couple of seconds by picking up her gloves and stuffing them in her skirt pocket before pulling her feet closer to her body for better balance. When she'd managed to draw them up only a few inches she realized the futility of that method. Instead, she awkwardly rolled over, then crawled up to her knees, hoping to be able to push herself up from that position.

Despite the aches and shaking in her uncooperative limbs she was making slow but steady progress when someone grabbed her waist from behind and yanked her to her feet.

She gasped as sharp pains stabbed up her legs. Then she felt hot, rank breath on her neck. *The scarface.* Frantically she ripped at his bony hands.

He tightened his grip and chuckled near her ear. Abruptly he released her but only long enough to capture her wrists. Then, trapping them in one of his hands, he cupped her breast with the other.

"Wormely." The half-breed's coal-black eyes seemed to drill holes in the other man as he strode toward them. "The woman will have to be able to make it on her own. We haven't got time to coddle her. Miss Jackson, if you can't keep up, we'll leave you to the buzzards." He said the words to her, but his eyes never left her tormentor. Chama continued to stare at Bert while shaking out a folded pair of soft cotton trousers like those the Mexican peons wore. He then shoved them into Carrie's hands.

Bert slowly uncurled the fingers holding her, his reluctance evident in their slight tremor before he finally broke away and stalked off.

Chama's gaze followed him for a moment, then shifted to Carrie. "Go over there, behind that rock." He pointed to a huge boulder about fifty yards down the sheer rock canyon. "Take care of your morning needs, then put the pants on under your skirt. They'll keep your legs from chafing any more."

When Carrie returned from behind the shielding stone with the long pants rolled at the ankles and tied firmly at the waist, all the horses were saddled and everything packed. The men stood warming themselves around the fire while munching on hard biscuits and finishing their coffee.

Chama pointed to a steaming cup and a bun that had been placed on a flat rock.

She tried to act casual as she deliberately circumvented the fire on the side opposite Bert to fetch the meager breakfast, and also when she moved to stand next to Chama. But as the strong aroma of coffee wafted up she forgot everything but it and the blaze that dispelled the morning chill. She took a sip of the revitalizing brew, then another, all the while wishing that the tin cup was sufficiently cooled to warm her hands on.

"Time to go." Chama tossed the dregs of his coffee into the fire and kicked sand over it, snuffing it.

Bert followed Chama to the horses, but Karl merely groaned, the sound a fitting match for the puffs under his eyes and the droop of his shoulders.

Perhaps Karl was waiting for her cup. Carrie gulped down the remainder of her now rapidly cooling drink and placed the cup in his trembling fingers. The big man, she mused, would probably have as much trouble riding today as she—if not for the same reason.

Carrie dropped her uneaten roll in a shirt pocket and walked stiff-legged to the bay she'd ridden the day before. Getting on that horse would be a monumental feat, she knew. Yet she would. Somehow.

She slid the reins around the horse's neck, then stretched up and caught the saddle horn. But the blasted stirrup seemed a mile high. Gritting her teeth, she managed to get a boot within it. She inhaled and steeled herself to spring up.

The half-breed stepped behind her as she did and tossed her onto the horse.

Thank heavens, the ordeal was over. She was even more relieved when no one came to tie her as the trio also mounted. She maneuvered her animal into position at the right and slightly behind Chama . . . and away from the other two. She no longer doubted that any hope of survival lay with the half-breed.

They traveled against an icy breeze that whistled past them in the sand-bottomed canyon, chilling Carrie until her teeth began to chatter. She rubbed her arms, trying to warm herself, then remembered the forgotten biscuit. She pulled it out and began to gnaw on it, hoping the act of eating would help warm her.

Chama reached behind him and withdrew a serape from his saddlebag and tossed it back to her.

Caught off-guard by the gesture, Carrie quickly dropped the blanketlike covering over her head and returned to eating her roll. She concentrated with her whole being on that piece of bread in an effort to stop the tears beginning to well in her eyes. After the way she'd been tied and neglected the day before, each of his small acts of kindness touched her deeply, no matter how casually given. As she chewed a bite, she found it increasingly hard to remember he was merely one more of the lawless renegades running free and terrorizing honest folk.

As they climbed deeper into the lower range, cactus and sage gave way to tufts of grass and spiked yuccas with their tall blossom stalks thrusting up among juniper and scrubby piñon trees. Hardy sparrows flitted among the branches, busily feeding their nestlings. Carrie also spotted several baby jackrabbits peeking around rock outcroppings. If it hadn't been for cowardly Bert looking back every few minutes and asking Chama if he thought they were being followed, the ride could have been almost pleasant, like one of the Sunday afternoon excursions she and her family used to take before the war, before everything that was good came to an end.

Carrie, of course, no longer bothered to watch for her father. After being tricked into riding south of Florida Mountain, she'd finally admitted to herself that it would be days, maybe weeks before he caught up.

By midmorning, the serape Carrie wore became too warm. Shrugging out of it, she nudged her animal forward until she rode abreast of Chama, then held it out to him.

"No, keep it for when it cools off again." He unhooked his canteen. "This, too. I don't drink that much."

The half-breed was truly an enigma. Why would such a kindhearted man be riding with someone as vile as Bert? And weren't Indians supposed to enjoy watching others suffer? This one also seemed to be as clever as he was kind—despite the fact that he resorted to robbing banks. Perhaps he would escape before her father got too close . . . perhaps. She found herself almost hoping he would.

Near noon, they crested a ridge upon which were scattered the first of the taller pines the Mexicans called ponderosas. To the north a cluster of clouds clung to the higher Black Mountains, and true to their name, the peaks now loomed even more darkly. Carrie's father had often mentioned how cool and green those mountains were in summer. She couldn't count the times she'd longed to be high up in them on sweltering afternoons. Now, she thought, considering the irony, it looked as if she were going to get her wish.

The men dismounted in a flat shady area.

"Get down," Chama said, striding toward her. "Your horse needs rest, too." Then before she'd scarcely lifted her stiff right leg out of the stirrup, he reached up and, encircling her waist, pulled her from the saddle. Setting her on her feet, he relaxed his grip, but didn't release her.

She felt his gaze upon her but dared not look up, dared not give him any sign of encouragement. She held her breath.

Abruptly, as if she were a hot stove, he let go. Then, reaching past her, he unhooked the canteen from the pommel and took a drink . . . his lips pressed to the same spot hers had touched only a few minutes before.

Wondering if he were dwelling on the same thought, she busied herself by stepping to the front of her horse on the pretext of checking its bit.

While she did, he rehung the canteen over her bay's saddle horn, then sauntered past her as if she didn't exist. He strode to a rocky outcropping and, with one hand shielding his eyes from the sun overhead, scanned the distant stretches of land to the south.

Remembering the other two, Carrie quickly glanced around. She didn't want to be caught off-guard again—she could still feel Bert's filthy hands on her. She spotted Karl lying in the new spring grass with his arms folded beneath his head and his eyes closed. *My, my,* she thought smugly. Her soreness had eased off considerably, but he looked worse than he had this morning. Red splotches now mottled his face. But where was Bert?

After a panicky moment, she saw him come from behind a tree, buttoning his trousers. His eyes met hers and a scar-twisted smile crooked across his face.

Feigning nonchalance, Carrie dropped her bay's reins and picked her way across the pile of crumbling rocks to where

Chama stood, his back to her. She strategically moved in front of him until he blocked her from Bert's view. Feeling much safer, she joined Chama in his survey of the vast and empty horizon far below.

Chama pretended not to notice her, but he couldn't help admiring her subtle maneuver. Most women in her place would already have worn themselves out crying and begging. She was a smart one, all right. Never moved a muscle during the time he'd had trouble letting go when he'd helped her down. He should take a lesson in control from her. And she was quiet, too, which was also to her credit.

Before turning to leave, he couldn't stop himself from studying her from behind. She was quite tall. Only three or four inches shorter than his own six feet. And he knew she was resilient, considering how well she'd rallied since the night before.

She turned her head, and he noticed red at the end of her slightly tipped nose and her chapped lips. "Come on," he said and started picking his way down the loose stones.

By the time the woman, still saddle-sore, reached him, Chama had found his flat tin of ointment. He unscrewed the lid and handed the container to her. "Here, Miss Jackson. Rub some of this on your nose and lips."

Carrie kept her gaze unwaveringly fixed to the ground while she smeared on some of the liniment that smelled strongly of camphor. But she was fully aware that he watched her every stroke since he stood no more than a foot away. The knowledge was very unnerving.

Finished, she handed back the salve.

As he took it, he dipped in a finger and with a smooth stroke spread more across her cheek.

His touch sent a lightning bolt straight to her heart, stopping it for a second. Surprised by her reaction to his touch, she forgot herself and met his eyes.

He seemed equally shocked by the exchange. He froze, forgetting what he was doing for a moment.

She wasn't sure who broke away first as she looked off to the side, and he resumed rubbing on the ointment.

He didn't stop until he'd covered both cheeks and her chin. Without a word, he returned to his horse, deposited the salve, and started leading the strikingly marked pony down the back side of the ridge.

Watching him go, she couldn't decide why he'd been so shocked until she considered her straggly appearance. Most likely, the addition of the slimy muck on her face made her so much more repugnant, it alone could scare crows out of a cornfield.

Carrie caught some movement out of the corner of her eye.

Bert sauntered toward her.

In his path lay Karl.

Bert poked at him with his boot until the Swede opened his eyes.

Carrie took advantage of Bert's shift of attention and retrieved her horse. Since they were between her and where Chama descended, she made a wide circle around the pair in her escape.

"Get up," she heard Bert snap. "Chama's already started down."

Covertly Carrie glanced to the side from beneath her bonnet bill and saw Karl sit up and stare blankly into space.

"The breed is gettin' real cozy with the woman," Bert continued, the menace in his voice sending a shiver of foreboding up Carrie's spine. "Just a minute ago, I saw him puttin' grease on her face real easylike. You'd think she was his own private property."

Tugging on her bay's reins, Carrie tried to get the weary animal to step livelier as she moved ahead of him off the crest. She didn't like the fact that she'd lost sight of Chama.

As she hurried off the ridge after him, she heard Karl answer Bert on a weary sigh. "I really don't give a damn. Hell, Wormely, last night you was ready to give her to any passing stranger."

"Changed my mind. And the only reason you don't want her is 'cause you already got an ol' lady. By tomorrow night you'll be all snuggled in. Well, I ain't got one. All I ever get is them two flabby whores at the cantina. And for *that* I gotta pay."

Carrie yanked on her animal's reins again as she sidestepped down the steep gravelly slope. Bert's every word spurred her to put more distance between them.

"Get up!" she heard him yell. "I lost sight of Chama and the woman. He's the only one who knows the way into the valley, and I'd sure hate to get left up in these Injun-infested mountains alone."

"Yeah," Karl's croaked. " 'Specially without a bottle."

5

ALL DAY CARRIE and her captors climbed higher and deeper into the Black Mountains. Much to her relief, Chama never left the group as he had the day before. And, thank heavens, the ugly one kept his distance. Although she often felt the heat of his leering gaze, she never looked back at him to verify her suspicions.

Instead, she soothed her sun-scorched eyes with a full palette of greens, from that of the soft new needles lacing the tips of pine boughs to the recently budded leaves of the craggy oaks. Within the shade of the tall trees, lacy ferns were unfurling. But most of all she reveled in the occasional grassy meadow sprinkled with tiny flowers of every delicate shape and hue. It had been years since she'd seen anything so welcoming, not since she was twelve and she and her family had been forced to come west.

Without her realizing, Carrie's mind drifted into thoughts she usually avoided, the beginning of the bad times when the army had refused to trust her father, a Union cavalry captain, to fight against the Confederacy—his superiors thought an officer who'd married into an influential Southern family was too much of a risk. They transferred him to Fort Cook in New Mexico, away from the chance for rank and glory the war would've made possible.

From that moment on, Wiley Jackson had considered his lovely, pampered wife and her offspring nothing but a millstone around his military-erect neck. And as much as Carrie hated to admit it, her father had been correct. Passed over several times for higher rank, he resigned after the war to become sheriff of La Mesilla.

"Same color as your eyes," Chama said, pulling her out of her reverie as he reined in beside her.

Confused by his comment, Carrie peered at him questioningly.

"The pond down there," he said, pointing past her to a small lake several hundred feet below.

She looked down the steep slope through a break in the trees and saw a small aqua-colored lake. A breathtakingly beautiful shimmering gem. And he thought her eyes were the same color.

Before she had time to ponder the possibilities of his casual statement, he nudged his horse forward up the narrow deer path they'd been following. She gave her bay his head until he'd caught up. With the ever-present threat of Bert, she didn't want to lose her place between Chama and the Swede.

An hour or so earlier, the sun had been blocked by a high ridge to the west, taking away its heat. As the cold began to seep through the worn cotton of her work shirt, she swung around to retrieve the serape she'd tied to her saddle. While working it loose, she glanced back at Bert, and as she'd suspected, he was staring at her.

"Need any help?" he called in a overly familiar tone as his vulgar gaze fairly undressed her.

She wrenched the serape free and spun back around, but couldn't avoid hearing his confident chuckle. When she tossed it over her head, it warmed her on the outside, but did little for the icy chill spreading within. Last night she had been mercifully oblivious when they'd stopped to camp, but this evening, even though she was bone-weary, she was very much awake. This time she had no doubt Bert would insist on having his way with her. And Chama had never actually said the ugly one couldn't have her once they were safe from danger. Had he?

In the fading light of dusk, Chama brought the group to a halt at the edge of a pine-framed boggy meadow that was sliced through by a swift mountain stream. The trees would provide protection from the clouds that had been gathering for the past hour, and the horses would have good grazing during the night. He dismounted, and as he did, the quiet woman with eyes of turquoise swung down, too, showing almost no leg at all considering she wore a skirt.

"Is this where we're campin'?" Wormely asked, slouching tiredly in his saddle as he brought his mount alongside Karl's.

"Yep." Chama reached beneath his pony to unwind its cinch strap.

"It's about damn time." Wormely lowered himself to the ground. "My butt feels like it's been drug over cactus all day."

"My whole body feels like that," Karl added.

Chama decided Karl looked more like he'd been pulled through a wringer. It was a damned shame the Swede was cursed with a need for firewater. If not for that, a man couldn't ask for a truer friend.

The beefy man eased his bulk off his horse with aching slowness, his saddle groaning almost as loud as he did.

Chama shook his head and smiled. But he had to admit, if it wasn't for Karl's weakness, the two of them would probably never have met. Karl would still be in Minnesota, pushing a plow for some wife and half a dozen youngsters instead of riding the outlaw trail to keep his belly full of swill.

Something moved beside him, and Chama turned to see the woman lead Hickory to the other side of his horse, then begin unsaddling the gelding with swift, sure moves. Again she stuck to him like a burr, as she had all day, following his every move. But he couldn't blame her. Bert was chomping at the bit to get at her.

Chama removed his saddle and blanket, then tossed them over a smooth boulder. The Jackson woman imitated his every move, placing her outfit beside his. Even when he led his horse into the saw grass, she followed with hers. She held both sets of reins while he hobbled them, then removed their bridles. He couldn't fault her assistance . . . and without either of them speaking a word. Women being natural-born talkers, he wondered how much longer she'd be able to hold her tongue.

On the way back to the trees, he gathered some wood from a busted fallen tree. She also gathered an armload. Then, while he nursed a fire to life with kindling and dry pine needles, she broke some larger twigs, then handed them to him when he needed them. No doubt, she was making herself as handy as possible.

Amused, he let a smile tickle the corners of his mouth as he strolled away from the fire and into the near darkness of a dense stand of young pines to relieve himself. In a matter of seconds he heard the crunch of her clumsy boots as she followed him across the pine debris. His smile grew. He turned to face her. "Lady, I usually take care of my business alone, but you're welcome to join me if that's your pleasure."

The woman's mouth gasped open. Just as swiftly, she slammed it shut. She spun around and made a hasty retreat.

Walking deeper into the woods, Chama chuckled, no longer able to suppress it.

On the way back, he found her no more than a few feet from where they'd parted, waiting within the veil of some low-hanging branches. As he passed, she stepped out and, like some pup, trailed him back to the brightly glowing campfire where the others were digging out the last of the foodstuff.

Bert looked up and pushed his roping hair aside to leer at the Jackson woman.

Her step faltered, and she placed herself, as she'd done all day, on the safe side of Chama. And, damn it all, how could he not admire her? She was fighting for her life the best way she knew how—in the same quiet way his mother had . . . for all the good it had done Spotted Fawn.

Chama's emotions seesawed between disgust with Wormely and an intense urge to protect the woman, stealing all other thought. With the realization, he knew he had to walk away from these unbidden passions. He couldn't let his compassion for a needy white woman—especially the daughter of an ex-soldier—stand between him and his vow.

"Chama," Shipstead said, catching his attention. "We'll be getting to the *rancheria* sometime tomorrow, won't we?"

"Yeah. Before dark if things go as smooth as they have so far."

"Good," he said, stabbing his knife into the top of a tin. "Canned beans and camp coffee ain't my idea of tasty vittles."

"That right?" Bert piped in on a chuckle as he threw a handful of coffee grounds into a pot. "Never heard no bottle of whiskey called vittles before."

"You never give up, do you?" Karl growled.

Bert's glance slid to the woman. "Not if I can help it."

Plate in hand, Carrie settled her weary body onto a sheared flat rock in Chama's shadow, feeling far more protected than she knew she should—nothing but a campfire separated her from Bert Wormely. After years of living with her most hated enemy, her father, never trusting him, never expecting anything but food and shelter in return for keeping his house, she wondered at how naturally she'd come to count on this outlaw leader to keep her safe from the nasty one who wanted to claim her. It made no sense, no sense at all. Concerned by this queer new allegiance, she began to lose her appetite after only a few bites.

But the men banged their spoons unceasingly against their tin plates. She peeked around at Bert and saw him happily shoveling food into his mouth. He seemed to be gaining strength with each bite while the fire's flickering blaze exaggerated his every scar. And his eyes fairly gleamed. With anticipation?

The thought drained any energy she had left. She could barely chew or swallow the food in her mouth as the dread of the night to come loomed before her.

Unable to eat anymore, Carrie set her half-finished meal on the rock beside her. She picked up her cup, steadying it with both hands, and concentrated with all her being on the flames reflected in the liquid in the hope of erasing Bert's mangled features from her mind.

Time passed in silence until Chama dipped his head and looked at her beneath the bill of her bonnet as he took the cup from her. "Better get your blankets and roll them out. I'm not putting you to bed again tonight."

The unscarred side of Bert's mouth lifted in a grin as he came to his feet. "I'd be glad to tuck her in."

His words stole Carrie's breath, and her heart began to pound wildly.

"I'm also not up to hearing you and her fighting all night," Chama returned. "Besides, if I let you have her now, she won't be fit to travel tomorrow." Chama rose to his feet and exhaled. "We brought our ace in the hole too far to leave her behind now."

"I'll be careful. I won't hurt her."

"Tomorrow, Bert. We'll discuss that tomorrow." Chama's tone was quiet but unyielding. "When we reach the *rancheria*. Tonight she gets her rest."

The muscles in Bert's jaw jumped, and his eyes narrowed. He flexed his fingers repeatedly as he lowered his right hand dangerously near his holstered gun.

Chama stepped away from Carrie, his body tensing, his attention riveted to the smaller man.

Bert stared back for several heartbeats, then, suddenly, threw up his hands. "Shit!" With jerky movements he went to sit on the log again beside Karl, then picked up his cup and slurped down a gulp of coffee.

Karl turned his head away from Bert and grinned, the first nongloomy expression Carrie had seen from him all day.

She, herself, felt a strong urge to cry she was so relieved, if she but dared. She'd been saved again, for one more night. Her pulse began settling to a slower rhythm as she walked to her saddle and retrieved the bedroll tied behind its cantle.

Chama argued with his good sense that his reasoning in stopping Bert yet another time had been sound. They all did need a good night's sleep. Including him. Putting some distance between him and the woman who caused him to act so strange, he also went to fetch his bedding.

Returning, he noticed the woman still stood with her blankets in her arms. When he unrolled his, she did the same . . . right alongside him.

48 / Elaine Crawford

Pretending to ignore her closeness, Chama sat down and tugged off his boots, then crawled into his bed and lay on his side . . . away from her.

Without removing her footwear, she lay down so near he felt her warm breath on the back of his neck. Didn't she know what that kind of closeness did to a man? How it could start a fire in a man's groin, a fire so fierce that only the musky, moist depths of her body could extinguish it?

In self-defense, he edged away slightly and pulled his shirt collar up around his neck. But a few seconds later she sighed softly, and he felt the betrayal of his body as he began to harden. Dirty Bert wasn't the only one who was going to have trouble sleeping tonight.

As he'd predicted, long after the others had fallen asleep, Chama still lay awake. Every time he started to doze, the woman's face would float before him, then dissolve into his mother's, jerking him awake. In too many ways the sheriff's daughter reminded him of Spotted Fawn, though the two certainly did not look alike. His mother had been Kiowa, and Miss Jackson was of English or northern European stock. The age of his mother at the time of her death would be the only similarity, both somewhere in their twenties.

Chama rolled over to examine the woman more closely. In the moonlight she looked almost comical. She had spread his serape over her cover and slept beneath both fully clothed, with her bonnet strings still tied beneath her chin and spots of the greasy salve catching the dim light. From the moment of her capture, she'd been very careful not to expose a single female curve or the blond hair he'd only glimpsed the night before. Not even the sound of her voice had she trusted to them.

He wondered if his mother had been as terrified when her father sold her for three jugs of whiskey to a fur trapper who had happened by their village along the Arkansas River. His mother had said the mountain man was on his way to winter in the Rockies, and a pretty young squaw would be good company during the long cold nights. His mother—for jugs of whiskey! But her father had grown to need the white man's firewater the same as Karl now did, and he'd already traded away all the wealth he had ever gained as a warrior. All he had left of value was his youngest daughter.

Chama tried to imagine how his mother must have felt, taken from her people and given to a man who cared so little for her that he lost her to an army sergeant in a card game before they ever reached the mountains. Lost her to Sergeant Joseph Wade Campbell, who would become father to Joseph Wade Campbell, Jr., half-breed.

Chama didn't remember him, but his mother had said that he was kind for a white man, and that he'd been the first to call her by the English translation of her name, Spotted Fawn. The sergeant took her with him along the Santa Fe Trail as his troop provided safe passage for the new settlers and traders traveling from the United States to New Mexico in the late 1840s. When she'd talked about him, she'd never failed to mention that this Sergeant Campbell backed down from no man, yet whenever they moved to a new post, he always insisted on helping her set up her tepee—woman's work.

Joseph Campbell was transferred back east before Chama was two, but before he left he sold Spotted Fawn to another soldier. Sold her as if she were nothing more than a slab of army beef and his own son even less. That alone would be justification for Chama's hatred of the bluecoats. Even if their trespasses didn't outnumber the stars.

An owl hooted in the distance, and the woman moaned softly, drawing Chama's attention to her again. That mouth, those full pouty lips, might not ask for anything, but the eyes, the eyes sought so much. To give her what she wanted would mean taking her from Wormely and maybe even some of the other Comancheros at the *rancheria*. He might be forced to leave the hidden valley before the gunrunners came. That mustn't happen. No one, no thing, could stand in the way of his vow.

But to turn over this wordless one with the magic eyes of turquoise to Wormely?

Chama recalled that his mother, too, had taken great care not to provoke whatever man owned her at the moment. Some of the other squaws who traveled with the bluecoats were not so wise. His first memory was of a woman screaming in the dark—much as he sometimes heard on a summer's night while lying in his cabin across the meadow from the *rancheria*. Once in a while, one of the camp followers would disappear. When he would ask his mother about the missing woman, she would warn him never to mention the woman's name again.

Although Spotted Fawn feared for her little Joe Joe's safety, most of the soldiers treated him like their mascot. And he looked up to them, *wanted to be one of them when he grew up*. What a fool he'd been. As if they would have ever let a half-breed enlist in the cavalry.

Chama's fists clenched as he recalled marching in step behind them on the parade ground, or begging for rides on their long-legged horses. Then, even more enraging, he remembered how proud he was the day they made him permanent Unofficial Flag Raiser. Most of the time he'd been far too young and innocent to be anything but happy . . . until the next drunken soldier beat his mother.

She always tried to pass it off as nothing. She would hug her little Joe Joe and tell him she wasn't hurt, that the man was sorry and wouldn't do it again.

By the time he was five or six, he'd become quite a linguist. Equally fluent in English and Kiowa, he could also understand quite a bit of Comanche. He always felt very superior when one of the soldiers asked him to interpret a conversation with a newly arrived Indian woman—one more thing he now bitterly regretted.

The only memories he could still take pleasure in were the times he and his mother walked out on the prairie, out across grass that the wind caused to ripple like a great sea. Spotted Fawn, in her graceful way, would tell him of the buffalo, the Sustainer of Life, and of the great hunts her people went on each spring. She told him of their history, of their migration from the north. She would recite tales of their strength and bravery in the face of their enemies. He became so proud to be Kiowa that it stung only a little when some drunken soldier told his mother to get her bastard breed out so they could be alone.

Then one day when he was seven, Spotted Fawn was dead—killed by a swill-bellied Irisher by the name of Corporal Sweeny.

After all these years, Chama could still picture her, crumpled and contorted in the corner of their hut. When he lifted her head, her neck had made a sickening cracking sound.

He'd taken a knife and tried to avenge her, but he was no match for the bluecoats then. They hog-tied him, threw him in the back of a wagon, hauled him over Raton Pass, and dumped him at an orphanage along the Chama River run by a Franciscan priest.

They may have counted themselves safe from their guilt and a little boy's rage, but Chama's need for vengeance still burned as hot now and had for all the years he spent with the Spanish padres, no matter how they tried to dissuade him. The soldiers would pay in full for that atrocity. And all the others. He would not lay down his weapons until the last bluecoat was driven from this land. Not until his mother's people and all the others who had been herded onto reservations of disease and hunger were free to roam again.

An icy breeze swept down from the snowcapped peaks, stealing the last lingering trace of warmth.

The woman edged closer.

Chama lifted his blanket, and she snuggled against his chest. He then pulled her covers over them both and pillowed her head on his arm. Her spirit, so like his mother's, drew his soul to her, tempting him to turn away from his sacred pledge. But he could not weaken. Particularly not for the daughter of Sheriff Jackson.

But still it gave him pleasure to know that for this one last night, he could keep her safe. Encircling her with his other arm, he drew her closer, felt her breasts mold themselves to the hard contours of his chest . . . her softness nested within his strength.

≫ 6 ≪

CARRIE'S EYES SHOT open at the sound of rapid banging. She attempted to rise, but found herself pinned.

"It's all right," Chama whispered in her ear. "Just a woodpecker."

The loud tapping started again.

Reaffirming the sound, Carrie relaxed, then became aware that she and the outlaw were curled together closer than two spoons, her bottom nudging his manhood. She tensed.

His chest vibrated against her back for a couple of seconds in a near-silent chuckle. "Can I have my arm?" he then asked and slid it from beneath her head as he unfolded himself from around her.

She quickly scooted away. Mortified, she stared into the distance until her eyes gradually focused on several deer grazing in the meadow beyond the horses. She tried desperately to concentrate on their grace and beauty in the predawn light, but neither they nor the gaily chirping birds overhead in the trees could prevent her from sensing Chama's every move as he sat up and put on his boots. She could even imagine the stretch of his shirt across muscles that would be rippling and bulging beneath it.

Pine needles crunched as he rose to his feet. She then heard the slap of leather as he apparently buckled on his holster. She knew she, too, should get up. But she didn't know how to face him after so brazenly sleeping with him. In his very arms!

He stepped near her head, then stopped beside her.

She had no choice but to look up.

The hint of a grin softened the precise etch of his bronze features. "Better straighten your bonnet. It's all cockeyed."

Then turning on his heels, he strode away.

With heat flaming her cheeks, Carrie swiftly sat up and stuffed hopelessly tangled stray hairs into her bonnet as she watched Chama gathering kindling. Pulling the blanket around her shoulders to ward off the damp cold beneath the trees, she glanced over to the two other wool-covered lumps on the far side of the campfire. With relief, she saw they both still slept.

After Chama had a small blaze going, he picked up the smoke-blackened coffeepot and walked out across the meadow seemingly unaware of her attention. He stopped at the swift stream that was no more than a yard wide.

The grazing deer, startled by the intrusion, darted into the forest. Carrie felt a moment's disappointment at the loss. It had been years since she'd seen any.

Chama, too, watched them flee before kneeling to fill the container with water.

Carrie couldn't stop herself from studying him as he splashed water onto his face, which crinkled against what was surely icy cold. Before returning, he pulled a comb from his back pocket and ran it through hair that hadn't seen a barber in some time. Of course, she reminded herself, barbers were probably hard to come by in his line of work.

At the thought, she remembered the robbery and wondered where her father was at this moment. Had he given up waiting for the outlaws at the border and returned to start the tedious task of tracking them? More than likely, he would've gone back to La Mesilla to recruit more deputies. She doubted he'd ride into the foreboding Black Mountains without a small army. Considering all the renegades and Comancheros who had taken refuge in them these past few summers, the steep and lofty range was not a safe place to venture.

And Chama was obviously counting on it. He strolled back to the fire without so much as a glance around. Her father would no doubt be several days behind them.

Chama placed the coffeepot on a flat stone, its edge licked by flames, then stood over the blaze himself, rubbing his arms. His gray-striped cotton shirt provided little protection against the cold.

Taking note of the many-colored serape trapped among her covers, she pulled it out and, with a blanket held tightly around her, rose and handed it to him.

He barely glanced at her as he took the serape and mumbled something she assumed voiced his thanks before he dropped it over his head.

Perhaps he was as embarrassed by the intimacy of their awakening as she. No, her common sense argued. After two days and nights without spending any time on herself, she was sure not even the hardiest of men could bear to look at her. As she stepped past Bert's sleeping form to fetch the sack of coffee, his stench puckered her nose. Holding her breath until she was upwind, an uplifting thought occurred. She cocked a brow and eyed the ugly one. *Pretty soon,* she mouthed, *not even the likes of you will want me.*

After pouring a measure of grounds into the pot, Carrie followed Chama into the spongy meadow to help him bridle and unhobble their horses. She sensed his appreciation, making the silence between them really quite companionable as they worked among the animals.

By the time they'd saddled them, Carrie could smell the boiling brew. She went to fetch the tin mugs and the last of the old biscuits. While she did, Chama woke the other two.

Chama sat down on a nearby log as he watched the Jackson woman pour coffee into two cups. He had no doubt one was for him or that she would serve him, then sit beside him.

She did exactly as he'd thought but with the warming addition of a shy smile. She also treated him to a brief view of her eyes before she took her place.

Her presence was becoming more enjoyable all the time, and he found himself hoping that he would again catch her snatching peeks at him from beneath her floppy bonnet as she had on the ride yesterday. She was a bedraggled dirty mess. But those eyes . . .

Chama suddenly realized he was mooning over the woman—one who'd just cost him half a night's sleep. Women sure did have a way of moving into a man's life, taking over. Robbing him of his power. He couldn't allow that. Wouldn't.

Karl kicked out of his twisted bedroll and lumbered to his feet, sporting swollen eyes and sallow skin that was veined with red. Two days without whiskey had taken its usual toll. Even his six-and-a-half-foot frame seemed shrunken. However, when he sighted the woman on the log, his manners came to the fore—he bobbed his head and cleared his throat. "Mornin', ma'am." Then, before she could respond, he turned and reached with trembling hands for the coffeepot.

Bert, on the other hand, sprang to his feet and danced over to the others in that jangly way of his. Displaying his scummy teeth, he bent before the woman in a deep mocking bow. His hand flicked out and pulled hers to his mouth, and before she could yank hers back, he slobbered on it.

On instinct, Chama lunged forward, ready to come to his feet, but caught himself.

Bert snickered and jigged away to retrieve his breakfast.

The idea that the little runt thought he'd backed down grated on Chama.

Nonetheless, Miss Jackson edged closer while spending a considerable amount of time wiping the back of her hand on her skirt. About the time Chama thought she would rub her skin off, she stopped and snatched her gloves from her pocket, then pulled them on.

Bert glided back, cup and biscuits in hand, and crowded down beside her on the log. "You sure," he asked, "we're gonna reach the hidden valley by nightfall?"

"Yeah." Chama leaned past the woman. He wanted to see Bert's face after he said the rest. "As long as those trackers don't pick up our trail."

"Trackers?" Cup to his mouth, coffee dribbled down Wormely's stubbly chin. *"What trackers?"*

"The ones Sheriff Jackson has out scouting. Yes, sir, that man must be real put out with you about now. Isn't that right, Karl?"

"Me?" Bert jumped to his feet, his beady eyes darting back and forth. "We're all in this together."

As Karl's belly bounced with a rumbly chuckle, Chama caught the corner of Miss Jackson's mouth lifting, though she didn't look up. She raised her cup, hiding her smile behind it.

"Don't you think it's time," Wormely said, effecting a brave strut as he moved to the far side of the fire, "we divvy up the money? I don't want them vultures back at the camp knowing how much we got, so's they can jack up the price of ever'thing."

Or, Chama thought to himself, *so you'll have some jingle in your pocket when you take off like a scared rabbit at the first sign of trouble.*

"Yeah, let's split it now," the Swede agreed. "Soon as we reach the valley, I want to get straight home to my little señorita. The baby was croupy when I left, and Esperanza was kinda worried."

"I been thinkin' on buyin' my own little señorita," Bert spouted. "Tacate and his Apaches brought in three just before we left. Stole 'em outta some whorehouse down in Ol' Mexico." He shot a glance at the Jackson woman, then, looking down at his coffee, took a quick sip before continuing. "One of 'em was real flirty. Smilin' and swishin' her tail around a lot. Tacate said if I still wanted her when I get back, I could have her for three hundred." He grinned and slapped his knee. "Whoo-ee, but I get plumb weak just thinkin' about climbin' into that sweet, soft body."

With the woman's shoulder touching his, Chama felt a shudder course through her body. He stopped himself from covering her hand to comfort her.

"Don't be sad, Miss Jackson," Bert said with his contorted grin. "I plan on doin' my duty by you, too. I got lots of me to go around."

The woman dropped her cup.

Karl didn't seem to notice as he spurted through his laughter, "Lessen the sheriff gets his knife after you."

Chama stood, snagging the cup as he rose. He handed it to her with a look he hoped would convey his sympathy. He then wheeled around to the men. "Think it's time we stopped yammering and started counting. There's gotta be seven or eight thousand, at least."

* * *

The shape of a live oak caught Carrie's attention as she and the others rode across a lettuce-green meadow. The tree, spreading its limbs wide over a meandering stream, triggered visions of another oak—one that was probably gone by now, she mused, along with the plantation.

More old Carolina memories flooded her thoughts, the sounds of laughter as she and her brother swung out across the water on the thick knotted rope. Splashing, playing. Picnics beneath the tree's massive branches—Mammy Dahlia always fixing a basket of her and Charly's favorite foods for when they'd exhausted themselves swimming. Stretching out in the warm sun, they'd gleefully gobble down the treats. Carrie's mouth watered at just the remembered taste of huckleberry jam and butter on fresh-baked bread, although it had been many years since she'd even seen a jar of those particular preserves.

Everything had been so pretty in South Carolina then, pretty as here. And warm and safe. But most of all, love had enveloped them. Back then, she and Charly and her mother had been wrapped in it. If only she'd treasured every precious moment instead of taking it all for granted.

Mournful tears formed and clouded Carrie's vision. She wiped them away to feast again on the oak. Soon she was peering into the forest beyond, imagining what would've lain just beyond it if she truly had been passing the tree of her childhood. She could almost see their sparkling white mansion with its stately columns. And if it hadn't been for that damned war and that bastard Sherman, it would all still be there. Grandma would be there, and Grandpa. Uncle Jason wouldn't have been killed at Gettysburg, and sweet, teasing Uncle Andy wouldn't have died of fever in some stinking Union prison.

Realizing where her thoughts were taking her, Carrie drew in a deep shuddering breath, then exhaled it. Recalling horrors of the past would cost her the enjoyment of today's alpine loveliness. She'd let it remind her only of the wonderful times before the war.

Sundays had always been her favorite, always such fun with everyone dressing in their finest. Grandma would fuss over each and every one of her "Sweet Caroline's" ringlets, never failing to call Carrie a little wiggle worm. Mama, of course, was absolutely beautiful as she stepped into the carriage for the ride to church, all creamy and blond and as fragile-looking as the porcelain doll Uncle Jason had brought her from Paris. And tiny . . . nothing like Carrie, her much taller and larger-framed daughter. Everyone always said Mama had been the belle of the county. They said beaux had come calling from miles around. But instead of picking one of those eager young swains, she'd chosen an army officer, the son of a mere Ohio shopkeeper.

Captain Wiley Jackson had been one of the young officers stationed at Fort Jackson who frequented the gatherings at their home just outside of Columbia. Mama said he'd stood out from all the rest, looking so dashing, so strong in his uniform, someone with whom she could always feel safe and cared for. And, of course, with the right word in the right ear, her father could see that Wiley was stationed in Washington from time to time—Washington, where the parties were endless. To Carrie's mother, it all seemed so exciting, so perfect. And it had been, too . . . until the South seceded and her father was banished to a remote post in New Mexico to rot away while his fellow officers were being brevetted majors and colonels.

Carrie's horse began vaulting up a steep gravelly incline, bringing her back to the moment. She lifted her weight over its withers to assist the animal, and noticed how achy her back felt as she stretched it. They'd been riding for hours, stopping only to rest the horses a few times. She glanced at the sun and found its rays streaking through the pines at a midafternoon slant.

As the ground beneath them leveled, Bert's tinny cry came from behind. "Chama. Ain't we never gettin' to that damned Comanchero camp?"

Comanchero camp! Oh, God, no. Icy shock raced through Carrie's veins and exploded behind her eyes. He'd just confirmed her most horrifying fear.

"It's not much farther," Chama called without slowing the pace or looking back.

Carrie glanced frantically down the steep mountain they'd been climbing at an angle. Her first instinct was to slam her heels into her mount's flanks and try to gallop down it. But as she clamped her fingers around the reins, she knew she'd only break her horse's neck as well as her own.

This is it. The end. I've lived for years in my father's hell. Now, I guess I'll be tortured and killed in an even worse one. She melted back into the saddle, feeling the utter depth of her helplessness. She knew the futility of looking skyward in yet another pleading prayer. *For years, she'd tried to believe, to hope, that she'd one day be saved. All for nothing.*

There was no God. No one she could count on. Even if her father did come, it wouldn't be to save her. He'd be coming for his pride's sake, to enforce his will over others.

Carrie swung her attention to Chama's back, another man of power. But why had this Comanchero bothered to save her from Bert when a far worse fate awaited her? A weakness on his part, perhaps? A crack in that strong, virile Indian facade? If so, there must be some way to use it to her advantage. She must if she were to survive.

7

For more than half an hour Carrie and her captors had been riding into a deep, damp, darkly shadowed trench, its walls becoming steadily closer together, and for the first time she questioned Chama's leadership. If the crack continued to narrow, soon they would be trapped, as trapped as her gnawing insides told her she was. Yet, as she viewed the relaxed posture of the half-breed, he certainly didn't seem concerned. Perhaps the trench ended in a crumbled landslide that could be easily climbed.

As the rugged granite walls crowded in until only one horse could barely squeeze through at a time, Chama pulled his rifle from its scabbard. He raised it overhead and, looking to the rim above, waved it to and fro.

Carrie followed his gaze and saw that he signaled a figure silhouetted against the setting sun. She watched the sentinel return Chama's greeting in the same manner.

Aware that the cursed Comanchero camp must be near, her throat constricted until each breath became a struggle. She still had yet to think of a way to get the half-breed to save her, none, that is, except falling at his feet and begging. And, with the same surety that she rode into the gravest danger of her life, she knew it would only turn him away from her. Pleading for mercy disgusted a proud man. It had only served to make her father revile her mother with even more venomous hatred.

Rounding a bend, light shafted toward her, and a warm breeze swept across her cheeks. She looked ahead and saw that the mountain walls stopped as abruptly as one comes to the end of a hall.

Emerging from it, Chama reined in his paint.

Carrie came alongside him and halted on a ledge that overlooked a valley far below. Sheer walls rose up a thousand feet or more from it and were cast in gold by the setting sun. They ran along both sides for several miles before curving to meet at the far end. Near the top of the eastern ridge a rainbow glistened across a sparkling waterfall that dropped in a foaming white rush to a deep pool below. Gorgeous! Carrie continued to stare for a long moment, finding it difficult to tear herself from such beauty.

"Pretty, ain't it."

Without her noticing, Bert had come up beside her. She nudged her bay forward a few steps, halting barely short of the precipice on the pretext of wanting a better view. Gazing downward to forests and meadows that created a lush patchwork of greens, it was hard to believe evil lurked below. She would've been consumed with joy to be going to such a paradise, this place the men had aptly referred to as the "hidden valley."

Chama guided his paint to one side of the shelf and started down a path that seemed no more than an extended slant of the ledge but much narrower, with a wall on one side and a precarious drop-off on the other.

As dangerous as the trail was, Chama's horse still became frisky, his feet prancing excitedly and his head in a strained arch against Chama's taut grip on the reins.

Carrie held her breath in fear while watching Chama's flexing muscles as he worked to retain control. His solid hold won out and the animal surrendered to a steady pace for the descent.

It was just as well that the bay followed the paint in a docile fashion without being directed, because Carrie doubted if she would've had the nerve to give the command had the decision been left to her. As her mount trudged along the rock-strewn path, she unwittingly glanced down to the sure death awaiting if the animal took the slightest misstep. After a few frozen seconds of staring and grasping the saddle horn with both hands, she closed her eyes and hoped with all her might the horse's surefootedness would see them to the bottom.

Minutes seemed like hours. Then she heard another horse move past her. She opened her eyes to see that they had reached the forest floor, and Karl had moved from the rear and now guided his horse next to Chama's.

"I'm going to ride on ahead. It's been kinda worryin' me, leaving Esperanza alone with a sick baby." The big Swede kicked his dun in the flanks, and the animal sprang into a gallop down the snaking trail, and within seconds he was swallowed up by the tall firs.

Bert trotted his horse alongside Carrie's. The stench of him caused her stomach to convulse as he turned his mangled face to her and gave her a roving look.

Her heart began to pound, and she felt a scream gathering in her lungs. If he but touched her, she knew she wouldn't be able to stifle it.

He slowly wagged his head, his stringy hair flapping sluggishly, then nudged his roan forward to where Chama rode. "I see ol' Karl just couldn't wait to get back to his jug," he sneered.

"He said he was worried about his woman and little one."

"Speakin' of women, you oughtta buy yourself one of them Mexican whores Tacate's got."

Carrie's gaze riveted onto the half-breed. Would he participate in the buying and selling of human beings? Cast her aside and purchase a more appealing captive?

But, thank heavens, Chama shook his head. "Not interested."

"Just 'cause Juanita was nothin' but a two-timin' *puta* don't mean you can't keep a woman in line if you put your mind to it. Stayin' alone out in that cabin way off to itself, why, that just ain't natural. Ain't good for the juices."

Carrie had noticed a slight stiffening in Chama's back when Wormely mentioned the name Juanita, but her mind quickly switched to the fact that he lived away from the camp *and alone*.

"I have other uses for my money," Chama said in a monotone.

"You mean like buyin' rifles for your damned Injun friends? Hell, if you get a gal off Tacate, he'll most likely spend the money on guns anyway, so's you'd be killin' two birds with one stone."

"More likely, he'd spend it on that rotgut Rodriguez is selling in his store."

"Well, suit yourself. But I think I'll ride on ahead and make sure Tacate's still holdin' that woman for me." Slapping the reins across his horse's neck, Bert sent the animal into a trot and bounced his raggedy self into the twilight shadows.

Carrie sagged into her saddle with relief. If the other woman pleased Bert enough, perhaps he would forget about her. Now if she could convince the half-breed to keep her for himself, she might be safe until she was rescued.

Safe? Had she lost her mind? The man robbed white men's banks to get money to buy guns—undoubtedly from white gunrunners—to give to Indians for killing white soldiers. And besides the army, lawmen all over the territory were no doubt after him for robbing the banks. It was all a senseless circle of violence. But, at the moment, convincing him to keep and protect her was the only option she could see.

As they continued on in silence, the beauty of the fragrant forest eased Carrie's anxiety somewhat. Crossing a small meadow, she spotted a doe and her fawn grazing while several blue jays flew above. Off to the side, a lone coyote lapped water from a streamlet as he slanted wary glances at them. It was hard to believe that a Comanchero camp could exist in all this enchantment. But then, for the most part, the Comancheros she'd been with had not harmed her. Maybe the terrifying stories of their evil ways were exaggerated.

Suddenly the coyote darted into the woods, and the deer bolted in the opposite direction.

Chama reined his paint to a stop and looked around.

Carrie did the same, but no matter how she strained, she neither saw nor heard anything save a few chirping birds and the breeze as it rustled the tops of the firs.

Chama soon seemed satisfied that all was safe and started ahead, leading her into the woods again.

Carrie did not relax so quickly. She began watching to the rear as often as she did each side. Several times the ever-deepening shadows tricked her into thinking they were being followed. She clutched the blanket she was using for a shawl tighter around her as she nudged her lagging horse closer to Chama's. This was not a safe place. The evil here was very real. Hadn't Bert just left them to go purchase a woman, *from a renegade savage?* She could be sold just as easily . . . if the nasty one didn't decide to keep her for himself.

Shuddering, she cast her gaze onto the half-breed's powerful-looking back and shoulders. He had protected her thus far. And she simply had to see that he continued.

A short time later the forest gave way to a much larger meadow than the last one. At the far edge of the clearing sprawled a settlement. Its size amazed Carrie. Thirty-five or forty cabins and wickiups stood in clusters near two larger buildings, one with several corrals and animal shelters attached. In the fading light of dusk, she also saw women cooking over open fires in front of their shanties. Men were scattered about in small groups, apparently visiting. To her amazement, she even saw several children playing a game with sticks and a ball. By all outward appearances it seemed a small, peaceful village.

Then Carrie jolted at the sight of a corpse hanging spread-eagled between two pines, his body pierced with lances and arrows. Even her father might've been appalled by such a bloody spectacle. The naked reality of her situation slammed into her full force. If she didn't act now, she would end up like that man, or worse, cribbed in some whorehouse down in Mexico after the men at the camp finished with her.

With ironlike resolve, Carrie straightened her back, lifted her chin, and brought her bay alongside Chama's pony. Then, determined not to allow the slightest concern ring in her voice, she spoke in a matter-of-fact tone. "I'm very dirty and most unpresentable. Would you mind taking me to your cabin to repair myself before I meet your friends?"

Taken by surprise, Chama reined Eagle Wings to a stop.

The woman did likewise and looked at him calmly as if this weren't the first time she'd spoken in the three days she'd been with him.

Then the absurdity of what she said struck him. "Did you say my friends? You want to be presentable for my friends?" He burst into laughter.

She flinched, but just for an instant, then continued to stare at him without any further sign of wavering.

As he watched this trapped, coarsely dressed woman trying so hard to be "the brave lady," he began to sober. As so often before on this trip, she reminded him of his long-dead mother. His compassion for her returned. "Sure, lady. I'll take you to my cabin so you can clean up." His voice sounded oddly gentle to his ear. He finished with more force. "I've got a few woman things there you might be able to use." And besides, he told himself, it wasn't as if he wasn't already headed there. He didn't enter that hellhole across the meadow any more often than necessary.

He reined his paint to the left and began veering across the clearing toward the shallow creek that edged it. He could almost feel the woman's relief as she moved Hickory abreast of Eagle Wings. He did catch her glancing toward the *rancheria* a time or two, though, before they reached the bank and crossed to the other side of the swift-moving water.

Once they climbed the opposite bank, the woman visibly relaxed and let her horse fall behind his as they took a deer trace that ran alongside the creek. Soon he caught a glimpse of his cabin nestled on its wooded knoll overlooking the meadow. Damn, it was a welcome sight. Three summers ago he'd built it with his own hands, the first place that had ever truly felt like his . . . like home. "There it is," he said, pointing to it through a break in the trees. He looked at the woman to see her reaction.

She closed her eyes and sighed, but it sounded like a pleased one.

He felt a warming around his heart as he led the way to a small pen behind the cabin and dismounted. As usual, she copied him. Then, she again worked with him to unsaddle the animals and rub them down with straw. Always the helpful one, making herself useful, trying never to be a burden.

Juanita, too, had been helpful at first, hadn't she? Maybe not quite so much. Her mouth had always done more working than anything else. That woman never would stop talking. She'd filled the air with her shrill chatter until there was no room left for a man to think. In fact, the woman had become so wearisome, he'd been glad when she found someone else more free with his time and money. Glad to have the cabin to himself again.

Chama eyed the Jackson woman as she draped a damp saddle blanket over a railing to dry. In her own way she could be just as devious as Juanita had been. Her helpfulness was surely just as much of a ploy as her silence had been. Give her a day or two to get over her fright, and she'd probably be every bit as talkative and naggy as Juanita ever had been.

He shot the woman another look while he picked up his saddle and slung it over a sawhorse. No sense chewing on it. Most likely, Bert would come to claim her tonight . . . or tomorrow if things went well with Tacate.

The woman stretched and placed a hand at the small of her back.

The trip had no doubt been very hard on her, he knew, and a goodly portion of compassion seeped into him again as he realized there was no way Juanita would've suffered in silence for that long. Maybe this one really was different. Maybe . . .

Maybe what? he scolded, coming to his senses. The woman wasn't his to keep *or* give away. She was the daughter of the sheriff of La Mesilla, and returning her to her father before Jackson got the whole territory out looking for her was the only sensible thing to do.

"Come on," he called to the woman and started around the cabin toward the door.

As Carrie followed Chama along the side of the log structure, she couldn't keep herself from looking through an opening in the trees to the Comanchero camp across the meadow. Although it lay a good quarter of a mile away, it seemed but a stone's throw. And the disgusting one was there this very minute, buying some poor soul from a savage.

At the unthinkable idea, Carrie quickly returned her attention to Chama. Somehow she would make him want to keep her here until her father rescued her. Just for a week or so. She could do it. Had to. At least this man's touch didn't make her skin crawl.

They rounded the corner to the front of the cabin and Carrie noticed a rock-ringed cooking spot with a large black kettle suspended on sturdy poles over it. Logs formed an L on two sides, creating a friendly atmosphere. Her gaze lingered.

"Ma'am."

She turned and saw Chama standing at the door, holding it open for her.

The first thing that caught Carrie's eye as she walked past the outlaw was a crude wood-framed bed.

It stared back at her from the far wall.

She quickly glanced away and determinedly concentrated on the room's other contents in the growing darkness.

Along one side ran a wide counter board with two shelves above stacked with pots and crockery. Sacks of flour, meal, and beans slumped below on the floor. Against the opposite wall sat three brass-hinged trunks, and above them hung a mirror evenly spaced between a couple more shelves. Everything sat neatly in its place. The man obviously took good care of himself *without a woman's help*.

She stopped before a rough-timbered table that took up most of the center of the room. Taking hold of its edge for support, she again stared at the bed.

Off to the side, she caught a flash of movement.

It was Chama, stooping down before one of the trunks. He unlatched it. "There's clothes and some other woman things in here." He then tilted his head upward. "There's soap and a towel up on the shelf. And outside, there's a washtub hanging on a spike at the side of the house. Water's in the creek. I'll bring some up and put it in the kettle to heat before I leave."

Leave? He was going to leave her here alone? What if Bert came while he was gone? Or other, worse, Comancheros?

"Don't worry," he said, coming to his feet. "They all know I like my privacy. No one will come snooping around."

Her expression must've betrayed her. She composed herself once again. "Then that would be very kind of you."

He scrunched his brow. "What would?"

"The hot water. I would very much appreciate a bath."

He grinned slowly, his gaze wandering away. "And some privacy, too, I'll bet." He nodded toward the counter board. "There's matches in that cup for the lantern." Then without another glance her way, he wheeled around and strode out the door. He closed it behind him, and the room fell into pitch-blackness. She tightened her grip on the table as she regained her bearings.

The realization resurfaced that he really was going to leave her there alone. She couldn't believe her good fortune. As soon as he was out of sight, she'd resaddle the horse and escape . . . No, she couldn't do that. The only entrance to the valley was guarded. But it *was* a fairly large valley. She brightened. Of course. She could easily hide out somewhere until her father came.

"Don't be a fool," she whispered on a sigh. Chama was part Indian . . . an expert tracker. He could find her with very little effort, and to make matters worse, he would probably be so enraged over her attempt, he might just turn her over to the animals at the camp.

"Oh, dammit! Damn them all!" she cursed in her frustration. "Damn every last one of them." Ripping at the ties at her throat, she tore off her bonnet, then felt her way across the planked floor in the dark to the counter board and swept it with her hand until she found the matches. Maybe she'd think clearer after a nice hot soak.

8

CHAMA WALKED ACROSS the meadow toward the scatterings of light for information about the anticipated arrival of the gunrunners and, of more interest at the moment, to get a ready-cooked meal for Miss Jackson and himself. After more than a week of trail grub, even Shorty's greasy cooking would taste good.

As he neared the oversize shack in which gimp-legged Juan Rodriguez had set up a store, Chama spotted several men lounging on the porch. In the glow of a hanging lantern, they relaxed on some of the mismatched old chairs that cluttered the porch.

"Come on over," Waco Bob beckoned. The red glow from the gunslinger's cigarette flared back and forth as he gestured. "Heard you been out havin' a high old time."

As Chama mounted the steps, the other shadowy figures chuckled.

"Is it true?" drawled a long-toothed Southerner Chama only knew by sight. "Dirty Bert says y'all robbed Jackson's bank and stole his daughter."

Bert and his big flapping mouth, Chama cursed inwardly as his hand instinctively came to rest on the butt of his .45. "Where is Wormely?"

"Oh, he's over at Tacate's camp," one of Three-Fingered Mike's boys said as he rose to his lanky height. Leaning against a porch post, he pulled out his makings.

"Yessah," added the Southerner, "he's over yonder, dickerin' with that red devil for some li'l ol' Mex gal."

"Well, is it true?" Waco Bob, dressed in his usual black garb, stretched out his legs while he readjusted one of the two gunbelts strapped around his hips. "About the sheriff's daughter?"

"I suppose so."

"Where is she?" a silhouetted figure asked, standing just outside the circle of light.

"Yeah, where you keeping her?" Waco Bob added. With an eager look on his blunt-angled face, he pulled in his legs again, ready to rise.

"Don't get excited, boys. She's not that much to look at. Fact is, Bert was real disappointed. Why do you think he's off trading with Tacate right now?"

Waco Bob's expression flattened. He flipped his cigarette butt out into the dirt and slumped back in his chair. "So, tell us, how did the job go? How much did you get?"

The lanky one struck a match across his britches and lit his newly rolled cigarette. "I don't think it was smart stealin' the woman. Sheriff Jackson's a rough hombre to mess with already. But with you stealin' his daughter . . ."

"Bean's right," the Southerner drawled, pushing back a battered Confederacy cap. "She's sure to bring a shit pile a trouble down on us. We always been safe here before, but from what I hear, Jackson used to be one of them damn Yankee officers. He might even be able to talk the army into comin' up here lookin' for us."

"Stop worrying. By the time the sheriff figures out I sent him on a wild goose chase down to Mexico, our trail will be too old to read." Chama swung around and started down the steps again. "Now, if you want to jaw anymore, you'll have to walk with me over to Shorty's Cantina. I'm hungry."

Apparently still interested, the men got up, their spurs scraping and jingling on the rough planks as they followed Chama off the porch toward the stone and log-built saloon.

A few yards from it, Chama slowed, allowing the others to catch up. "Has anyone heard anything about the gunrunners?"

"No," Waco Bob said. "But, who knows, with all the trouble in Sioux country, maybe they thought they could do better up Dakota way."

"No," differed another. "They wouldn't take a chance like that. Not while hundreds of soldiers are chargin' all over them prairies this spring. Leastwise that's what they're saying down at Fort Seldon."

Chama hated hearing that. But he knew his fierce "brothers" to the north had the brave strength of their buffalo and the cunning of the mountain cat. They would not tuck their tails between their legs for the bluecoats any more than old Nana or Geronimo.

Reaching the heavy-beamed door of the cantina, Chama swung it open and strode into the dimly lit room. Only three customers sat at one of the dozen or so tables, giving the place a cavelike feeling.

At the far end, Shorty, the balding owner who was almost as wide as he was tall, waddled from around the bar, wiping his hands on his apron. A big smile puffed his already fat cheeks even more. "How you doing, Chama? Hear tell you boys did real fine."

"Fine enough to buy drinks for the house." With only eight customers, counting himself, he didn't mind too much buying the expected round of drinks after a successful robbery. But never would he waste another cent of his rifle money on more than one.

The other men joined his group. Then while Chama shoveled in two bowls of chile beans along with a half dozen tortillas, he gave an abbreviated account of the robbery. Soon the conversation shifted as the others began to brag about their own lawless exploits. As usual, Chama maintained a stoic expression. It would be at cross-purposes to his quest if they knew his opinion of their shabby, senseless lives, devoid of all honor or meaning.

Just as Chama finished his meal, Bert ambled in, hugging a short, wide-hipped Mexican woman to him. The two were laughing and talking at the same time, but in different languages. Upon seeing Chama, Bert headed toward the table. When he reached it, he pulled the woman tighter to him and leered down into the gaping neckline of her peasant blouse. "Ain't she a beaut?"

The woman, now only inches from Chama, giggled, and he smelled the distinct odor of mescal on her breath. Wryly, he noticed that she couldn't seem to focus on one spot. Probably for the best. Getting a good look at her new man would sober the worst swillbelly.

Bert pulled up a chair from the next table and dropped into it, bringing the whore down on top of him. He slung an arm across her thighs and took a handful. "Now, this is the kinda saddle a man can climb into and ride all day an' all night. And that's just what I plan to do after I've had one more whiskey." He swung toward the bar. "Shorty! Your best. All around. And make it quick."

Waco Bob slapped Wormely on the back, but the grin rounding his square face didn't reach his deep-set eyes. "That's my kinda talk. But, Bert, you said you had two women to take care of tonight. Looks to me like you're gonna need a little help. I'd be glad to take this one off your hands."

Bert's own grin vanished. "I'm doin' just fine, Bob. If you're willin' to part with some of that money you stole off those miners last week, I'm sure Tacate can fix you right up, just like me. He's got two more. Speaking of women"—he turned to Chama—"where's the sheriff's daughter?"

"I left her at my cabin."

Wormely draped his other hand over the whore's shoulder and slid it into her blouse, grasping a breast.

She jumped, then giggled and reached for a drink from a tray that Shorty was lowering to the table at that instant.

"Well," Bert said, his mouth grazing her neck, "you tell Miz Jackson I'm gonna be a little busy tonight. But I'll be sure and get to her first thing tomorrow."

As Wormely slobbered over the drunken whore, the others snickered and looked on with the lusting eyes of a pack of dogs on the scent of a bitch.

Chama's stomach began to churn. He came to his feet. "Speaking of the Jackson woman, I'd better take her some food." Wheeling around, he left the rank bunch behind and headed for the kitchen.

* * *

Chama crossed the meadow beneath a moonless, diamond-studded sky on practiced feet, balancing a cloth-covered plate. But he couldn't enjoy the stars' frozen beauty. The bitter taste of the scene he'd just left behind kept intruding. About halfway across he began muttering curses. Finally, he shook his head and spoke out loud. "White men. The whole damned lot of 'em aren't fit for crow bait." The words finally said, his temper began to mellow. By the time he jumped across a narrow spot in the creek and started up his hill, he'd calmed enough to even grant that Karl was a passable white man. And so was Farmer. He missed the good-natured cowpoke who'd robbed a couple of mine payrolls with him last year. By far a better choice than Bert Wormely. But Farmer had taken off at the first sign of snow last winter, and Chama hadn't seen him since. His friend would probably pop up soon, though, if he hadn't gotten himself shot or thrown in jail.

Chama reached the door of the cabin and noticed light seeping through the cracks, but he heard no sound. He rapped a couple of times with his free hand and pushed it open.

At his first glimpse, all he saw was hair. Long, silky. It fell in the softest waves, shimmering silver and gold as the woman brushed down its length. As she slowly turned toward him in the amber glow of the lantern, his heart careened crazily.

She dropped her hands to her sides and looked at him with those incredible eyes that now seemed much darker, wider. They held no hint of fear. Only a welcome.

No doubt he was having a vision, and after only one drink. He closed his eyes. When he reopened them, she remained as before. He reached out and touched an arm. Smooth. And it radiated the warmth of flesh. This couldn't be a ghost. This was a beautiful woman. And she stood waiting in his cabin, wearing nothing but a sleeveless night shift that stretched tight across a most generous display of breasts. The deeply scooped neckline revealed much of their swell. Chama's breath caught as his gaze lingered there, the palms of his hands tingling with his desire to touch them, hold them.

The woman's own breathing quickened.

His attention drifted downward, and he noted the looseness of the muslin gown as it dropped past her waist, then tightened somewhat again as it spilled over her hips before stopping a good foot above the floor. And damn, but the woman did have legs . . . long, handsomely turned. And trim, as were her ankles and feet.

This was impossible. The woman couldn't possibly be this gorgeous.

He sent his gaze on a return trip up her figure. If anything, he viewed even more loveliness. Hell's own fire, if she wasn't the most beautiful woman he'd ever seen.

Gone was the bonnet, the dirty canvas gloves, the work boots. That faded shirt and heavy limp skirt. And from that heap of rags had emerged a glorious golden butterfly. Yet there was more. Much more. Her loveliness had a strength to it. Even in the slender turn of her arms and neck he saw it.

His gaze traveled upward to her face, and again as always, her mystical eyes captivated him as they held his. After a long moment, he managed to leave them and begin a visual tracing of her other features, the brows that flared wide, the defined cheekbones accenting a delicately curved jaw, but most of all, he savored the lips, generous and vulnerable in their softness.

He'd been with her for three days, he'd even put salve on that face. How could he have been so blind? Hell, he'd even slept next to her, had wrapped himself all around her.

At the last thought, he felt himself begin to harden.

"The food you're carrying, is it for me?" Her voice came out in a feathery whisper.

"Food? Oh, yeah. I thought you might be hungry." Then realizing he'd been staring at her with his tongue practically hanging out, Chama lowered his eyes to the plate in his hand. He placed it on the table. But his gaze chased back to her again, and he began once more to take in every curve of her body, every silken tendril of hair.

She remained achingly still as he tarried . . .

. . . *until his predicament suddenly struck him.* "I have to go! I have some business to take care of."

The woman's lips parted in surprise.
One last look, then he swung away, starting out the door.

She'd stood before him as brazenly as any saloon girl and almost as naked as a holiday turkey. Carrie didn't think she could've given a more blatant invitation without actually speaking the unspeakable. *And he had looked interested.* He had. Those intense coal-black eyes of his had fairly glowed as they burned paths across her skin before he actually reached out and touched her. Yet, strangely, it had been with only two fingers, and ever so lightly. His chest, however, seemed to double in size. And couldn't she see those muscled arms beneath his sleeves ready themselves to take her?

Carrie heaved a long ragged breath and closed her eyes. When he'd touched her, every taut nerve within her had cried to fly for the door. Remaining still had taken every ounce of will she could gather. For all the good it had done her. Her "brave and fearless" captor beat her to it. What now? If she couldn't lure him to stay in the same room for more than a minute at a time, how would she ever entice him into keeping her?

Remembering the brush in her hand, she picked up a hank of hair and yanked the bristles through it in frustrated fervor until she felt a cold draft wash over her feet. She noticed that the door had not latched. It stood open a few inches. She went to close it.

As her hand touched wood, a gunshot rang out across the clearing. Then another. The echoes bounced back and forth across the valley until they eventually disappeared into the distant night.

More sounds followed—men's laughter and the shrieking titter of a woman.

Carrie's hand went to her breast.

9

CHAMA SPRINTED ACROSS the field. He was filled with a tremendous urgency to reach the cantina before Wormely left for the night with his new woman. He burst through the door and, to his relief, found Bert seated at the table, his hands still kneading the whore's plump flesh.

She seemed to be enjoying the attention as she lolled her head on his shoulder and smiled drunkenly.

And the rest of the little party continued to look at her with those same leers while the Southerner gave the lurid details of his last visit to a Juarez bordello.

Bert saw Chama approach. His grin widened and he picked up his glass. "Thought you left. Sit down, have another drink. I'm buyin'." He slapped the empty seat next to him while yelling at the bartender for another round.

Aware that the scrawny runt was in high spirits, Chama felt he would have no trouble getting Bert to agree to his proposal. "Watching you there, so happy with your new gal, got me to thinking," he began, swinging around the empty chair and straddling it. "I know the Jackson woman isn't much to look at, but she's real quiet. I don't think she'd be too much bother to keep around. Besides, like you said, it isn't good for a man to stay to himself all the time."

"You mean it ain't good for a man to *sleep* alone all the time." Chuckling, Bert grabbed one of the woman's plump breasts and jiggled it.

She yipped and slapped playfully at his hand.

Waco Bob scooted his chair closer as he tittered along with Bert and the others. Most likely there'd be blood spilled over the woman before the night was spent.

"Well," Chama said, pulling a fold of bills from his pocket, "I never was one for sharing a woman, so how about I buy you out of your third. Say, for two hundred." He peeled off the correct number of bank notes and fanned them out on the table in front of Bert.

The woman grabbed them up and stuffed them down the wide neck of her gathered blouse. "He have me. Is plenty."

Bert wasted no time diving after the wad while she giggled and bobbed around. Succeeding within a few seconds, he brought out the cash and counted it. He then looked up at Chama with a pleased scar-jagged grin and shoved the money into the woman's blouse again. "You must want the sheriff's daughter purty bad. She just cost you two of those precious rifles you're always buying. And you still got the Swede's share to go."

"That's right. Guess I'd better go take care of that right now." He stood up and gave a short nod, then turned toward the door. "See you boys later."

While Chama walked to the entrance, Bert's raised voice chased after him. "Here's to the bravest man in the territory! The man who's gonna bed Jackson's daughter! Wonder just how sharp the sheriff keeps that knife of his."

The following loud laughter and clink of toasting glasses irritated Chama as he strode out the door. Yet he couldn't deny the fact that as long as he kept the woman, Jackson never would give up the search.

Cutting through an encampment of wickiups, the vision of the willowy woman standing in a sunny swirl of waist-length hair told him she was worth the risk. And, besides, he reassured himself, no white man had ever found this valley on his own. As long as she was kept safely tucked away here, Chama would have nothing to fear from her father.

After passing several more clusters of dwellings, mostly dimly lit shanties and tents, Chama reached the cabin Karl Shipstead had rented from Rodriguez for the summer. It huddled with others around a common yard where in the daytime women staying at the *rancheria* came to share a large beehive-shaped oven and the latest gossip. The fact that the women continued to perform the ordinary chores of daily life in this otherwise lawless place had often been a wonderment to Chama. Would the sheriff's daughter, ripped from her home and everything she held dear, also soon join the others as if nothing had ever happened to her?

As Chama rapped on their door, he thought of Karl's young, sweet-faced Esperanza, who was not much past a child. Not only had she readily adjusted to life with an outlaw after being abducted by Apaches, but anyone could see she loved her big Swede.

A very pregnant Esperanza answered his knock. Upon recognizing him, a lively smile dimpled her cheeks. "Señor José, *es mucho* long time since you *entrada la casa* of *mi* husband. You *es muy* welcome." She turned to Karl, who sat slumped in a rocking chair in the corner.

He didn't seem to notice anyone had come in as he lazily rocked his small sleeping child in one arm while holding a jar of whiskey in his free hand.

"Karl," she called in a merry voice. "See who comes."

Shipstead's chin bobbed upward, and his gaze settled on Chama. "What brings you here tonight? Is something wrong?"

"No. I knew you were worried about your little Ingacita, so I dropped by to see how she is." Ingacita. Chama always found the name hard to say with a straight face. Only in a mixed-up place like a Comanchero camp would one hear a Swedish name with a Spanish endearment tacked on the end. But then, he supposed with a snort, it couldn't be any odder than what the Apaches called him—Chamasay—their version of Chama José, the nickname given him during his days at the orphanage. Since there had been two other Josés—the Spanish translation of Joseph—and since he kept wandering off to the nearby river, the priest had added the stream's name to his.

"Oh, the baby!" Esperanza said, beaming. "She *es mucho* better. She had *mucho fiebre* . . . fever. I think maybe she die. I am so . . . how you say . . . afraid. But then I remember Baby Jésus." She pointed to the small carving of a Madonna with child resting on a shelf beside the door. "I know He loves babies, even in this bad place. So I light a candle and say the *rosario* many times. And I make *la promesa*. I say, 'Baby Jésús, if you make *mi pocacita* better, we go from this bad place and no come back. We take our little ones and go.' And he did! Baby Jesús make the miracle. Ingacita, she was *muy* hot. And just like this"—she snapped her fingers—"the fever, she is gone. It is big miracle!"

"That's wonderful." Chama couldn't help matching her happy grin as he looked from her to Karl, who scrunched one cheek and shrugged.

Suddenly remembering her manners, Esperanza asked in a rush, "You want something to drink? Coffee?"

"*Gracias*, no. I just stopped by for a minute." He turned to his whiskey-mellowed friend. "Karl, you don't mind if I keep the Jackson woman for myself, do you? I just bought out Dirty Bert for two hundred dollars. I'd be willing to do the same for you."

"Glad to hear you've decided to keep Wormely away from her," Karl said as he settled the tot more comfortably on his lap. "I never did hold with what happens to women who get brought here."

"Then you'll take the two hundred for your share of her?"

"Keep your money. Instead, when Esperanza has the new baby and can travel again, I'd be beholden to you if you'd guide us outta here and down to Chihuahua. That's where Esperanza's kinfolks is. And with the kinda money we got robbin' Jackson's bank, I hear a man can live like a king down there. Besides," he added with a sheepish grin, "she's got her heart set on leavin'. And I sorta promised."

Chama kept his own face straight as he answered. It wouldn't do to let Karl see that he knew how henpecked his friend had become. All the tiny little señorita had to do was look up at Karl with those big sad eyes and he'd do anything she asked just to make her smile again. "Sure thing. Be glad to. Anytime you're ready, just let me know." He took a backward step. "Well, guess I'd better be going. Good night. Give Ingacita a big kiss for me when she wakes up."

Chama couldn't remember when he'd had a lighter heart as he returned to his cabin on the hill. A woman had been delivered to him as if from the sky above, and on her way to him, she'd captured all the brilliance of the sun in her hair, and all the magic of the turquoise in her eyes. Ysun, the Apache's Creator of Life, must have given her to him for helping his people. Yes, she was a most wondrous gift.

His hands trembled with anticipation as he lifted the latch and walked inside. The soft glow of the turned-down lamp met him . . . and nothing else! *She was missing.* His heart began pumping hard against his ribs as he glanced swiftly around the shadowy room. Then, looking down, he found her lying in his bed at the far end. Exhaling a pent-up breath, he moved past the table toward her.

Her eyes were closed, and she seemed to be asleep. In that peaceful state, she looked even more beautiful, if that were possible. She lay pillowed in a swirl of her magnificent hair, one of her hands resting against her cheek. The coarseness of his gray army blanket stopping just below her shoulders made her skin appear even more delicate, more creamy, more touchable.

Something white caught his eye—her night shift. It covered the footboard. *Not her body.*

He felt the lurch of his heart all the way to his groin.

Driven by urgency, he wheeled away to his clothing trunk and pulled out a pair of soft cotton trousers and his moccasins. From the shelf above, he snatched soap and a towel and rushed outside.

At the slam of the door, Carrie's eyes flew open. He'd left again! How much more of this torturous waiting could she take? Short of forfeiting what was left of her pride by opening her arms to him, what else could she have done? After all, she'd climbed into his bed, for heaven's sake.

She eased up onto her elbow, stiff with anxiety, and scanned the area where she'd heard him rummaging about. On the shelf by the mirror she noticed the soap was missing from its dish, and the towel she'd left hooked on a nail beside it was also gone. Perhaps she'd been too quick to think the worst. Maybe all the man had done was go down to the stream to wash.

"Yes, he's washing up," she sighed and lay back down. And she really should be grateful. Not only was this darkly handsome outlaw pleasing to look at—in a frightening sort of way—he'd always been considerate of her, *and* he valued his cleanliness, something she'd rarely seen among the saddle tramps who'd been roaming up and down the Rio Grande Valley since the war. And as for the Indian side of him, the Apaches she'd seen looked, more often than not, as if they'd just blown in on a dust storm. Yes, there was no denying it, she really should be grateful.

Nonetheless, the tension in her spread into another anxious quiver as it traveled to her farthest reaches at the mere thought of him lying with her. Clutching the blanket to her, she pulled it up to her neck. To be touched by this man, any man after the last time with Michael. And it had been years ago. Seven, hadn't it? She'd been much younger then, eighteen, when for a few short weeks he'd brought new hope into her life. And love.

Carrie slipped her hands beneath the cover and smoothed them over her body. A delicious tingle warmed every place she touched at the remembrance of the handful of sweet times when she and Michael had been together. Closing her eyes, she envisioned, as she hadn't let herself do in years, that buoyant Irish smile of his and his bowler tilted to a jaunty slant, that hat that could never even begin to contain his riot of red curls. She would never forget the first day she saw him.

She'd just pulled the wagon team to a stop in front of the general store when he came strutting across the boardwalk to her. He'd tipped his hat and flashed that grin. His whole face lit up, freckles and all.

"Might I have the supreme pleasure," he'd asked in his lilting brogue, "o' helpin' down the fairest maiden of the realm?"

And by the time he had, she'd fallen in love with the very first brave knight willing to approach her and risk the wrath of her violent-tempered father.

As it turned out, Michael was new to the territory, brought in from New York by a mining company, and hadn't heard of the sheriff's reputation. By the time he did, he was already too much in love to give up his Caroline. And they had been careful. So careful. Michael never ventured out to her house unless he was sure Father was detained in town.

Carrie could feel his arms around her even now, feel his whispered words at her ear as he told her time and again how they would elope as soon as he had enough cash saved. How they would run away to Wyoming where homestead land was just waiting for the asking.

Then it happened. One month, almost to the day, before they were set to leave. Just one more month before she would've escaped. Been free. Would've had a life.

Carrie's heart filled with the same old bitterness, regret, and the same hatred she also felt for her own cowardice. After all the weeks, months, the years she spent dreaming of various ways to torture her father, kill him for Michael's sake as well as all his other atrocities, she'd never mustered the nerve to do it. No matter how viciously she berated herself for her failure while he was away, each time he walked in the door, his steely alertness, the authority in his eyes overpowered her as they raked over her. Even now, here, Carrie shuddered. And, of course, there'd also been the fear of being cast into another hell—the eternal one.

"So, Father," Carrie whispered wearily as she curled onto her side, "you won again. Like always. No matter how many of us you destroy." And he was surely on his way. Not so much to save her, she knew, but to take back all that the outlaws had stolen from him. To make certain everyone knew that no one messed with the sheriff of La Mesilla, the future governor of New Mexico.

Realizing the hateful depths to which her memories had taken her, Carrie wrenched her thoughts back to this afternoon and when she'd first seen the beauty of this secret valley. She imagined herself standing again on the ledge, looking across to the spectacular waterfall, the rainbow shimmering in an arc before it, the walls turned golden by the slanting sun . . .

The door creaked open.

Chama.

With her pulse throbbing at her temples, Carrie feigned sleep again as he stepped almost soundlessly into the room. Hearing him replace the soap in its dish, she peeked at him through a veil of lashes.

Naked to the waist, his moist back took on a lustrous glow in the lamplight, accentuating his superbly muscled build. Her gaze fixed on to his powerful shoulders as he hung up the towel . . . a towel that had no more than two hours before dried her own dripping body. In that instance of realization, a shiver of anticipation sped from her heart down to an inner hunger—a hunger she thought had died so long ago with Michael.

Chama turned toward her.

She quickly closed her eyes and waited, hoping desperately he couldn't see the pounding of her heart beneath the covers. For the longest moment there was no sound, no movement, and she knew he looked at her.

She thought her heart would explode before she finally heard him lift the glass chimney and blow out the flame. Daring to open her eyes, she was met by a blackness so complete, she could scarcely discern his form as he removed the soft cotton trousers and moccasins he'd worn on his return to the cabin.

He took hold of the blanket and turned it back.

He was naked, and he was climbing into her bed. She lost her breath.

The man slid his cool, moist body down alongside her own hot one and rolled to face her.

The moment had arrived. Her one chance to bind this man to her before Bert came. Swallowing down her fear, she found herself feeling a passion that had been buried for far too long. She reached up and brushed across his jaw with tingling fingers, then laced them into his hair.

Surprised but very pleased by her overture, Chama took the woman into his arms and pulled her close. As her warmth melted into him, he buried his face in the hair at her neck, reveling in its luxuriant softness and the clean scent of soap. He then slowly, very slowly, began to nuzzle her throat, not wanting to move too fast and frighten her. He didn't kid himself. He knew she was offering herself to him in the desperate hope he would save her from Wormely.

Guilt began to seep into his spirit. Had his lust for this woman driven him to become the same as those men at the cantina or those who had degraded and finally killed his mother? With unparalleled disappointment he knew he could not take advantage of her, do this to her. He would have to tell her that Bert wouldn't be coming.

"Chama," the Jackson woman sighed softly, causing his heart to kick. She moved a hand to the back of his head, drew him closer while her other hand began tracing up and down his back until all logical thought and every honorable intention spilled away.

There was nothing but the feel of her breasts pressed against his chest, her leg wedged against his hardening arousal, the feathery pants of her breath at his temple.

He began blazing a trail of kisses up to her cheek, across to one eye, then the other. The tip of her nose. Each corner of her mouth.

Carrie never dreamed any man could make love with such tender passion, let alone a savage Comanchero. Her mind began to fuzz, then became even more muddled with each of his new ventures until clear thought became impossible. Yet her hands seemed to know instinctively where they needed to be as they explored the smooth hard planes of his back and downward.

She felt the muscles along his spine tense beneath her hands as he pressed harder against her body, as his embrace became more urgent and his mouth fully claimed hers. And she felt the strength of his pounding heart against her breast, his desire.

She was sure he could feel hers, too, as he deepened the kiss, his tongue entering her mouth, exploring, seeking.

For no more than a second she hesitated, then joined him in a fiery duel. She quickly reached the same peak of hunger, a hunger so intense, every sensitive spot on her body clamored for the same. She began moving her hips against him in an age-old invitation.

His kiss became even more insistent as he lowered a hand to her bottom and held her tightly against the length of his desire.

The feel of its smooth throbbing hardness, knowing where it would soon be, so inflamed her, she had to break away from his lips to take in more air.

Chama knew she wanted him as much as he did her from the sound of her ragged breathing, the swiftness of her electrifying hands as they moved up and down his back, and the path she opened to him as she moved one leg up and over his. But logic told him he must be having a peyote-induced dream, because this vision could be no other than the Apaches' White Painted Woman, wrapped in her clothing of light. A goddess, coming to him on a bolt of lightning.

He parted from her just enough to cup the full roundness of a breast.

She gasped as he did and pressed harder against his engorged shaft.

He, too, groaned at the sweet pain, but would not be rushed. There was so much yet to discover. He ran his thumb over her nipple and reveled in the way it hardened into a tight nub. He took it into his mouth and drew on it deeply.

A tremor coursed her body, and her hands flew up to his head, hugging him closer to her breast. Then she stopped breathing. Froze.

When he began to tease her crest with his tongue, she started to pant again, and one of her hands left his hair and slid along his side, then slipped down to his belly, continuing downward, until he found himself freezing into waiting stillness.

She touched that most sensitive part of him, and he, too, caught his breath.

Her hand encased his length and began to move back and forth, driving him to the edge of sanity, and he knew exploring every inch of her lush body would have to wait—for his impatient seed would not. He rolled her onto her back and moved over her.

She parted herself for him in a welcoming invitation, sparking in him unbridled pleasure as he guided himself into her. With every ounce of willpower, he restrained from taking her swiftly. Instead, he slid inward with deliberate yet agonizing slowness, wanting to feel every moist, hot inch of her as she closed around him.

She arched recklessly against him, swiftly, taking him all the way inside her.

He remained deep within her for a moment, fully sheathed in her pulsating passion, reveling in their oneness. Then he closed his mouth over hers and began to withdraw.

As he did, Carrie felt utterly empty where his immense manhood had been. Her throat caught on a sob, and she knew she was crying. But it had been so long since . . . So very, very long. And Chama was so gentle, so giving.

Her body clamored for his return. She begged for more by returning his kiss with fevered urgency.

His tongue thrust into her mouth. At the same instant he dove into her.

She met him with matching ardor, arching to take him deeper with each joining, wanting more, ever more. She wrapped her arms and legs around him, taking him again and again as he came into her with increasing swiftness until she felt him become so engorged, she thought she'd die from ecstasy. Suddenly she exploded into a thousand pieces, melting all around him. And from somewhere in the distance, she heard herself cry out.

An answering shudder ran through him as he, too, erupted within her, sending her into another dazzling explosion that rained heavenly fire through her, over her.

Then, on the longest groan, he stopped moving and settled his weight over her. He encircled her head with his arms and kissed her neck, her shoulder, an ear, a cheek . . .

Abruptly he stopped. "You're crying. Did I hurt you?"

Feeling foolish, she removed one of the hands she was using to caress his back and swiped at her tears. "No, not in the least. You were—you—" Her words became lost on a sob she tried desperately to smother.

He tensed and started to raise up.

She reached for him and brought him back. "Please, stay," she whispered, then swallowed and tried again to explain, despite the tears that refused to stop streaming down her face. "It's just . . . I—I've been alone for a very long time. It's been so long. I . . ."

Whatever else she might have said was lost as he blanketed himself over her again and began to kiss away each and every teardrop.

❧ 10 ❧

CHAMA AWAKENED TO something tickling his nose. He brushed it away, and a wisp of silky hair teased his fingertips. Smiling lazily, he opened his eyes to the dim slices of light peeking past the edges of the door and the board shutters. One touched the blond head on his shoulder. His woman from the sky was still with him. He drank in the softness of her warm body as he curled snugly around it. Then remembering the previous night's fiery passion, his heart leapt.

Filled to near bursting with emotion, he stopped himself just short of giving her a big squeeze. She looked so peaceful after the hard three days she'd just spent. She needed her rest . . . for a few more minutes, anyway, he thought as he considered the pleasure of taking her again this morning. Slowly, this time very slowly.

At the thought, he began to harden against her tender rounded bottom. He raised up on an elbow. As he did, the blanket slid down far enough to expose a creamy shoulder and the upper swell of her breasts. "God Almighty," he whispered, his gaze traveling up to the delicate curve of her jaw, her slightly tipped nose, the amber lashes. She was so beautiful. Absolutely perfect. Yet, from her response last night, she'd been sorely neglected.

Then an ugly picture intruded, one of Bert's scrawny grasping hands. Chama's stomach clinched, followed by the hottest rage. Not in a hundred seasons would he let the mangy bastard lay hands on her again. Never. He'd kill him first.

The woman sighed and snuggled closer.

When she did, he could feel all the fury leave him as if she were drawing it away, absorbing it into herself.

As the realization took hold, a wariness filled Chama. Even in her sleep, this one could take his power. Maybe having her here wasn't such a good idea after all.

Pondering that thought, Chama slipped his arm from under her and eased out of bed. As he placed his feet on the icy floor he noticed the blanket had slipped down to the woman's waist. A lock of hair curled carelessly over her lush endowments. Even in disarray, she looked gorgeous. He reached down to cover her against the morning chill and when he did, he couldn't resist running his fingers through the silky strand.

Catching himself beginning to fall under her spell again, Chama quickly located his white cotton pantalones and pulled them on, then slipped into his moccasins. After putting on a matching loose shirt, he belted the comfortable outfit with a colorful woven tie. Then with one last look at the sleeping woman, he grabbed the sack of coffee grounds from beneath the counter board and went outside.

A pine-scented crystalline morning greeted him.

Taking a deep breath, he felt himself also filling with a deep sense of well-being. He couldn't remember when he'd felt so good.

The rich aroma of freshly brewed coffee awakened Carrie. She let her eyes drift open and, stretching languidly, smiled as she became aware of her surroundings and the source of the coffee. Chama had obviously made it. For her? Her thoughts swung to the night before, and winds of excitement swept across every wondrous place he'd touched . . . entered.

Just as suddenly, the hottest embarrassment turned her cheeks to flame. How could she have been so utterly wanton? Even with Michael she'd always had to be coaxed.

But, my, hadn't it been wonderful? she thought as joy spiraled through her once more. And if she wasn't mistaken, hadn't he even told her she was beautiful afterward when he kissed and held her until she'd fallen asleep?

Carrie hugged herself at the realization of this tenderest yet of his gestures. A man like that wouldn't give her to Bert. Chama couldn't, even if he did rob banks for a living—*her father's bank, no less.* She envisioned the strangled expression her father would have if he knew how much she'd relished letting a Comanchero touch her. *Let him? I begged him.* The memory brought on another wave of shame. She quickly climbed out of bed, feeling a need to clothe herself. Then on a lighter thought, she smiled. *But wouldn't I just love to see Father's face if I told him that.*

She retrieved the night shift from the foot rail and tossed it on, then ran the brush through her hair, the one she'd found the night before in the trunk of woman's clothes.

Another woman. Someone else had slept in this bed, known his touch.

She forced aside the unsettling thought, not wanting anything to steal her newfound joy.

After untangling her locks and combing through their length until they shone, she picked up a piece of twine lying on the shelf and moved to the looking glass to tie back the weighty mass. But, suddenly, it seemed a shame to entrap it, even if her father always did say only slovenly, wanton women let their hair go undressed.

"And women who were out from under their father's thumb," she added aloud, speaking with triumph into the mirror. "Besides, I do feel wanton this morning. Deliciously wanton." With a jaunty grin, she turned her head from side to side, watching her tresses flow and swirl all around her. The grin bubbled into laughter as she moved away and fairly floated past the table to the kitchen shelves. Fetching a tin cup, she sauntered outside for some of her considerate lover's coffee.

The sunlight danced with the woman, fluttering among the gently blowing waves of her hair as she moved in long lissome strides toward him on bare feet. As she walked into the shade, the sun followed, silhouetting her flowing grace within its halo.

Chama didn't move from his seat by the fire. He couldn't bring himself to intrude on the woman's morning song with the sun.

A distant clanging echoed across the meadow from the *rancheria,* jerking him back to his senses. Instantly he tossed aside his half-full cup and, springing to his feet, charged around the campfire.

The woman's eyes widened. She cringed and thrust out her hands to ward him off.

He grabbed an arm and dragged her back into the cabin, not noticing how hard he breathed until the door was safely shut behind them and he stood over her. "Are you crazy? Don't you know where you are?"

Her eyes held the fear of a trapped deer. She opened her mouth, but a long second passed before anything emerged. "I was just—"

"You was just!" he shot back, his anger mounting. "You were just about to show yourself off to the whole damned camp!" He emphasized his words by clutching her shoulders. Then, inhaling deeply to regain control of himself, he continued. "This is a Comanchero camp. Most of the men who come through here rape and kill for the sport of it. And worse, they run in packs. One look at you, and they'll be on you like dogs fighting over a juicy bone."

"But, I—"

"No buts. You listen to me. I told those men last night I was keeping you for myself. But I also said you weren't much to look at."

"You told them you were keeping me for yourself?" The storm in her aqua eyes calmed to less-troubled pools.

He refused to let them sway him, though he did notice his voice softened slightly with his next words. "Yes, but if they get a good look at you, I'll have to stand guard over you day and night. And, believe me, that isn't the way I plan to spend the rest of the summer."

"The rest of the summer?" She didn't sound nearly as relieved as he thought she'd be. *"You're keeping me here till autumn?"*

"It's either the men over there or me." Instantly wishing he hadn't retorted in such a heartless manner, he added, "I thought that was what you wanted."

She lowered her lashes. "With the Comancheros just across the meadow, they're bound to see me. Or do you plan to keep me locked up in this cabin?"

"No," Chama said, raising her chin. "But I do want you to get your own clothes on again."

"But they're—"

"And the bonnet," he interrupted with force. "I don't ever want to catch you out of this cabin without it hiding your hair." He reached out and touched a strand. Then, feeling himself weakening, he quickly retrieved his fingers and straightened to his full height. "And I want you back in those floppy old boots."

"The boots, too?" she wailed.

"Yes." Glancing around the room, he couldn't find any of her things. "Where are your clothes?"

"Everything was so filthy. I washed them last night and hung them on some bushes out back."

"I'll go get 'em." He released her and started for the door. But when he reached it, he turned back. Feeling a little embarrassed, he couldn't help his grin as he asked, "By the way, what's your given name?"

She tilted her head, and a smile lifted one corner of her mouth. "Carrie. My name's Carrie."

When Chama returned with her clothes, she noticed all trace of humor in his expression had disappeared. "The only thing I can find for breakfast," she said, hoping to lighten the mood again, "is the makings for biscuits and some beef jerky. I could boil it a few minutes to soften it, if you like."

He slowly surveyed the storage area before returning to her. "Sure. Anything's fine." Then, without another word, he strode outside again.

His abruptness disturbed her. She hoped he was simply being a gentleman by allowing her time to change—yet she doubted it.

After she'd prepared their meager breakfast over the campfire and brought it inside, Chama followed with the coffee and sat on the opposite bench from her. On occasion while they ate, she felt his eyes on her, but he never spoke. It was as if he'd withdrawn completely. Uncertain of where she stood with him, she also kept her thoughts, her anxieties, to herself.

Toward the end of the meal, Carrie's gaze drifted to the trunk of women's clothing, and another disturbing question snatched at her. Why had the woman, Juanita, run off in such a hurry that she'd even left behind her personal things?

Finishing his plateful, Chama gulped down the last of his coffee and rose to his feet, then started for the door. "I'm going over to the store for supplies. You stay inside while I'm gone."

Carrie stood up and followed him as far as the door, but he didn't look back as he strode down the hill. At the bottom, he leapt with ease across the narrow but swift stream, and her gaze swept past him to the *rancheria*. She felt more tension building in her chest.

"No. I won't let myself think about that," she said out loud, banishing any thought that he'd decided not to keep her after all, and was going to that terrible place to tell Bert. "He said he was going there for supplies, and he hasn't lied yet."

She firmly closed the door, determined not to worry another second. Spotting the dirty dishes, she started clearing the table.

Upon reaching the far side of the meadow, Chama turned and looked back at the wooded knoll and especially the small clearing in front of the cabin door. Taking into account the distance and the scattering of trees between him and the hill, he knew a clear view of the woman would have been difficult from the *rancheria*, and the anxiety that had been nagging at him since she'd exposed herself eased off. Feeling far more relaxed, he swung back and walked the rest of the way to Rodriguez's store.

The same men plus a couple more sat on the porch just as they had the night before. Some sat in chairs while others squatted on the steps or lounged against the posts. Their talk ran free as usual.

A couple of the heavily armed men noticed Chama and touched their hat brims in greeting.

Another who'd been facing the opposite direction turned around. "Well," he said, his whisker-stubbled jaw slanting into a sneer as he stuck his thumbs in his belt, "if it ain't the generous benefactor of the noble red man."

Chama bristled at the remark. He had no use for Stiles, Three-Fingered Mike's second in command. He wouldn't mind in the least taking the sneaky son of a bitch down a notch or two.

"A few minutes ago," Waco Bob said, coming to his feet, "a bunch of Injuns come riding in here asking for you."

"Leastways," Stiles said, nosing in again, "we think it was you they was asking for. They said they was looking for the man with many tongues. Open your mouth," he jeered. "If you got more than one wagging around in there, you're it."

Chama hardly noticed the other men's laughter as he strode, fists ready, up the steps toward Stiles.

The lanky one who'd been with the others the night before shoved away from the post he'd been leaning against and moved into Chama's path. "They looked like Plains Indians. Kiowa. Or maybe Comanche. The fame of your generosity must be spreading far and wide, 'cause they said they was here for them rifles you hand out. You know, like rock candy."

"I'll tell you one thing for sure," Waco Bob declared from around a stubby cigar jammed in his mouth as he lifted his black-clad frame up from his chair, "if one of them redskins ever takes a shot at me, I'll be looking for you."

Chama noted that the men's laughter had ceased. Surly expressions now replaced their humor as they began to bristle. Eight-to-one odds were not good. His "brothers" had great need of him—too great to risk getting killed. Also, after last night with the woman ... No, it was not a good time to die. He relaxed his stance and managed a nonchalant one-sided smile. "You planning on joining the army anytime soon?"

"Hell, no." Waco Bob spit out the smelly butt. "They'd as soon hang me as look at me."

"Well then, just stay out of the way and you won't have anything to worry about. It's the army we're at war with."

Chama returned his attention to the long-shanked one. "Which way did the braves go?"

The man settled against the post again and pointed upstream. "I shooed 'em on outta here. Sent 'em back yonder, where them two Kwahadis pitched them prairie tents. Told 'em I'd let you know they was here."

"Thanks." Glad to leave the men behind, Chama veered across to the west end of the meadow, then walked a half mile or so deeper into the thickly forested valley until he neared a small clearing. Seeing the buffalo-hide tepees with their owners' deeds painted proudly on them, he paused. The rare sight of a tepee in Apache territory reminded him of the most exciting days of his young years, the times when he and his mother followed behind the soldiers to yet another outpost along the Santa Fe Trail. Each evening, he remembered, he would help her pitch one. During those trips, his mother always seemed more alive, too, and she would tell him of the great buffalo hunts her people went on each summer.

As Chama watched the new arrivals busily clearing the ground and cutting poles to support the tepees they would raise alongside their brothers', Two Bears, one of the Kwahadis in fringed deerskin, saw him and lifted a hand.

Chama smiled and returned the greeting. He had a special respect for men from this last tribe of the Comanche nation to surrender to the army. In the four years since the American government had managed to force them onto the reservation north of Red River, it was not uncommon for Chama to come across two or three runaway braves heading west toward the shrinking remains of Apacheria.

Chama approached camp, and the newcomers, who looked as if they'd been traveling for quite a while, stopped work and eyed him guardedly. But when Two Bears strode up, grinning, and gave Chama a big hug and a slap on the back, the others relaxed.

Two Bears introduced him to the six strangers as Chamasay, the one of many tongues.

In a friendly manner, Chama smiled and nodded at the first five Comanches, who dressed far more resplendently in their feathers and beaded buckskins than their Apache cousins. When the last one introduced himself in the dialect of Chama's mother, Chama was so thrilled he grabbed the man and gave him a resounding hug. Then, stepping back, he spoke in the same tongue to the surprised one. "I, too, am Kiowa. We are 'brothers.' "

At his statement, a joyful grin spread across the young brave's face, and he returned Chama's embrace with equal fervor.

Chama spent the remainder of the morning with the renegades, and while the other Kwahadi, Strong Hand, roasted chunks of venison over a small fire, Chama listened raptly to the braves reminisce in their own dialects about the days when they were free to roam, the days when they pitched their tepees wherever the setting sun found them. Then, as usual around the campfire, each of them began to brag about his past feats against the shaggy-coated buffalo and to recite the various heroic acts against the enemy that had earned him each feather he wore. Whenever a tale would become too tall, too brave, the others laughed and poked fun.

Later, after the men had eaten their fill, the conversation shifted to talk of the white devils who kept coming, chopping down their trees, plowing up the prairie grass. The easy laughter ceased, and the men grew quiet as one of the Comanches mentioned the deliberate wasteful slaughter of the buffalo by the white eyes. Now the great animals that had been beyond number came no more . . . these buffalo that in the past had provided everything for them—from tools to food, to shelter, clothes, fuel, and so much more. Chama could see from the steely glint of the men's eyes the extent of their hatred for this new enemy. This enemy who now came beyond number. Hunger now drove the people onto the reservations of those who had caused their hunger in the first place. They were left to eat rancid meat or starve.

One of the youngest Comanche braves sprang to his feet in a fighting crouch. He pulled his knife and jabbed as if the enemy were before him. "I, Spotted Horse," he proclaimed in a loud voice, "vow I will take no wife until all white dogs are driven from our hunting grounds and the Great Spirit again sends the buffalo across our land."

Two others jumped up and pulled their own blades.

A man in his thirties, easily the oldest in the group, remained seated. He eyed the rash younger ones, then turned to Chama. "We were traveling south to Mexico where the long knives do not follow. We crossed trails with a Mimbre Apache hunting party. We admired their new rifles. They say a man, Chamasay, makes a gift of them during the summer moons at the *rancheria* of the Comanchero. They ride with us, show us the path through the high walls. Now we are here to ask Chamasay if the Mimbres speak truth."

The younger braves, their interest obvious, dropped down to the ground again and rejoined the circle.

"Did they tell you," Chama asked, "that you must vow to kill two bluecoats for the gift of a rifle?"

"Yes. And it will be done with great pleasure."

Chama looked around the circle, including them all. "Then you will each receive a repeater rifle and two hundred rounds of ammunition when the gunrunners arrive. They should be here very soon, so you will not have long to wait."

Every face brightened at the prospect of receiving the coveted repeaters. Their spirits darkened only slightly by Chama's next words.

"Stay away from the store and the cantina. Most of the men here have evil spirits in them. Do not trust them. If you need something, come to my cabin, and I will get it for you. It is the one downstream from here." As he pointed in that direction, Chama remembered his new woman and envisioned her eyes of turquoise, eyes he hoped would be waiting for him alone. With a sudden, undeniable urge to return to her, he rose to his feet.

≈ 11 ≈

JUST OUTSIDE, A twig snapped.

Carrie swung toward the opening and listened.

Needles crunched. Again. Someone was sneaking up to the side of the house.

Fighting down her panic, Carrie backed on silent feet to the table. Without taking her eyes off the window, she felt around until her hand bumped into the paring knife she'd used to scrape off some table splinters. She picked it up, then edged toward the side of the window.

Hearing the heavy breathing of the skulker, Carrie held her own as she flattened herself against the wall, knife raised. Could it be Bert? Or someone even more horrible?

A brown head jutted in.

Carrie lunged forward. Stopped. "A deer!"

The startled animal reared up, then crashed away in a swift retreat through the undergrowth, disappearing into the forest.

With a sputter of relieved laughter, Carrie placed her empty hand to her racing heart as she moved on wobbly legs toward the nearest bench.

As she reached it, the latch at the entrance rattled.

She whirled toward the sound.

The door swung wide . . . and Chama filled the opening.

Profoundly relieved, Carrie dropped the knife from her hand. It clanged onto the bare wood floor.

Chama stepped inside, then stooped and picked up the utensil. As he rose, his eyes seemed blacker than ever as he looked from it to her.

"I'm sorry," she stammered. "I thought . . ."

"No need to apologize. It's a good thing to be careful." He tossed the weapon onto the counter board, then pulled the nearest bench away from the table and sat down. Reaching out, he touched the pot sitting in the center. "The coffee, it feels hot."

"I made it just a few minutes ago." She hurried to a shelf and fetched him a metal cup. As she returned and filled it, she realized he'd come from the store empty-handed, and he'd been gone for hours—*long enough for her to cook a pot of pinto beans.* "I have some beans outside. Would you like some?"

"Just a little," he answered, then raised the cup to his lips as he glanced around the room she'd just spent the morning scrubbing and cleaning. "I already shared a shank of venison with some Comanches camped upstream. This place sure looks neat."

Comanches! What were Comanches doing this far west? Uncertain whether or not to ask, she walked to the kitchen shelf and picked up a tin plate. Then making sure no straggles had escaped her bonnet, she went outside to the blackened iron pot suspended over smoldering coals. After she scooped up a plateful, she couldn't resist stepping to the edge of the knoll and searching upstream for any sign of the Indian encampment. After a hundred yards or so, the small riverlet disappeared into the darkness of the woods. Her gaze swung to the Comanchero camp on the other side of the clearing. She'd never felt so surrounded. And the half-breed inside, her supposed protector, had just dined with one of the groups of ravaging marauders.

Remembering the food in her hand, she returned inside. Then, after fetching a spoon, she set the plate before him and stepped back.

"Sit down. Join me," he said, motioning with his head.

Doing as she was told, she slid onto the opposite bench. "I already ate, but I'd be glad to keep you company while you do." Then, feeling the need to occupy herself, she picked up the coffeepot and poured herself a cup.

"Yeah," he said, looking up at her. "Guess I was gone quite a spell." He continued to stare, his meal seemingly forgotten.

100 / Elaine Crawford

As he did, his hand wandered up to the piece of turquoise at his throat.

Carrie didn't know whether to look away, speak, or what. Finally, she picked up her tin cup and took a sip.

"You know," he said, shattering the long silence, "you don't have to wear that ugly old bonnet when you're inside."

Knowing he thought her desirable again, she untied the ribbons under her chin and removed the sunbonnet. As her hair began to tumble, she tossed her head a couple of times, helping the tawny mass to fall freely around her shoulders.

His expression enlivened, giving her a renewed sense of power. For a second Carrie thought he might even smile.

But, instead, he shifted his attention to the beans before him, scooping up a spoonful. "I didn't get a chance to buy anything at the store," he said after swallowing. "I'll go back when I'm finished. Is there anything in particular you want? Rodriguez doesn't have much, but I'll see what I can do."

His consideration warmed her as usual, and she smiled.

He brightened even more. His cheeks dimpled, giving the planes of his face an almost boyish charm.

"Well," she said, reluctant to tear her eyes from him as she looked behind her to inventory the meager food stores. "These beans sure could've used some salt pork for flavoring. And if the storekeeper has any potatoes or other vegetables. Eggs or some fresh meat would be really nice, too."

As she swung back, she saw Chama's eyes following the flight of her trailing hair. As it settled, he slowly lifted his gaze to meet hers.

The space between them became charged with excitement. Her arms turned to gooseflesh at the intensity of his desire. Shyness eventually overtook her, and she lowered her gaze to his lips. Firm, forceful. Yet as she knew from last night, so very giving, so very tender. They slackened. Any second now, he would reach for her. Take her as he'd done before.

He lunged to his feet.

Carrie held her breath. Her heart picked up its pace.

He pushed back his bench and moved to the end of the table . . . and kept right on going to the door. He was leaving?

Now? "I won't be too long," he shot over his shoulder on his way out. But at the entrance, he paused. "Why don't you bar the door while I'm gone."

By the time she reached it, he'd already jogged halfway down the knoll. "Always in a hurry to escape," she muttered as she picked up a piece of timber leaning against the wall.

But she'd been so sure he was about to— "To what?" she demanded of herself and slammed the board into the braces on either side of the jamb. Why in heaven's name was she so determined to turn a renegade outlaw into her Prince Charming? There could never be one for her—not him, not any man. She was no Snow White, pure of name and soul. She was the daughter of the devil, and he was coming. He would be here soon . . . for them both.

Chama crossed the meadow with a filled gunny sack slung over his shoulder. On his return from the store, he reminded himself as he had done all the way to Rodriguez's that the woman was nothing like his mother. His mother was Kiowa, born of a noble people. This woman was the offspring of the most ruthless lawman along the Rio Grande. And, before Jackson became sheriff of La Mesilla, he'd been an army officer. Perhaps one of the very soldiers who had patrolled the Santa Fe Trail when Chama was a babe.

Further reason to never let the woman's eyes bewitch him again. Or her tears. And he mustn't let himself listen to the hunger in her body. Or his own.

Always, he must keep the wise words of Walking Bear before him. Yes, remember Walking Bear . . .

Chama's heart warmed at the memory of the gnarled and crooked old medicine man. Then, recalling the words the ancient one had most often taught, he recited them now as if he were still a child forced to sit in some padre's classroom. "Keep your thoughts pure. Seek your vision and follow it. For no honor is gained, no victory won, while lying in a woman's bed."

Chama smiled and shook his head. Late at night the old outcast would sneak onto the mission grounds and encourage the Apache boys to disregard the strict rules of the padre. Instead, he would have them listen to the way of the people. Even after Walking Bear was caught and beaten, he would not be stopped from coming.

Looking back, Chama now realized the old man's devotion to the boys' instruction must have been his way of regaining some of his lost honor, honor of which he never spoke. And since Walking Bear never failed to warn them against the pitfalls of giving their souls to a woman, one had to have been the cause of his shame.

At the knock on the door, Carrie hurried to it. "Who's there?" she called, though she had little doubt Chama would answer.

"It's me."

Knowing the smooth deep timbre could be no other's, Carrie lifted the bar and swung open the door.

Chama breezed past her, lugging a tote sack over his broad shoulder. He lowered it to the floor below the counter board, then straightened and looked at her with the same stern expression she'd seen when he'd reprimanded Bert and Karl for drinking. "I bought a fresh supply of flour and coffee and beans, and a slab of salt pork like you wanted. I got a few potatoes, too, and some carrots and onions."

"That's wonderful. I'll put a chunk of pork in that pot of beans right now. By tonight, it should taste a whole lot better."

Some of the harshness eased from Chama's demeanor. Then, as he reached into his pants pocket, a grin stole across his face, and that boyish look reappeared. He withdrew three eggs. "The money-grubbing thief charged four bits apiece for these, so treat 'em like gold."

She matched his smile with a warm one of her own, then took each of them from his palm with care. As she did, she noticed his hand trembled slightly. She wondered if her closeness to him was the cause, then dismissed the notion as foolish. After all, it wasn't as if she were unavailable. Nonetheless, while she placed the eggs in a wooden bowl and emptied the gunny sack, she was sure his eyes followed her every move, especially since he remained rooted in the same spot.

"Rodriguez didn't have any fresh meat," he said as she placed the last sack on the floor. "So I thought I'd mosey up the valley a ways and maybe shoot a deer. I can usually get one toward evening when they come out to graze."

A ride into the beautiful forest? She whirled around. "Please, may I come, too? I'd love to go."

He looked as if he were more than willing to take her, then, surprisingly, his expression hardened again. "I've only got two horses. One's gotta pack the carcass."

"I see," she said, trying to hide her disappointment. "It's just that this is such a pretty valley, I would've enjoyed seeing more of it."

He glanced away and shifted his stance. "It would be real uncomfortable for you if you went. You'd have to ride the bay bareback on the way out—I'd give you the paint, but he takes some handling. Then, coming back, you'd have to double up with me."

"I wouldn't mind. And I'll be so quiet you won't even know I'm there."

He still looked unsure, then finally he let out a long breath. "All right. I'll go saddle up."

As he turned to leave she stayed him with her hand. "Thank you, Mr.—uh—Chama."

"Forget the formalities," he said, eyeing her hand on his arm. Then, looking up, he quirked one side of his mouth into a knowing grin. "I think we know each other too well for that."

A most intimate picture of their coupling flashed through her mind, and she flushed. Quickly lowering her gaze, she released his arm and turned away.

Obviously noticing her discomfort, he chuckled. Then, to her astonishment, he patted her behind as he passed her on his way to the door.

On reflex, she jumped and whirled toward him, her face growing even redder.

But, thank goodness, he didn't look back. "Don't forget to put that bonnet on before you come outside," he said as he walked out.

Within a few minutes Carrie rode along the stream bank behind Chama, her pleasure diminishing as she kept a wary eye on the *rancheria*, a mere two hundred yards to her right. She saw nothing more than a few lines of smoke and a couple of people moving about. If it hadn't been for the arrow-studded corpse still hung out in the open for all to see, it would have seemed as calm and quiet as siesta time in La Mesilla on a hot summer's day. She was more than grateful when they entered the trees, and the evil place became lost from view.

She began to relax as she absorbed the beauty surrounding her . . . a softly shadowed wilderness where the sun broke through rarely, and then only in feathery shafts. The breeze, fresh and cool, brushed her face and treated her nose to the fragrance of cedar and pine. She imagined how the unfurling ferns would soon look as they spread their fronds to cover the forest floor with frills of light green. At this altitude, it was also too early for the profusion of flowers that would spring up in the sunny patches, but a few hardy plants foretold the coming event with their clusters of tiny yellow and purple blooms.

Then she spotted a dogwood tree, her childhood favorite in South Carolina. Yet to bloom, it was still outstanding with sprinkles of sunlight sparkling like dancing diamonds through its large bright leaves.

So engrossed in the beauty she rode through, Carrie wasn't aware she'd followed Chama into an Indian encampment until it was too late.

Several men stared boldly at her without speaking.

An eerie chill ran down her spine. She wasn't accustomed to seeing Indians, let alone a war party. A few stray Apaches had come into La Mesilla a few years ago when she'd been in for supplies, but her father had run them out. Her one harrowing experience had happened soon after she and her family arrived in the territory. A hunting party had stopped at the ranch for water while her father was on duty at Fort Cummings, miles away. Hiding in the cellar with her mother and brother, she'd been frightened then, too, as she'd watched the lethal-looking men through a crack in the slanted door. As it turned out, they never even bothered to come up to the house, just took turns quenching their thirst and that of their rough-coated horses from the well.

But these Indians appeared different from any she'd seen before, fancier, with feathers decorating their braided hair and beads in threaded designs dangling from their buckskin clothing. Actually, they were really quite striking to look at, their bearing proud and strong. But their eyes held the same hardness she'd seen in those of the local Indians.

Chama spoke to them in a strange tongue, and the men closed in on both sides as they addressed him in what seemed a friendly manner.

One moved in close to Carrie's mount. He looked up at her, smiling, and spoke directly to her.

Not knowing what he said, she attempted a cheerful expression, then sat motionless in the thin hope no further notice would be taken of her.

As Chama spoke again, drawing the Indians' attention to him, Carrie glanced quickly about her and saw several tepees. She'd never actually seen any before, just pictures, but she knew they were used by Plains Indians. The colorfully painted drawings of animals and strange-looking signs on the covering of stretched skin surprised her. They were really quite attractive—a far cry from the woven-branch wickiups of the Apache. These men had to be the Comanches Chama had spoken of earlier.

One of the men broke out of the cluster and ran into a tepee. Within seconds he returned with a large fringed pouch and ran to the side of Chama's pony. From the bag he withdrew a long mass of golden hair. *And, God in heaven, it was attached to a piece of skin.*

The blood drained from Carrie's face, and her eyes lost focus. She grasped a handful of her horse's mane and nudged the bay gelding closer to Chama's.

Chama turned and reached out to her. But, instead of reassuring her as she'd expected, he snagged one of her bonnet strings and ripped loose the bow under her chin, tearing the covering from her head.

She gasped and looked wildly about her as the men crowded close to watch her own blond tresses tumble down around her.

A chorus of *ahhs* came from the bucks' open mouths as they shoved closer, their hands stretching up on both sides, touching, fingering locks of her hair.

A scream formed deep within her and threatened to burst from her throat.

Then Chama said something to the savages, and as if by magic, they melted away from her, taking with them their pillaging hands.

Carrie found herself breathing again in harsh, painful breaths.

Then, without warning, Chama caught hold of the bay's bridle and, nudging his own horse into a walk, led Carrie out of the camp. And not until they'd left the savages far behind did he let go and allow her to guide her own animal again.

In that space of time, Carrie's terror had turned into rage and found its just target. She jerked roughly on the gelding's reins and guided the animal up beside Chama's. "How could you do such a thing?" she cried in a high-pitched shout. "How could you? They might've scalped me. Did you want them to—to—" She would have continued her tirade—she wanted nothing more—but she choked on a sob, and the fire in her eyes drowned in a pool of tears.

Even through the blur, she could see his indignation.

"Oh, damn you," she sputtered past a sob. "Damn you." She swiped hard at the blasted tears, then slamming her heels into the bay's flanks, she sent the animal into a swift gallop up the trail, away from her new keeper, one who'd turned out to be just as heartless as her father.

※ 12 ※

EAGLE WINGS STRAINED against the reins, forcing Chama to tighten his grip as he watched the fool woman gallop away. She fled along the creek trace, hugging close to the bay's body. Without a saddle, she'd most likely fall off soon and break her fool neck. Perhaps it would be for the best. He had no time to coddle a female, particularly a temperamental one.

Then the vision of her tear-flooded eyes emerged, touching his spirit, and he began to weaken. The men shouldn't have crowded in on her like that. They'd scared her half to death.

But, then, who could blame them? One look at all that hair unloosed would drive anyone over the edge. Wasn't he proof of that? Strong Hand had said the color and the way it moved reminded him of buffalo grass bending with an autumn breeze. Thinking back to his early childhood, Chama, too, could see the likeness.

Eagle Wings continued to prance in place, eager to race after the other horse.

"All right," Chama grumbled, more at himself than the pony. He looped the strings of Carrie's bonnet around the saddle horn, then gave Eagle Wings his head. "Guess we'd better catch her before she kills herself."

Chasing after the woman at full speed, Chama caught sight of her within a couple of minutes as he crested a small rise. She'd slowed Hickory to a walk and rode in a forlorn-looking droop on his back. She undoubtedly understood nothing of what had just taken place at the Comanche camp. But a man shouldn't have to account for his every move. Well, maybe, just this once . . . He nudged the paint into a trot and overtook her.

She surely heard him approach—her back straightened, stiffened. But she didn't turn around, halt her horse, or do one blasted thing to acknowledge his arrival. She was obviously still all head-up. Probably expecting some kind of an apology. From what he'd heard, white women were stubborn that way. Well, she wouldn't get one from him. He would explain his actions, nothing more. Pulling alongside her, he allowed Eagle Wings to match the bay's pace. "The men back there needed to get a good look at you."

The woman shot him a quick glance, then looked straight ahead again.

"They're my Comanche and Kiowa 'brothers.' If there's trouble in the next few days and I'm not around, you're to go to them."

She opened her mouth as if to speak, then closed it, choosing to ignore him.

"For your information," he said in a much stronger voice, "you'd be a helluva lot safer with them than any of that scum at the *rancheria*. As long as you're my woman you'll always be welcome with my people."

To his dismay, a tear slipped down her cheek. She quickly rubbed it away, but the sight still tore at his gut, and he had to fight the urge to take her in his arms and comfort her as he'd done the night before.

Noticing the bonnet hanging from his pommel and grateful for its distraction, he lifted it off and handed it to her. "Cover your head," he rasped and nudged his pony into a faster pace.

Following behind, Carrie knew she'd made a complete mess of things. First, she'd begged to come with him, then thrown a screaming tantrum, and now had ended up showing herself for a silly female again by crying. She was starting to lose all control. She'd better take hold again.

Chama turned off the narrow path and headed into the woods, making his own trail past trees and thick patches of undergrowth. Occasionally, they would come to a small meadow in which Carrie thought deer might soon come to graze, but Chama never stopped. For more than an hour, he traveled without once looking back. Not until they neared the sheer wall at the far end of the valley did he slow.

From the roar of water, Carrie knew they were approaching the waterfall even before she could see it. Then as she broke out of the trees into a meadow, its cool spray breezed over her. Her gaze soared upward for several hundred feet and she marveled at its majesty as she followed its downward spill from one giant stone step to the next before its final long drop to the bottom. There it churned and sprayed over a cascade of rocks, then, as if by magic, poured gently over a wide smooth shelf into a glassy pond that reflected myriad shades of green from the hovering pines.

To reach the water, they crossed the small clearing and halted at a gently sloping beach of sand. Carrie looked about her once more. It was all so perfect, so inviting, like a fanciful fairy-tale painting.

"It'll be a while before the deer come out to feed," Chama said, dismounting, "so I thought we'd take a swim first."

His brazen suggestion stunned her. A grown woman didn't go swimming with a man . . . unclothed . . . in broad daylight.

But before she could find the words to object, he walked to the side of her horse and lifted her down.

Her gaze swept from him to the pond and back again.

Chama, however, acted as if he'd just mentioned that the sky was blue or the grass green. With maddening nonchalance, he led the horses to an oak and secured their reins. Walking back, he halted and frowned. "You can swim, can't you?"

"Yes, of course—I mean, I think so. I could when I was a child, back home. But, naturally, I haven't been swimming since."

"Back home," he said, ignoring her last remark. "Where do you come from?"

"Forrest Hills in South Carolina." She looked about her again, dismissing his proposal for a moment. "Your valley reminds me of it. I'd forgotten how beautiful and green a place could be."

He nodded, then gestured toward the water. "Get undressed

and let's see if you can still swim." He began untying the colorful belt at his waist.

He really was a savage if he expected her to strip off and blithely walk naked into the water with him in the middle of the day. He must think she was just another whore like that Juanita person.

Well, I won't do it, she decided with finality. *I can't.*

She shot a glance in his direction and saw he'd already removed his shirt to display his muscular bronze back. It virtually gleamed in the afternoon sun. At the heady sight her resolve began to slip, sending her into a mental debate over the advisability of causing yet another scene today. And, well, it wasn't as if she hadn't stood before him yesterday in nothing save a skimpy shift. And they'd already been as intimate as any man and woman could be. In the dark maybe—but intimate nonetheless.

She sneaked another peek as he let his cotton trousers fall to his ankles. That same bronze color smoothed over his thighs and down his long yet perfectly sculpted legs.

With a toss of his shaggy black mane, he looked over his shoulder and caught her staring.

She quickly averted her gaze.

"Well, are you coming?"

"Yes." Without meeting his eyes, the word came out more as a question than an answer. Then, attempting a brave front, she held her chin high and started for a big boulder a few yards away. If she had to do it, she'd do it with as much dignity as possible.

She heard a loud splash, a gasp, then the rapid sloshing of water.

From the noise Chama made, Carrie realized the pond must be almost as cold as the melting snow that had created it. She slowly shed her clothing. Fear knotted her stomach, turned her fingers to clumsy stubs. Stalling, she folded each garment she removed with exact precision, then stacked it neatly on the rock.

Too soon she was down to her last shoe. As she untied it, she could hardly keep herself from snatching up her belongings and putting them on again. Then, after placing the last item on the pile, she could delay no more. She peeked around the boulder.

Chama, swimming across the pond with smooth strong strokes, seemed to be thoroughly at ease.

He caught her watching him. Dropping down onto his feet, he stood and motioned for her to join him.

The sight of water sheeting off his shoulders and chest sent a thrill to Carrie's depths, but she couldn't just walk toward him as buck naked as the day she was born. "Would you please turn around," she hollered.

"What?" He hadn't heard her above the roar of the falls.

She quickly repeated her request while exposing one arm and making a circle with it.

He placed his hands on his hips and tilted his head. With his black eyes sparkling and that boyish grin dimpling his chiseled features, he stared boldly for a moment before turning slowly around.

Carrie watched his back for a few seconds to see if he would stay put. When he did, a sudden thought of what her father would think flashed across her mind. Then, taking a wickedly exhilarating breath, she ran pell-mell into the pond and dove beneath the icy water. Undaunted by the cold, she glided submerged until she ran out of breath and a sizable portion of her courage. She prayed desperately that she would be at least chest-deep when she surfaced. Dropping her feet to the sandy bottom, she found to her relief that with only a slight bending of the knees, the surface was above nipples that she knew had shriveled from the cold. Or anticipation? She didn't dare to guess which.

Chama swam over and rose up before her, grinning. "Well, it looks like you still know how to swim." Then his eyes locked with hers and his smile slowly died as his attention wandered down to her lips. Then, abruptly, he looked away and stepped back.

Carrie had a sudden, hurtful feeling of rejection.

"Oh, what the hell." He reached out and ripped her through the water to him, flattening her against his chest.

She stiffened at his roughness.

The strength of his hold lessened, and he leaned down. "Relax," he whispered into her ear, then began to tease it with his tongue while a hand played through her floating hair. "It's just you and me, like last night."

At his soft words, the tension flowed from her, and the cold water lost its bite as her flesh melded with his. *Yes, what the deuce,* she thought as her heart began to keep pace with his, and her tongue found the tender indentation at the base of his neck.

He groaned and slid his hands to her bottom, then lifted her up. As the water swirled about them, he moved her back and forth across his hardening manhood.

"Oh, yes," she heard herself whisper on a husky breath. "Give me last night again." Circling his neck with her arms, she wrapped her legs around him, teasing his shaft by pressing the pathway to her own need against it.

When she did, he moved his hands up her sides and took her face in his palms. "Look at me. This time I want to see your eyes."

She lifted lashes she hadn't realized were shut and saw sultry warmth in his own liquid gaze.

Steadily beholding her, he let his hands move downward again, down her throat, along her shoulders, over her breasts as if he were memorizing every curve. While his hands explored, his gaze wandered from her eyes to her hair, then gradually returned. "Woman from the sky," he whispered. "My beautiful woman from the sky. A gift to be treasured, not denied."

Woman from the sky? What did he mean by that? And why did he consider her a gift instead of the hostage she was?

Before she could ponder his words any further, he covered her lips with his, and when he did, his hands cupped her breasts, his thumbs teasing their tight buds.

The kiss deepened, and his mouth rode hard across hers. His tongue gained entrance, thrusting around hers, with hers.

With each of his increasingly frantic entreaties, Carrie felt his manhood press harder against her own tender flesh. She answered by digging her fingers deeper into his hair and tightening her legs around his waist and moving against him.

He tore his mouth from hers and groaned, "Not yet." He pulled her hands from his neck and kissed each of her palms; then, taking her wrists, he spread her arms apart and began trailing his lips along the tender underside of one with agonizing slowness.

Carrie thought she would scream with unfulfilled desire as he held out her wrists, preventing her from touching him, too. She could hear herself pant, then gasp as his mouth reached a breast and closed over it, tasting, nibbling, drawing. She tried to free her hands, to taunt his body as he did hers.

Chama tightened his grip, holding her fast as he removed his mouth from her nipple. For the longest time, he studied one breast, then the other as they floated just above the surface. Continuing the sweet torture, his gaze lazily roved upward until it met hers. "The turquoise has deepened. It tells me of your desire for me."

"You're driving me crazy. Please let me touch you again."

"If I do, I won't be able to hold back any longer."

"Please."

After a long second he gave in and released her wrists. As he did, he caught her head in his hands and kissed her full on the lips, grinding hard against them.

She clutched at his hair, answering him with her own urgency. Then, driven by some primeval instinct, she loosened the grip of her legs until his manhood floated free. Gliding through the water herself, she teased his tip with her hungering entrance. Taunted him as she moved in a tiny circle around it until little by little she began taking him within.

She felt tension in the hands holding her head as his lips parted from hers, saw the rapt passion in his eyes building as he kept his body still, very still, letting her do what she would.

Continuing to watch his expression, she pressed forward until she'd taken his satinlike tip a safe distance inside, then moved away with agonizing slowness until it withdrew to the very edge.

Just as she began to slide forward again, he groaned and, clutching her hips, drove himself into her to the very hilt.

Her breath whooshed out on a relieved chuckle, and she wrapped herself around him again, arms and legs. She hugged herself to him and rode him as she would a magnificent wild stallion.

Chama knew this had to be a dream. Someone this perfect couldn't be real. The woman, her hands, her hair, the water, swirled all around him. Fire and ice. Ice and fire. Taking him beyond thinking until there was nothing but the feel of her hot silken passageway taking his hungering length ever deeper, ever faster as he held her to him and drove into her again and again.

A moan escaped her lips, then another, telling him of her pleasure . . . intensifying his own. Then suddenly she arched her back and cried out.

Chama slowed his impassioned assault as he felt her melt deep inside. The fullest measure of pleasure filled his chest at knowing he'd brought her to the height of rapture.

On a sigh, she fell against him and began dropping hurried kisses over his face and neck as she started moving against his painfully ready manhood once more in an erotic dance older than time.

He thrust into her hard and swift, overtaking his own passion, bursting forth in the sweetest pain. Holding her tighter, he burrowed even deeper until he poured the last of his seed into her innermost reaches. Making her his, now and forever.

If he wasn't dreaming. If she was truly real.

She became limp, and her legs drifted from around him.

Sated exhaustion weakened his own limbs. Pulling her over him, he glided through the water with her, letting its cooling fingers caress and buoy their spent bodies.

As his lips found hers in a lingering kiss, one that threatened to steal his soul, her hair blanketed them like spun sunshine. This gift from the sky.

Or the most wonderful dream he'd ever had.

13

CARRIE LAY PILLOWED on Chama's arm, listening to the steady breathing of his slumber. The peaceful sound mingled with the distant roar of the waterfall and the chirping of a pair of birds overhead. The two sparrows busily hopped on their twiglike legs, fluttering about a nest to which they added bits of dried grass.

She smiled lazily at the sweet sight. A young couple, she mused, just married and building their first home together.

Rising up on an elbow, she looked down at the nest of petticoats she and Chama had hastily made amid their laughter after he'd carried her out of the pond. He'd even joked about it, saying they'd better put something between them and the sand, just in case he wasn't dreaming.

Her smile flashed wider, then settled into a fully satisfied one as she thought of the magic he began to work on her after he'd laid her down. No longer driven by uncontrollable passion, he'd explored every inch of her, teaching every part of her body to desire his touch. Even her fingers and toes had not been deprived of his attention before he moved inside her.

It would be so easy to love this man. So easy, she thought, her gaze wandering across his face. It centered on his lips, so firm-looking, yet so capable of bestowing the most sensual of pleasures. Then, leaving his mouth behind, she took a long-spun time roving the length of his body until she came to the delectable conclusion that he had to be the most beautiful man in the world. If it weren't for a small scar along one rib, he would've made the perfect model for those old Renaissance statues she'd once seen in a book of Michelangelo's works.

Carrie chuckled, remembering the long-ago day when her mother had come into the library at Forrest Hills and caught her ogling a drawing of the completely nude statue of David from the Bible. But, she thought, scanning Chama again, her "David" was by far superior to the old master's. From the rich brown of his skin, to the deep chest that was bare of the unsightly wiry hair that covered her father's, he was truly magnificent.

Knowing she shouldn't, she let her gaze skip down to that intimate part of him. Her heart thumped hard at the forbidden sight, and she quickly glanced up to his eyes to see if he'd caught her looking.

Thank goodness, he still slept. Even if he hadn't minded, she would've been mortified. She made herself concentrate on his facial features, lest her eyes betray her again. It amazed her now that she could have ever thought them menacing. But his thatch of shaggy hair sure could've used a trip to the barber a good month ago. But nonetheless, she loved running her fingers through its midnight thickness.

One of the birds swooped down to the ground a few feet from her, drawing her attention. As it picked up a pine needle and flew away, she looked upward, catching sight of the waterfall again, its magnificence thrilling her. She spent the next several minutes watching shooting streams plummet past each other in their race to explode onto the boulders at the bottom. Smiling, her gaze followed the water as it spilled smooth as a glassy wave over the last ledge into the pond.

Such an idyllic spot to be brought to by her lover. And he'd been beyond compare. If only they could have a lifetime of afternoons like this . . .

But, she reminded herself sternly, this was just a fairy-tale interlude or a dream as Chama had mentioned more than once. She must not allow herself to forget that soon it would all come to an end. She was the hostage of a bank robber who was on the run from her father.

Profound emptiness stole her joy.

No, she scolded silently. *I'll not let Father ruin this day, too. Today is mine. Chama's and mine.*

She focused again on the lovely emerald lake.

A movement on the other side caught her eye.

A deer. Majestic in his gait, he came to the edge and lowered his head for a drink. As he did, Carrie noticed that the buck's spread of horns was close to a yard wide. He'd seen many winters in these mountains.

A deer.

Suddenly remembering the reason she and Chama had come, Carrie deftly, silently, rose from the ground, watching the buck all the while, lest he bolted. Fortunately, the animal took no notice of her as she crept to Chama's pony. She slipped the rifle from its scabbard and, with slow fluid movements, raised it to her shoulder. Taking careful aim at the point where the stag's neck and shoulder met, she squeezed the trigger.

The deer dropped instantly from where he'd stood.

"Good shot!" she congratulated herself and grinned in triumph.

In her next breath the rifle was wrenched from her hands and her feet knocked out from under her. Landing bare-bottomed on the sand, she looked up to find Chama standing over her.

He reached down and yanked her to her feet.

"Deer!" she screamed with terror. "A deer. I shot a deer."

His thunderous glower began to lessen as her words soaked in. He shifted his gaze to where she motioned with her head. After a second, he loosened his bruising grip on her arm. "I thought—" He gave her an apologetic shrug and released her. Then, reaching out, he began brushing off the sand that had plastered itself to her bare back and limbs . . . brushing away the evidence of his mistreatment of her. "You should've warned me."

Her own ire building, she stepped back and glared up at him. "I saw the stag. If I'd taken the time to get you up, he might've bolted."

He moved close and swept a strand of hair from her brow. "I know." His whispered words were almost soundless as he pulled her into his arms. Gently, he kissed the tip of her nose, her chin, then taking a shuddering breath, he buried his face in the hollow of her neck and hugged her to him.

118 / Elaine Crawford

How could she stay angry? And he was right, she should have warned him. She wrapped her arms around his neck and returned his embrace.

Too soon, Chama gave her an added squeeze and stepped back. He looked across the pond again. One side of his mouth lifted into a cocky grin. "So, I see you got yourself a big buck. I like that, 'specially since that makes it your job to dress him out."

"What?" Carrie shot a glance to the crumpled animal, whose size seemed to have doubled since she last looked.

From Chama's animated expression, he was obviously enjoying her distress. "You killed him, Sunlight, he's all yours."

Defiant pride took the fore. He probably thought she couldn't do it. Well, she'd show him. After all, it wasn't like her father hadn't run off any number of times, leaving her to finish butchering a barely started hog. She walked toward the packhorse . . . then realized she was still nude. She turned back and gathered up her petticoats, then started for her other clothes.

"I wouldn't bother dressing if I were you," Chama said blandly. "You'd just get 'em all dirty."

Oh, isn't he the clever one. Carrie swung around to find him grinning at her, and without a stitch of his own on, no less. He certainly was turning into quite the joker. *So, it's games he wants to play, is it? Fine, we'll just see who comes out of this one the winner.*

Carrie dropped her petticoat on top of her other clothes, then sweeping her hair back so it no longer veiled her breasts, she strode undaunted to the packhorse. Then, without giving Chama even the merest glance, she untied the bay's reins and began leading him around the lake.

Chama watched her go, taking full pleasure in her long fluid strides, which were enhanced by her shimmering reflection as it moved along the water's edge with her. Not until she reached the far side did he tear his eyes from her loveliness and gather up his clothes. He dressed in supreme haste, not even caring that a little sand remained on his feet as he tugged on his boots. His Woman From The Sky was putting on a show for him, and he didn't want to miss a second of it. Mounting Eagle Wings, he rode through the marshy grass edging the pond to where she worked.

She'd already tied the buck's hind legs together with one end of his rope, and was now trying to toss the other end over a thick branch, high in an ancient oak.

"Here, hand it up to me," he offered, "and I'll throw it over for you."

She turned toward him, giving him a full view of every one of her seductive curves. One brow, however, was raised, suggesting she wasn't all that pleased with him. "That won't be necessary," she said with a stilted smile, then squatted. She picked up a good-sized rock and tied the rope around it, then pitched it, clearing the limb on her first try. Then, with more know-how than he'd expected, she removed the stone and looped the line through a ring in the horse's pack harness and led the animal away from the oak.

Once the rope became taut, the deer started lifting from the ground. When it reached a sufficient height, she secured the rope around the tree trunk, then began rummaging around the bay's tack.

"What are you looking for?" he asked.

"The knife."

"I keep it here with me." He pulled his prized bowie from the leather sheath strapped to his saddle.

As she came for it, she very casually flipped back some hair that trailed over her breasts, and Chama wondered if she was deliberately taunting him. When she reached up for the knife, her hand rested on his and lingered a moment before sliding up to take the bone handle, and he had no doubt she was.

And, damn her, it was working. He heard himself take in a ragged breath.

As she turned away, Chama could swear she swayed her hips more than usual, too.

It was hard to believe that only a couple of hours ago she'd been hiding behind a rock, too modest to come out. Who could figure a woman? Or maybe it was just this one—Juanita hadn't been at all hard to outguess. Treat Juanita to pretty baubles and nights of drinking and dancing and she dripped with the sweetness of warm honey, but only then. He'd been warned against taking up with the whore, but some things a man just had to learn for himself.

But this woman amazed him at every turn. One minute she acted as shy as a bride, the next she blossomed into a most passionate enchantress. Then there were the times when she acted as comfortable with him as if they'd been together for years. But never did she act like what she really was... his captive. She'd had his rifle. They were far from anyone else. Why hadn't she blown his head off and run like hell?

Could she truly want to stay with him? "Carrie?"

On the verge of slicing the stag's neck, she released his horns and turned toward him with an expectant look. "Yes?"

"No white man has ever found this place on his own. Only a few can even find their way to the crack in the canyon wall after they've been led to it over and over. That's why it's such a safe hideout."

She simply stared up at him, unfazed.

"Your father won't be able to find the entrance. That I know. But I don't know how long he'll search these mountains before he gives up."

The turquoise of her eyes took on a brittleness as she answered. "He won't give up."

"He puts that much store in you."

"No."

Not expecting her blunt confession, Chama's gaze faltered, and he fell speechless for a moment. The leather beneath him creaked loudly in the silence as he shifted his weight. "Then why won't he give up?"

Her own gaze never wavered as she tilted her chin. "You made it personal."

"Personal?"

"Yes. If you'd just ridden into La Mesilla, robbed the bank, and rode out, he would've done anything within reason to catch you. I remember once a few years ago, he lost a fugitive's trail and finally gave up. But that will never happen this time. You came into his house and took something that belonged to him.

It's like you dared him to try and catch you. And there's no prouder or more determined man on the face of this earth. Like I said, he'll never give up." Her expression took on a bleak sadness that matched the hopeless sound of her last words.

So, what he had begun to suspect was really true—she didn't want to go back to her father. He may have captured her, but he was starting to believe he was her rescuer. Things must have been mighty bad if she preferred being kept by a half-breed renegade in a Comanchero camp.

Karl's story about the castration crossed Chama's mind and he concluded it may very well have happened, that it wasn't just some drunken saloon talk. And from the hungry passion of Carrie's response to him last night, she'd surely been deprived of any gesture of love or kindness for years.

As she turned back to her chore, Chama noted that her posture had lost its proud straightness. He dismounted, his need to protect and care for her surging forth with a new earnestness. He took the knife from her hand. "I'll do this. You go get dressed."

"But, I thought you said—"

"I was just teasing," he interrupted. Reaching out, he caressed her cheek with his thumb. "Go on now, before I change my mind."

Once Chama had dressed out the deer and packed the venison onto Hickory, he returned with the two horses to the other side of the pond.

Carrie, now dressed and sitting on a slab plaiting her hair, greeted him with a smile.

. . . the same loving smile his mother had given him countless times when as a small child he'd come in from playing. And how many times had he awakened in the morning to see Spotted Fawn twining her hair? "Almost ready?" he asked Carrie with a tender smile of his own.

"Yes," she said, tying a piece of string around the end of her braid.

Chama dismounted and walked to the side of the packhorse. He unlashed the rack of horns he'd taken from the buck and held them out. "I thought you might want to keep these."

She brightened. "Thank you. I've shot a few rabbits before, but this is my first deer."

"When we get home," he said as he secured the horns to the harness again, "I'll nail them over the door."

"I'd like that."

From the warmth in her voice, he knew she really meant it. And nothing could've pleased him more. Even if Sheriff Jackson never gave up trying to track them down, this woman was worth it.

14

WITH DISMAY, CARRIE watched Chama stroll across the meadow on his way to the *rancheria* as he'd done every day for the past week. He went each time seeking news of the cursed gunrunners, days overdue, and also to purchase and deliver supplies to the ever-increasing number of Indians camped elsewhere in the valley. He said the less contact his people had with the depraved misfits the better.

On his return she knew he would tell about the latest arrivals of renegades, mostly Apache, and if they'd come from Mexico or the San Carlos reservation. His pride in them was always evident, and she knew he thought he was doing a great service by furnishing them with weapons.

Never did he acknowledge the white half of his heritage, but she could hardly blame him. The Indians judged him by his deeds, the white man by the color of his skin. No telling what manner of abuse he'd suffered—he'd never spoken of his childhood. But then, she never spoke about her past, either. It was probably best not to disturb their little slice of happiness. Too soon it would end.

Carrie looked up to the distant crack in the wall where her father would be coming. With a heavy-hearted sigh, she turned away and went to the campfire to check on her simmering venison stew. She and Chama had so little time—why did he have to remind her every day that he, too, was a man of violence?

Yet, aside from his trips to the *rancheria*, they couldn't have shared a more perfect bliss. Even when they weren't wrapped in each other's arms through the night, they'd fallen into such a pleasant routine of sharing chores in the morning and spending afternoons sometimes hunting, sometimes exploring the secrets of the valley . . . and each other.

Carrie's lips meandered into a smile at the thought as she picked up a long wooden spoon to stir the stew.

A gunshot exploded across the clearing.

Jumping at the loud crack, Carrie looked across to the encampment, wondering if someone was now sprawled in the dirt over there, bleeding and dying. If so, would anyone help the person? Would Chama? Her heart plummeted. *Chama.* Maybe someone had shot him.

No, don't do that to yourself. She reassured herself further by recounting the number of gunshots that rang out each day, and especially at night.

Deliberately she turned her back to the meadow and looked at the evidence of all the work she and Chama had accomplished that week. Spread in accordion fashion across a number of drying racks lay the venison from three deer. He'd seemed to really enjoy teaching her the Indian way of preserving meat, and she'd taken particular comfort in the fact that they were storing food for the future—something she knew he had not done here before, since he'd had to build the drying racks.

"We could be so happy together," she mumbled, slipping the spoon into the savory-smelling stew to stir it. "If only he'd leave all this gun business behind."

But there was still her father.

He would come prepared. Considering his leadership ability, that perfect mix of authority and comradeship, he could easily recruit fifty, maybe even a hundred men. There were plenty who'd cashiered out of the army from the territorial forts, men at loose ends with nothing better to do than go help him save his *poor* daughter.

Over the years, Carrie had become accustomed to keeping her thoughts and opinions to herself, but with Chama, maybe she should speak out, convince him to take her far away, now, before it was too late.

A ground-shaking rumble caught Carrie's attention, and she swung around.

Three Indians rode through the meadow toward her at a full gallop.

She shot a glance at the cabin. If she ran fast, she might make it. She dropped the spoon and snatched up her skirts, then hesitated. Chama had told her often enough that she could trust his *brothers*.

Feigning a calmness that her hands belied, she plucked the utensil from off the ground and wiped it clean on her apron as she watched them charging toward her. Holding her head high, she refused to so much as flinch as they raced up the hill.

Mere feet before running her down, they reined their unshod ponies to a sliding halt, engulfing her in a cloud of dust, then glared down at her with hate-filled eyes.

Carrie had the strongest urge to run—these Indians were not in the least like the Comanches she had previously met, no feathers and braids. No smiles. Their hair fell just above the shoulder in the blunt cut of the Apache and was held in place by a strip of cloth wrapped around their foreheads. One wore a store-bought shirt, the other two had on loose-fitting peon blouses. But below their belted waists only breechcloths flapped above knee-high moccasins. Very savage-looking. Very deadly.

They looked about them and mumbled a few unintelligible words. They obviously were looking for Chama.

She couldn't imagine why—they were already heavily armed with an array of rifles and pistols. They even had full ammunition belts crisscrossing their chests.

The Indians turned, stony-faced, and studied her again.

Her own gaze didn't waver, but she had never been so glad in her life that the bonnet hid her hair. These renegades looked quite capable of scalping her on the spot.

One motioned to the cabin and spoke in clipped tones. "Cha-ma-say."

She hesitated, not wanting to tell them he wasn't there, that she was alone. She gripped the ladle more firmly, her sorely lacking weapon, then took a deep breath and pointed the spoon in the direction of the clearing. "*Rancheria*. Chamasay. *Rancheria*."

Without another word, the frightening savages whipped their steeds around and galloped off the hill, leaving her once again in a haze of dust.

Regaining her courage, Carrie's temper flared at their rude disregard for her or the stew simmering in the open kettle. "It would serve them right," she muttered as she attempted to skim off the silt settling on the broth, "if Chama invited them to noon with us. I'd purely enjoy serving them this dirty mess. In fact, I might even throw in an extra pinch or two for good measure."

There was something particularly enchanting about the way a woman's hips moved when she walked barefooted, especially when her waist-length hair swayed just above her rounded bottom. Coffee cup in hand, Chama leaned both elbows on the table and took a sip while studying Carrie as she placed three small flapjacks from the skillet onto his plate, then watched her saunter around to her side of the table and do the same.

She picked up her spoon and smiled questioningly. "Is something wrong?"

"No. Just enjoying the view." He picked up a pancake and took a bite. It was hard to believe that two people who slept intertwined, who if they drifted apart during the night sensed the separation and reached out for one another, knew so little about each other. No one who just happened by would've guessed it, for more with each passing day they'd come to laugh and tease each other as they worked together. When near her, Chama had begun the practice of draping his arm around her. And Carrie would brush his hair from his forehead or pick a pine needle off his shirt with natural ease. But when it came to things close to their hearts, their past, their feelings, their hopes for the future, Carrie was as silent as he. Chama had come to believe that she, too, made a practice of hiding her inner thoughts—perhaps for as long as he had.

The rapid crunch of footsteps, followed by hard pounding on the door, sent Carrie to her feet. She grabbed her bonnet off the bedpost and began stuffing her hair within it.

Chama walked to the door but waited until she'd finished before he opened it.

A young Mexican boy stood there, gasping for breath. He slid a sombrero from his head and gushed, "Señor José. They here! The gunrunners, they here! They say for you to come."

At last! "Tell them I'll be there after I finish supper."

"*Sí*, señor," the lad said while craning his neck to look past Chama.

The boy must have heard the men talking about the infamous sheriff's daughter, Chama realized. And now the squirt wanted to see why a loner half-breed would pay so much for her. Well, he could just keep wondering. Chama placed one hand on each doorjamb to block the boy's view even more and glared down at him. "Is that all you came for, *muchacho*?"

The kid's dark eyes widened as he looked up. Spinning around, he sprinted away and down the hill.

Chama turned back to the table and looked at Carrie. "It's sure taken long enough. I was beginning to think they'd been stopped by the army."

She said nothing, just stared up at him as if she were scared half to death.

He couldn't imagine why some harmless young kid knocking on the door would disturb her, and right now he didn't have time to worry about it. Remaining standing, he grabbed a pancake and, after rolling it up, stuffed it whole into his mouth. He washed it down with a big gulp of coffee as he turned to stoop before the middle chest. Feeling around behind until he found the small lever, he pushed it down.

The secret drawer at the bottom sprang open.

From it he took the four large rolls of greenbacks and banknotes, enjoying the weight in his hands—it had taken all winter to collect them. He shoved them inside his blouse shirt until they rested securely just above his woven belt. Standing up again, he readjusted the tuck of his shirt until the rolls were concealed in its folds. He'd just as soon no one noticed them until they were needed. He then lifted his gunbelt from off a wall hook and buckled it on . . . all the while feeling Carrie's eyes on him.

Deciding it would be best to pretend he didn't notice, Chama started for the entrance. "Bar the door," he said as he opened it. "I'll be real late."

She whispered something he couldn't make out.

He turned. "What?"

She swallowed hard and stood up. "I said, don't go."

"I have to go now if I want first pick. Then I'll be staying to translate. I'm the only one who understands all the languages."

"You're going there to buy guns for the Indians," she said in an accusing tone. "Guns they'll use to—"

"Buying guns for my people is what I do." The woman was meddling in his business, trying to stop him. Without giving her a chance to say another word, Chama wheeled around and slammed out the door.

By the time he reached the *rancheria* in the fading light of dusk, the entire male population had already gathered in front of the trading store. The Apaches who had been arriving for the past two weeks far outnumbered the mix of other tribes, Mexicans, whites, Negroes, and half-breeds. Jugs of mescal and bottles of whiskey passed freely from hand to hand, heightening the air of excitement as the men surrounded stacks of wooden crates.

Chama shoved his way toward the center and saw that two boxes had been pried open and several rifles were being examined by the customers. From one box came single-shot Springfield carbines, the same as those used by the cavalry; from the other, Winchester repeaters. The latter drew the most interest, since the newer style was harder to come by.

Chama listened to the men as they discussed the merits and shortcomings of each. He heard one man point out that the single shot easily outdistanced the repeater. Then another argued that by the time his enemy stopped to reload, he could close the distance and shoot the pants off the bushwhacker. From the affirming rumble, Chama could tell most of the men agreed with the second man.

The two gunrunners got up from the crates they sat on when they saw Chama. Both stepped forward, wearing business suits with stiffly starched collars and greedy smiles on their faces. If Chama didn't know better, he would've taken them for well-fed bankers or merchants. He had no doubt they'd stopped their mule train shortly before reaching the valley to bathe and dress in their finery, knowing that a prosperous appearance would give them an edge when bargaining.

Mr. Humphries, the taller one with pop eyes set in a narrow face, shook Chama's hand with solid sincerity. "Why don't you join Mr. Whetsler and myself for a drink at your little establishment over there while our boys here show the rest of these good customers our wares." The *boys* Mr. Humphries referred to were eight of the biggest, meanest-looking men the territory had ever seen and the best possible insurance the two gunrunners could buy in this risky business.

Mr. Whetsler stepped up and shook Chama's hand with equal sincerity, his small blue eyes lighting up his square, beefy face. "Yes, we sure could use a drink about now. A more private drink."

"Be glad to." Chama knew without a doubt why, when a hundred men clamored about, he was given preferential treatment. He'd aided them considerably in the past with his ability to translate the various languages. But more importantly, for the last four years he'd been their single best customer. He cut through the crowd with Whetsler, while Humphries delayed long enough to inform a Negro with arms like tree stumps of their departure before following Chama and Whetsler to the cantina.

The saloon was empty except for Shorty and one of his whores who'd passed her prime at least ten years ago.

In a fluttery rush, she stuffed a drooping wisp of dark brown hair up into the knot at the back of her head. She then smoothed skintight red satin over her bulging hips and slinked over to the table to where Chama and the two *gentlemen* seated themselves. She smiled too brightly, too desperately. "What'll you gents be havin'?"

"Why, you, of course," Whetsler said, his meaty hand grabbing her rear.

"Not now," Humphries growled.

Whetsler gave the whore an extra squeeze, then let her go with a knowing grin. "Later."

"Mr. Whetsler and I will have some of your best whiskey, miss," Humphries said to the woman, then turned to Chama. "And what's your pleasure, Mr.—uh—Chama?"

"The same," he answered, amused by the other's fumbling attempt to perform the social graces of a white businessman.

The woman left to fetch the drinks and Chama settled back in his chair for what he knew could be a lengthy bargaining process. "What took you so long?" he asked, wanting to get the pleasantries out of the way so they could get down to dickering. "You were due here over a week ago."

"We've had a lot of trouble getting through unnoticed," Humphries said. "The whole territory is swarming with bounty-hunting posses, and we heard tell the army is likely to be called in."

"And that's a damned shame," Whetsler added. "It's been real easy traveling up into these mountains since all those Mimbreno Apaches got shipped off to San Carlos, taking all them troops with 'em. It's a damn shame."

The whore returned, interrupting their conversation. She bent low over the table.

From the glint in Whetsler's eyes, she'd obviously given him a choice view of her swinging breasts. He rewarded her by pinching one.

She giggled and sashayed back to the bar, undoubtedly to wait until the men concluded their business.

"I take it they've heard about Geronimo and his band coming up from Mexico," Chama said, drawing the men back to the subject. "Has Geronimo been raiding along the Rio Grande?"

"No, it's nothing like that." Humphries took a sip of his drink, then continued. "Some fools robbed Sheriff Jackson's bank in La Mesilla and stole his daughter. And he's put five thousand on each of their heads. He's got posses riding out of his town, Lordsburg, Silver City, and—where else did they say?"

Whetsler, who had yet to take his eyes off the whore, swiveled around to face them. "The sheriff telegraphed Las Palomas for a posse to ride into the mountains from the north. From what we heard, if they don't turn up anything, he's going to Fort Seldon to talk to the army. And if anyone will know how to cut through all that crap about jurisdiction and orders, it's Wiley Jackson. There's sure to be pony soldiers swarming all over these mountains before the month is out."

"Well, gentlemen, what can I say?" Chama grinned and gave them a helpless shrug. "You're looking at the fool who's got the sheriff's daughter."

Both men's mouths dropped wide open, and the identical words tumbled out. "How could you do such a stupid thing?"

"Don't you know," Humphries added, leaning closer, "you can't mess with the likes of Jackson?"

"Fact is, when I was planning the robbery, most everyone was still down in the low country, and Wormely was the only stray gun I could rustle up. But when he heard it was Jackson's bank, he wouldn't go unless we took the sheriff's daughter hostage. He thought if Jackson caught up to us he wouldn't be quite so willing to rush us. I didn't like the idea, but that was the only way Wormely would go."

"No, it was absolutely *not* a good idea," Humphries said, puffing out his thin chest. "What you've done is stir up the biggest damned hornet's nest I ever saw."

"Yeah," Whetsler chimed in with a leering grin. "You know how much we white folk enjoy saving a damsel in distress, even one no one's seen hide nor hair of since—"

"Well," Humphries drawled, overriding his partner's words. "The way Jackson's going about it, I don't think he's all that worried about the girl's safety. He appears a whole lot more interested in the men who robbed his bank and stole her. Dead or alive."

Whetsler's tiny eyes brightened, and he slammed a beefy fist onto the table. "Mr. Humphries. There still may be light at the end of the tunnel."

"What do you mean?"

"Since Mr. Chama, here, possesses the female in question . . ." He swiveled to Chama. "You did say you had her, didn't you?"

"Yes."

"Then all we have to do is see her safely returned to the sheriff. That should calm the waters considerably."

"But he'll still be after the bank robbers," Humphries argued.

"Yes," Whetsler said, picking up his drink. "But it'll take the wind out of his sails, so to speak. Jackson won't be able to keep the *good citizens* all stirred up over just some two-bit robbery. And more important, it'll take the matter out of the army's jurisdiction. They won't be mounting up if the girl is returned. It's the perfect solution. Wouldn't you say, Mr. Chama?"

"Except for one thing." Chama looked from one starched-up fraud to the other. "I'm not giving her back."

"What?" bawled Humphries, his bulging eyes nearly popping out of their sockets. "Why the hell not?"

"If it's just a woman you want," offered Whetsler, "we'll get you another. Hell, we'll get you two. Keller over in Tucson has a China doll he'd let go for a price. And if you like 'em light, Sanchez down in Nogales has a pretty little blonde he bought off the Apaches. She's real young, too."

In the aftermath of the gunrunners' depraved proposal, Chama stared at them with deadly calm as he moved the hand hidden beneath the table until it covered his pistol butt, then downed the remainder of his whiskey before answering. "The woman belongs to me now, and I'm not giving her back."

Whetsler's neck swelled at his collar. His face turned purple, and he started to rise.

Humphries placed a steadying hand on his partner's arm. "Forget it. It's not worth it." Then he turned to Chama with a businesslike expression. "About the rifles, how many will you be needing this time?"

Half an hour later, the disagreement apparently forgotten, Chama walked outside again with the other two, who seemed content with the bargain they'd struck. He, too, was satisfied.

He'd be getting forty-five rifles, five more than the going price, plus ammunition for his four thousand dollars.

Lanterns now hung from pegs on the store's porch and a few men also carried torches to light the darkness. Within the overlapping glow, Chama noticed that the crowd now stood in clusters, separated into the various gangs and bands. Spotting the returning gunrunners, they came together again, circling the crates.

As Chama wedged through to the center, he looked about him until he saw a Mexican with a serape draped over his shoulder and asked to borrow it. Then, kneeling, Chama spread it on the ground and displayed some of the rifles he'd just bought.

Several Indians at a time squatted down before him, their eyes alight as they ran their hands over the smooth metal, tested the weight, the balance, and the fit of the wood stock to their shoulders. After each brave chose the one he liked, Chama extracted from him in his own dialect the promise to shoot two "long knives" for the weapon and two cartons of cartridges.

When Chama had distributed about half the rifles, he stood to stretch his legs. As he did, he announced in Apache, "The long knives at Fort Seldon may leave their walls soon and ride into these mountains. Their blue coats will make fine targets. Good hunting."

The Apaches thrust their rifles overhead. *"Yizithee, yizithee,"* they yelled. Kill, kill. They started dancing to their chant, and a few discharged their weapons into the air.

After a few seconds Chama noticed that the outlaws and *bandidos* had begun to back away and reach for their own weapons. Sensing a fracas about to erupt, Chama raised his hand and yelled above the noise in English. "It's all right, men. Relax."

When the Apaches settled down again, Chama offered an explanation for their excitement. "The Apache are happy because I told them where to find some fresh game."

Most of the Comancheros' faces, Mexican and American, mirrored their doubt, but no one chose to challenge Chama's word since the Indians had calmed, and those already in possession of their prized gifts were beginning to drift back to their own camps upstream.

After Chama finished with his own business, he remained to act as translator for the gunrunners who traded off remaining rifles for either cash money or any kind of valuable object. And from the look of the spoils on the serape by the time the trading was almost over, Humphries and Whetsler could have opened a jewelry store. Pocket watches, rings, necklaces, ear bobs, as well as an array of other stolen items covered the striped wool.

Then a member of the most bloodthirsty gang to terrorize the border towns tossed a large golden crucifix down, one obviously taken from a church.

Several Mexican *bandidos* grabbed the scrawny white man, lifting him till his feet dangled inches from the ground. One held a razor-sharp knife at his throat.

Before any of Bull Dolan's other men could rescue him, the always-ready *boys* of the gunrunners knocked the blade from the one Mexican's hand and ripped the others away from their intended victim.

Unwilling to take on the notorious guards, yet with tempers still ablaze over the sacrilege, the *bandidos* stalked off into the darkness, cursing anyone else who touched the sacred cross.

Carrie huddled on a stump with Chama's serape tented over most of her in an attempt to ward off the evening chill as well as her apprehension. Never taking her eyes from the distant Comanchero camp, she'd waited in the dark for hours. With as many as twenty torches aflame, she could easily see, as well as hear, the noisy, milling mob.

Compared to this night, the *ranchería* had been relatively quiet since she'd arrived. In the past, the only sounds that had pierced the silence were an occasional cry of a babe or a more unsettling scream or yell. Every night or so she'd also heard angry shouts punctuated by gunshots, always followed by an eerie stillness that Chama dissipated by drawing her closer.

But tonight was different.

All evening the drone of voices had been constant, except when it exploded into shouts. Guns had been fired by the dozen, their sharp cracks echoing off the canyon walls and turning her nauseous with fear. If Chama were killed she would be alone again, and at the mercy of all those vicious animals.

A couple of times she'd thought she saw men break away from the other silhouetted figures and head in her direction. Each time panic had gripped her until she gradually realized her eyes were only playing tricks.

Finally, overcome by mental as well as physical exhaustion, she could no longer hold up her head to keep watch. Hugging the serape more tightly to her, she got up and trudged to the cabin.

Once inside the inky room, she wasted no time locating the door bar and dropping it into place, securing her haven. Yet still she couldn't stop the feeling that evil lurked within every shadow.

She undressed quickly and climbed into bed, pulling the blankets up past her chin. She curled into a tight ball, surrounding herself in comforting warmth as best she could. But as time slowly passed, sleep continued to elude her. She missed the warmth of Chama's body next to hers, the safety of his sure arms enfolding her. When she finally dropped off, it was fitful. At every sound, real or imagined, she awakened. With so many milling about and Chama occupied with trading, one of the marauders could easily slip across the meadow unnoticed. Come take for himself the sheriff's infamous daughter.

15

By the time the last rifle had been haggled over, Chama's mouth felt as dry as a desert wind. He needed a drink. And besides, he was in the mood for a little celebrating. Maybe forty-five rifles wouldn't fill a post arsenal, but in the right hands they could inflict a lot of damage.

As he rose to his feet, one of Dolan's gang caught his shoulder. "You're joinin' us at Shorty's, ain'tcha?"

Remembering how upset Carrie had been when he left, Chama looked across the clearing. He saw no light burning. She must have already gone to bed. Without him. "Sure," he said to the outlaw. "Why not?"

The cantina was already alive with clamor and smoke as men jostled up to the bar for service. After Chama managed to reach the counter and buy a drink, he put one hand over the top to prevent it from spilling while he pushed back through the crowd to an empty corner. Leaning against the wall, he scanned the room and figured there had to be fifty or more white men stuffed into the place, plus a good twenty Mexicans.

It was hard to believe how much the number of men being shown the way to the hidden valley had increased with each summer since he'd first been led into it four years ago. Too many.

And to prove him right, Bert Wormely sauntered up. Along with him came Jack Potfeld, a hard, lean man who'd first arrived in the valley two summers ago. Kid Lightning, the strutting young gunslinger who looked as silly as the name he used, swaggered beside them, a poorly rolled cigarette dangling from his lip.

Bert glanced back over his shoulder, then shook his head and grinned. "Ain't this one helluva hoop-dee-do? Shit, man, we oughtta hoist our own flag and start us our own country."

Jack Potfeld didn't share Bert's enthusiasm. Thumbs hooked in his pants pockets, he stared steely-eyed at Chama. "The gunrunner they call Bone says they had trouble gettin' in here 'cuz of that woman you boys took. It's been real nice havin' this place to come to. I'd sure hate to lose it over some fool daughter of that blasted sheriff."

"Yeah," the Kid said, bristling like some feisty little dog. "You pack her off, now, or we're gonna do it for you."

Chama eyed the smart-mouthed fledgling, and though he felt like stuffing the squirt's bright yellow bandanna down his throat, he bared his teeth in a grin. "What's the matter, Kid? Thought you weren't scared of anything."

"I ain't," he bawled, his bravado deflating.

Chama looked back at Potfeld, the real threat. "I agree. It's been real nice having this hideout as long as we have. But too many people know how to get here now. Sooner or later the army will find it . . . unless," he said with a slight smile, "my Indian brothers get to them first."

The Kid elbowed Wormely in the ribs.

Bert flinched. "All right," he said, giving the skinny lad a sour look. "Some of the fellas has been comin' up to me tonight, wantin' us to do somethin' about the woman. I say what the hell. Why not just send her back." He fanned his hands and grinned hopefully. "She sure ain't worth all this fuss."

"I see." *So, the little weasel didn't think she was worth a fuss, did he?* Chama took a step back. There was a good chance he'd be needing more elbowroom. "Well, I'll tell you what, Bert. I'll think about it if you give back the two hundred I paid you for her. And for good measure, why don't you throw in that soft little whore you bought last week."

Wormely started stammering, "But I don't—I can't—no, I—"

Leaving him floundering, Chama shifted his attention to Potfeld. "And, Jack, I take a real fancy to that Acoma woman of yours. How about you throwing her in, too?"

Potfeld's sinewy body stiffened. He reached for his gun.

Chama grabbed his wrist before he could pull it.

The muscles in Potfeld's jaw knotted and his eyes narrowed. "Uletee is *my* woman. She's carrying *my* child, and I'll have no man talkin' like she's just some worthless sack of dirt."

"Well," Chama said lightly, contrary to his battle-ready stance, "I guess the deal's off then."

"Wait a min—"

"No, you wait," Chama grated as he stepped within inches of Potfeld's face. "First man to come anywhere near my woman, I'll kill. You got that?" Knocking past Potfeld and the Kid, he started for the entrance, then swung back. "And don't forget to tell your friends. The first man I see coming up my hill is dead."

Shoving through the crowd toward the door, Chama heard Bert's tinny voice ring out. "Naw, there ain't no trouble. It's just the breed's got kinda attached to Sheriff Jackson's daughter. Lord knows why. And, well, he sorta started threatenin' to shoot us if we try an' take her. But it don't mean nothin'. He's just all worked up right now."

"I'll bet I could take him," Chama heard the Kid bluster.

Chama was tempted to go back and give him his chance. But there was more at stake than taking some young buck down a notch or two. If something happened to him, Carrie would be left to the mercy of those animals. Squelching his fierce urge to smash in a few faces, he slammed out the door.

He ranted at the impudence of the bastards as he tromped through grass wet with night dew. "They're nothing but a bunch of sniveling cowards. If they even look at her crossways, that sheriff will be the least of their worries.

"What am I saying?" Chama halted at the insanity of his words, of the stand he'd just taken. For the daughter of an ex-officer of the army, he was risking his life? And the lives of every Indian who sought refuge in the valley?

But then Carrie's face intruded into his thoughts, her eyes brittle-bright, her chin tilted with defiance. He would never forget her brave front the day she told him her father would never give up the search. Chama had taken something from his home. Not some*one*. Some*thing*.

Chama's lungs tightened at the thought of the years of shame she must've suffered after her father's brutal castration of her young lover. The guilt. And from the way she acted, her father had never forgiven her, yet he'd never let her go. That first time when Chama had lain with Carrie, her hunger for a loving touch had been so great it had torn at his soul as nothing before in his life. He could never send her back to Jackson if she didn't want to go. And especially not for that cowardly trash at the *rancheria*.

His resolve firmly restored, he started walking again.

Something dashed across his path.

Years of training brought him to a halt until he identified the sound of the creature's midnight flight. Just a rabbit.

Picking up the pace, his mind swung back to the standoff at Shorty's. "Potfeld didn't see any reason at all why I couldn't just give Carrie up . . . until I turned the tables on him. Carrying on about his woman being pregnant. Hell, for all I know, so's mine."

At the idea, Chama's anger dissipated again as he mulled over the possibility of a baby, his baby, snugged deep inside Carrie. He pictured her as her belly began to swell, then when she'd grown ripe with child. He envisioned her cradling the tiny new life to her breast, her hair veiled about them in a sunny glimmer.

Slowing, Chama breathed in the scents of the night. A child born of his own seed. His gaze wandered up to the glory of the starry heavens. For the first time he fully felt a oneness with it and the burgeoning earth beneath his feet. From his seed a new life would begin. Carrie would feed and nurture it. And within the protection of his watchful eye, the child would grow tall and strong and beautiful.

"And free," he vowed. "My son will be free to walk wherever his feet take him."

Carrie jerked awake at the sound of knocking. Tossing back the blankets, she sprang out of bed and ran to the door in the dim glow of the turned-down lantern. She grasped the wooden bar, then froze. What if it wasn't Chama?

"Carrie, it's me." His voice came from the other side. "Let me in."

Vastly relieved, she unbarred the entrance and stepped back.

Entering, Chama closed the door behind him, then took the stud from her hands and dropped it into the slots again.

"Did everything go all right?" Carrie couldn't help asking while returning to bed, despite the fact she hated the whole gun business.

He looked up from unbuckling his holster, something he strapped on only when he went to that cursed Comanchero camp. "Pretty much."

Carrie noticed a tightness in his reply and sensed things had not gone well at all. The same uneasiness she'd had all evening gripped her again, and when he didn't say anything else, she hesitated to question him further.

As she lay waiting, too anxious to close her eyes, Chama removed his clothes, then blew out the lamp and joined her in bed. He pulled her to him and wrapped himself around her, holding her tight.

She felt the tension in his arms, in his body, and knew something was terribly wrong. Something that threatened them both. "Tell me," she managed in the faintest whisper.

He took a deep breath and relaxed his grip somewhat. "The gunrunners were late because they had to dodge around several big posses that are searching the mountains. It seems your father has the whole territory stirred up over us taking you. And to make sure they keep at it till we're caught, he's put a high price on our heads."

Carrie went rigid. The end was near.

Chama pulled her close again and nuzzled her temple. "Some of the men around here think the posses might give up sooner if I send you back to your father."

Back? Carrie's heart began to thud with such force, she could barely form the words. "Are you going to?"

"No!"

The impact of his strong answer punched into her fear. He

would keep her, protect her. Tears flooded her eyes as she pressed her face into the hollow of his neck and breathed deeply of the musky scent that was his alone.

"But if you want to go back to him, I won't keep you against your will."

She wrenched away and tried to see his expression in the inky darkness. "I could never go back to him after being with you."

"Surely he couldn't blame you. Not this time."

"No, that's not what I mean. I don't ever want to go back. I hate him. From the moment the first shots were fired in South Carolina, he started blaming us for ruining his army career—his Southern family. And he never stopped. He crushed my mother's spirit so badly, she just went to bed. She stayed there till she died. And poor Charly . . ." Her throat clogging, Carrie forced a swallow. "My brother, Charly. Father always called him a whine-bag sissy. You see, he wasn't up to being a bully or kicking stray dogs. No, sir, he was never going to live up to what Father expected. Demanded. Thank God, he ran away. I just wish he would've taken me with him."

"Where's your brother now?"

"I don't know. He was just a kid when he escaped. Fourteen. I never heard from him after that. I just pray he's alive. And happy."

Chama drew her close again, cupping the back of her head with his hand. "Your father never went after him?"

"No. Said he didn't think Charly was worth the effort."

"Well, maybe that's a good sign. Who's to say he won't eventually feel the same way about you?"

"Don't fool yourself. I told you before, his coming is not about me. It's about him . . . and you. And mark my words, he *is* coming. Tomorrow. Next week." Tears flowed now with free abandon as she clutched him fiercely. Why wouldn't he understand?

"I believe you, Carrie," he crooned, his hand rubbing up and down her back, soothing the stiffness from her muscles. "But you have to trust me, too. You're my woman now, my gift from the sky. I will protect you."

❦ 16 ❦

ALL THE NEXT day Chama kept his rifle close by just in case someone decided to take him up on his challenge. But as the late-afternoon shadows stretched across the meadow, he saw nothing from his hilltop vantage except a few picketed horses grazing just this side of the *rancheria*. The Comanchero camp, itself, seemed as peaceful as any Rio Grande village on a Sunday afternoon.

Chama's gaze wandered to Carrie the way it always did since she'd come to stay with him. She stood at the campfire, turning a venison roast suspended on a spit. She'd seemed much calmer since he'd vowed to protect her. Nonetheless, she still jumped at the slightest snap of a twig or any varmint that scampered into their small clearing. And though she pretended not to, she'd kept as close a watch as he had. But her frequent glances were usually directed toward the valley's entrance. It was hard for him to believe that she could be more afraid her father would come than a mob of Comancheros.

She raised her hand to brush a fallen pine frond from her bonnet bill, and a lush breast pressed upward against her work shirt.

Even in those ugly clothes the sight caused his heart to pump strong with desire. Maybe he'd ask her if she'd like to go inside for a little *nap*.

His mouth dropped into a slack smile as he scanned the meadow once more and still found nothing suspicious. Turning, he sauntered up behind her and wrapped his arms around her, snugging her against the hardness of his growing arousal.

"Stop that!" She giggled and tried to pull away. "If I don't keep a close watch on the meat now, it'll burn."

Nuzzling the nape of her bare neck, he whispered, "I like burnt meat."

"That's what you say now." She pulled at his fingers laced across her waist. "Go tend the horses. By the time they're fed and you give them a good brushing, supper will be on the table."

"Food is *not* what I'm hungry for," he teased and blew a breath of warm air across her cheek.

"Go!"

Reluctantly, he released her and trudged around the back of the cabin to the shed.

Chama had fed and watered both horses and was brushing the tangles out of Hickory's black mane when the bay perked his ears outward.

Chama stopped working and listened for whatever had caught the animal's attention. He heard nothing, but both horses obviously did. Both had their heads hiked high and their nostrils flared wide.

Dropping the currycomb, Chama ran to the entrance—and collided with Carrie. He caught her by the arms. "What is it?"

"Two people are headed this way, and because of what you said last night, I thought . . ."

Not waiting for her to finish, he sprinted around to the front, grabbing his carelessly abandoned rifle as he went. When he reached an opening in the trees, he shaded his eyes against the dipping sun and searched the meadow, quickly spotting the intruders coming at about a hundred yards. Almost instantly he recognized them and relaxed. It was Karl, toting his toddler, and Esperanza.

Carrie, running close behind Chama, stopped at his side and clutched the sleeve of his cotton *camisa* while she caught her breath.

He wrapped an arm around her and gave her a reassuring hug. "It's only Karl and his woman—his wife—I mean, sort of."

"That doesn't make sense. What are you trying to say?"

"Nothing really. It's just— Well, you wouldn't think it would bother her in this hellhole, but it shames Esperanza to have anyone know she's living with Karl out of wedlock. So I act like they're married to make her feel better. She's really such an innocent little thing. Anyway, looks like they've decided to pay us a visit. Do you have enough food on the fire? I'd like to invite them to supper."

Carrie stepped out of his hold. Then with a curious smile, she picked up his hand and kissed the palm. "You know," she said, loving him with her eyes, "you really are a very nice man." She released him and started away. "I'll go peel some more potatoes to put in the pot."

The emotion swelling inside Chama at her unexpected gesture overflowed into a wide grin and the hearty handshake he gave Karl after the overweight man lumbered up the hill. He then took Ingacita from Karl and swung her around while planting loud sloppy kisses on one cheek, then the other.

By the time he stopped and stood the wiggly, giggling tot on the ground, her mother and father were laughing, too, obviously enjoying the attention Chama paid the little one as much as she did.

Ingacita spun around in a wobbly sort of way, then took off at a teetering run.

"Don' go near the fire," Esperanza warned as her urchin scampered onto one of the logs that made an L for seating around the open flames.

The dark-haired tot looked back with large stubborn eyes for a second, then swung them to her father. Her defiance collapsed, and she slid off the rough bark, then ran to Karl, grabbing him around the leg.

Esperanza stepped up to Chama and offered a small cloth-covered bundle. "I bring bread. I know this place, she has no oven. You like?"

"We sure do." Chama held it to his nose and took a whiff. *"Muchas gracias."*

Just then, Carrie came out the door with a bowl of cubed potatoes.

Chama held out the freshly baked gift as she neared. "Look,

Carrie, Señora Shipstead brought us a loaf of bread."

"How wonderful." She paused long enough to smile warmly at Esperanza before continuing on to the pot that now hung over the center of the fire. "I didn't know anyone up here had an oven," she tossed over her shoulder as she dumped in the vegetables and set the bowl on a flat stone. Then, wiping her hands on her apron, she walked up to Karl and stretched out her hand to take his.

His mouth stood agape, but he managed to thrust out his.

Since Carrie still wore the same unrevealing outfit she'd worn on the trip here, it took a moment for Chama to realize why the Swede looked so stunned—he'd never heard her speak.

"How nice to see you, Mr. Shipstead. It's been too long. And is this lovely lady the wife you spoke so highly of?" Carrie added as she turned her gracious smile to Esperanza.

The Swede eventually found his voice. "It's nice to see you, too, Miss Jackson." He reached back and pulled Esperanza up beside him. "Sweety, this here is Miss Jackson, the lady I told you about."

Tiny Esperanza, with her large lovely eyes and a ballooning belly, waddled forward. She took Carrie's hand into both of hers and looked up. "I am *muy* happy to meet you." Then her expression changed to one of concern. "You are good, no?"

Carrie covered Esperanza's hands with her own and gave her a look that Chama wished held no doubt. "Yes, Mrs. Shipstead, I'm fine. Very fine, thank you." Turning back to Karl, she looked down at Ingacita. "And who is this darling little creature who's turned your leg into a maypole?"

It was a tight squeeze, but Karl and Esperanza managed to fit on one of the benches while Carrie sat beside Chama on the opposite one. And Ingacita, Chama noted, seemed quite happy, squatting on the floor in front of a trunk. With a filled plate before her, she already had a handful of mashed-up potatoes stuffed into her mouth.

"Chama," Carrie said, handing him a butcher knife, "would

you please cut some slices of roast for our guests?"

Our guests. He liked the sound of that. "Sure."

"Pardone me." Esperanza held up her hand and turned a beseeching gaze up to her man. "Karl, he say the blessing first, no?"

The Swede's cheeks flushed to beet-red as he shot a glance at Chama and opened his mouth, but nothing came out.

"Yes, Mr. Shipstead," Carrie said, filling the gap of silence, "that would be very nice."

Chama did his best not to smile as Karl bowed his neatly trimmed blond head. "May God bless this food," he mumbled almost inaudibly, "this house, and all within it. Amen." Then, looking up at Chama, he grinned sheepishly. "That's another thing Spranza promised we'd do if Ingacita was healed."

During the meal, as if it had been prearranged, conversation never once strayed from the safe subjects of the various wonders of the valley and the exceptionally warm and dry weather they were experiencing for this time of year. Then about halfway through, Esperanza stopped eating and stared at Carrie.

"The hat," she said after a moment and pointed to the bonnet on Carrie's head. "He is still on the head."

"Oh, yes." Carrie fingered its floppy bill. "I usually keep it on because . . ." Pausing, she looked with hopeful eyes to Chama.

He knew he shouldn't let her remove it, but couldn't resist showing her off. He nodded.

As her flaxen hair came tumbling down like a shimmering waterfall, both Karl and Esperanza gasped. And the Swede's dumb stare was priceless.

Esperanza spoke first. "The hair, she is *muy bonita.*"

"Thank you, but then so is yours," Carrie replied, complimenting Esperanza's shiny black braids.

Karl's head turned toward Chama, but his eyes stayed with Carrie for another couple of seconds before following. His mouth dropped into a slack grin. "You sly old wolf. So, tell me again how you was doin' me and Wormely a favor by takin' her off our hands."

Chama tried to keep a straight face, but failed. "It seemed like the thing to do at the time."

"I'll bet," Karl sputtered and roared into laughter.

Chama joined him, laughing until tears formed in his eyes. Then, when he'd regained most of his control, he brushed the wetness away to see a full-blown smile on Carrie's face—a coveted sight. But in Esperanza's eyes, he saw only confusion.

Karl wiped away his own tears and took her tiny hand in his. "When we get home, sweety, I'll explain." He then looked from Carrie to Chama and burst out laughing again.

Supper over, Karl wanted a smoke, so Chama accompanied him outside. Settling on one of the fallen logs, Chama enjoyed the warmth of the dying coals and the fresh scent of pine while this friend he'd grown to care for over these past three summers rolled a paper square around a sprinkling of tobacco.

After Karl ran his tongue along one edge of the paper, he said, "Thought you oughtta know, some men come by to see me today all fired up. I told 'em I'd come see you."

"They want me to give Carrie up. Right?"

"Yeah. But now I understand why you won't. I wouldn't neither if she was mine, no matter how many posses was chasin' me. Your lady, she's real . . ." He paused, searching for the right word. " . . . special."

"I know. But, then, so is Esperanza."

"Yeah," Karl drawled and nodded absently several times. "Funny, ain't it, that a couple of rough cobs like us could end up with ladies like them. Guess it could only happen in a place like this. Anywhere else, and they wouldn'ta given us a second look."

"You may not believe this, but I think Carrie really wants to stay with me. I know she doesn't want to go back to her father."

Karl gave him a pat on the knee and nodded. "That's not hard to believe. He's a real mean hombre when he wants to be. And worse, he's good at makin' folks think he has the right to do whatever he wants. And Miss Jackson, she's acting real happy now. Smilin' all the time, like you two was on your honeymoon or somethin'. By the way, how is it, anyway?"

"How's what?" Chama said, pretending not to understand.

"You know," Karl singsonged.

"Oh, that!" Chama replied in mock surprise. "I've got no complaints." Hoping to distract Karl, he picked up a twig, set it ablaze on a hot coal, then lifted it up to light Karl's ready cigarette.

In a companionable silence, Chama and Karl enjoyed the twilight peace for a few minutes, till Karl finished his smoke. He flicked the butt into the campfire, then pointed to the distant Comanchero camp. "If it looks like trouble, I'll be over here in a flash."

"Thanks, old friend."

"You'd do the same for me." Karl rose to his feet and stretched. "Well, I guess I'd better gather up my little family and head for home before it's too dark to see. Besides," he said with a grin, "I left my bottle at home, and you never keep anything on hand to quench a man's thirst."

"I promise," Chama said, standing up, "the next time you come, I'll have something here for you."

Chama sat at the table, repairing a harness strap, while Carrie did the dishes. He hummed a simple little tune as he worked, one she didn't recognize but enjoyed a lot. In fact, she thought as she dried the last of the tin plates, the entire evening had been most pleasant . . . so pleasant, she'd hated to see the Shipsteads leave. They were such a delightful little family. Too bad Karl couldn't find them a safer home. Or Chama for her, for that matter.

Carrie glanced back at him, her happy glow fading. If he truly cared, he would. He didn't even have the gunrunners for an excuse any longer. She wanted desperately to approach him again about it, but he'd been so adamant last night when he'd insisted they were safe here. Yet if that were so, why had he kept his rifle at his side all day?

Finished with her task, she draped her towel to dry over the edge of the counter board and turned toward Chama. She'd held her tongue all day—she couldn't any longer. "Esperanza is such a sweet young girl. Why would Karl bring her to such a place?"

"He didn't exactly. She got here the first time the same way you did."

"You mean, you and Karl make a habit of kidnapping women?"

"No," he said with a chuckle. "She was captured by some Chiricahuas down in Old Mexico and brought here. Karl had never seen an Apache captive who'd been run for several days. Esperanza was almost dead, and she was a real mess, so I know he didn't buy her for her looks. He just couldn't stand to watch the way they were treating her. He nursed her till she was well. And as you can see, they took to one another. She's been with him ever since."

"If he loves her so much, why didn't he take her back to her people? From what Esperanza told me, she misses them very much."

"I guess maybe he was scared he'd lose her if he did. But he is taking her back after she has her baby and they're able to travel."

"I see," Carrie said, but she really didn't. It was hard to believe either man she'd supped with this evening could take a young woman captive or prevent a loved one from seeing her family. Or, she thought, an icy chill traversing her spine, stand by and let any young girl be mistreated. "How many other female captives have been brought here like us? Are there more living here right now?"

"Carrie, this isn't anyone's home. It's a rendezvous and a summer hideout." He lowered his gaze to the table again and picked up a new piece of leather.

Carrie came and sat down across from him. "That doesn't answer my question. How many captives are here? What's going to happen to them? I remember Wormely saying he was going to buy one. Did he?"

Chama looked up at her and sighed. Reaching across the table, he took her hands in his. "Listen to me. You must never think about the things that go on over there. I can't do anything about it and neither can you."

"But—"

"No buts. Ugly things happen during a war. You're from the South, you know that."

"But we're not at war."

"The hell we're not."

17

CHAMA SLEPT VERY little as the following days dragged by. Not wishing to alarm Carrie any more than she already was, he would retire with her as usual, then lay awake listening for any suspicious sounds. After she fell asleep, he'd ease out of bed and go outside to check the perimeter of the knoll. And, thereafter, during the night, he would do the same at least once an hour.

Standing in the shrouding shade of a pine in the wee hours of the ninth day, he looked across the meadow and wondered why no one had come. Most of the low-life bastards thrived on trouble—especially if they were causing it. Looking through a moonlit haze, he was drawn toward the narrow pass as more questions plagued him. Were posses still in the mountains, searching for Carrie? Had the army been called in? Someone at the Comanchero camp was sure to know. But he couldn't take the chance of going there for information—not for another week at least. For if by some miracle things had died down, he certainly didn't want to stir them up again.

Yes, she'd cost him a lot of sleep, all right. But she was worth it. Still, he had to make sure this hunger for her didn't grow so strong he would turn his back on his people just to please her. He must never let her bewitch him to that extent.

Through the trees he saw a new light flicker to life in the camp, bringing his attention back to the muted sounds of the late-night carousers—sounds punctuated by an occasional drunken shout or the shrieking laughter of one of the whores.

Chama didn't like being near the bloodthirsty scum any more than she did. But he had to stay where he could recruit men to ride with him. It would take two, maybe three robberies to collect enough money for when the gunrunners returned in late August. And if there was ever a time to arm the Apaches, it was now.

From what he'd heard when he passed through Doña Ana, the Cheyenne had joined with the Sioux to drive the bluecoats out of the Dakotas. And quite a number of soldiers from the forts here in New Mexico had been transferred north to strengthen their own forces.

Chama slammed a fist in his hand. *With the ranks low here, now would be the time for us to strike. If I could get the tribes down here to come together like those in the north, we might be able to free our own lands. Again be free to hunt and rest our heads wherever the setting sun finds us. And Carrie and I could be together without having to watch our trail every minute.*

A faint glow lit the eastern horizon, and Chama knew morning was not far behind. Soon he would take Carrie and spend yet another day away from the cabin in some secluded hideaway where he could nap in peace. Exhaling wearily, he trudged up the rise to start the morning coffee.

Drifting awake, Carrie found Chama bending over her, looking as dangerously handsome as ever.

He stared down at her from eyes so piercingly black yet so richly warm.

Unable to resist the lure, she smiled lazily and reached up.

As he knelt down, the edges of his own lips curled just before they found hers in a tender, lingering kiss.

As he pulled away, she caught a whiff of coffee, then noticed he was fully dressed. "Did I oversleep?"

"No, everything's fine." He brushed a strand of hair from her shoulder, then traced the spot with his fingers before rising to his feet again. "Breakfast is ready. By the time you get dressed, I should have the horses saddled."

As she watched him leave, she read the tiredness in his slow departure, and her heart ached for him. How many more days would he be able to stay up all night, then rest for only a few hours during the day? And all the time pretending there was nothing amiss.

Yes, she thought, he was quite a man. Not only was he ready to lay down his life for her, she mused while donning her clothes, he answered her every hungering need, wish, or whimsy. And she loved pleasing him as well, every inch of his magnificence, from his shining jet hair down to his Indian moccasins. And, besides, how many other men would have breakfast waiting for his woman?

But he was no henpecked sissy. No sir. He'd backed Bert down every time. And Karl, anyone could see how much the big Swede respected and admired him. In fact, she thought while buttoning her skirt, if he wanted, he could be leading a bunch of his own right now, like that marauder, Bull Dolan, she'd heard so much about, or one of the other gangs.

Shuddering at the loathsome thought, she sat down and grabbed up one of her old "clodhoppers." No, he could never be one of them. Even his lawlessness had an honorable intent—at least by his standards.

Realizing she was dwelling on a situation that was hopeless, she closed her mind to the grim inevitability before it could eat at her anymore. Deliberately, she diverted her attention to their rumpled bed, and in her mind she replayed their coming together the night before.

A tingle coursed through her body.

Grinning wickedly, she put on her last cumbersome shoe and tied it, then stood up, spread the blankets over their bed, and started out the door. "My, yes," she mumbled, "just the thought of him touching me, and I melt down to my toes."

"What?" Chama stood bent over a few feet away, tightening Hickory's girth.

"Nothing," she said, embarrassed that she'd been speaking such things aloud. "By the time you finish saddling Eagle Wings, I should be ready."

As he returned to his task, Carrie noticed him pat the bay on the neck. And that, she asserted silently in her final defense, was the best of all reasons to care for him. Not once had she seen him be anything but kind to his animals. And for his striking pony she knew he held a particular fondness. Every evening he brushed the stallion's coat until it gleamed.

Yes, he had nothing but the finest qualities. They could have built a happy life together. Had sweet babies like little Ingacita. If only . . .

Feeling herself starting to fall into a pit of melancholy again, she tore her eyes from him and headed for the campfire.

Carrie sat, as she had for a couple of hours, leaning against the sheer granite of the north wall, the rifle in her lap. After Chama had fallen asleep beneath the live oak a few yards away, she'd retrieved it *and would return it before awakening him*. He wasn't the only one playing the game.

She glanced skyward and watched with idle fascination as burgeoning thunderheads began to float toward them from over the southern rim. Most likely the clouds would bring only the third rainfall since the day of her arrival. And from their ominous darkness, a heavy downpour.

She glanced at Chama, lying on his side, his head resting on his hands. He looked so peaceful, almost childlike. It would be a shame to wake him for another couple of hours. Undecided, she shifted her gaze to the horses picketed and grazing in a small glen tucked within the dense forest in which she and Chama hid. Their mounts seemed to take no notice of the dropping temperature any more than the squirrels frolicking in and out of a landslide of shale slabs off to her right. If the animals weren't worried about getting a little water on them, why should she be?

A rapid tapping startled her. On instinct she clutched the rifle and quickly scanned the area before realizing it was just a woodpecker. Relieved, she resumed her guard duty by methodically scanning her entire circumference, starting with the wall at her left and ending at her right. Of course there'd been no unusual movement. The creatures of the woods and the horses would have reacted if anyone were sneaking about.

She relaxed her grip on her weapon and leaned her head against the sun-warmed stone to listen to the welcome sounds of an undisturbed forest.

LOVE SO WILD / 155

A sudden chill wind blew across her face, and at the same time it started a whirring sound through the pines. She looked up and saw the tips swaying in its force.

An ill wind. The first ominous words of an old adage stole her thoughts, gripping her with a keen sense of imminent foreboding. Like an evil wind, she knew as surely as she sat there, her father was on his way. In the rumble of the storm clouds overhead, she could imagine the thunder of his horse's hooves and the dozens more that would be following his lead. She and Chama had to escape this valley now, today, before he was taken, brutally slain.

Scrambling to her feet, she ran to where he lay and shook his arm. "Wake up. We have to leave here."

His eyes sprang open and he leapt up. "What? Who? Where are they?"

"No, no. I'm sorry. Nobody's here. We're safe."

Still only half awake, he looked wildly about him, then swung his attention back to her. "But didn't you just say—"

Carrie shushed him by putting her fingers to his lips. "I'm sorry I frightened you. It's just that I suddenly had this terrible premonition. My father is very close. You must listen to me this time. If you care anything about me—for your own life—we must leave this valley and go far away from here. California. I always wanted to see the Pacific. Please, let's go to California."

Chama looked at her for the longest moment, then, instead of answering her, he reached under her chin and untied her bonnet and removed it. As her hair fell, he spent an inordinate amount of time fanning it over her shoulders.

His gaze held her like a magnet, drawing her close until her lips met his. Losing herself in it, she shared the tenderest of kisses with him as they leisurely nipped and nibbled on each other.

It wasn't until they parted that Carrie's mind began to unfog. To help support her passion-weakened legs, she grasped his shoulders. "Chama, we must leave. We can't wait any longer. My father will have fifty, maybe a hundred men with him. Our only chance is to get far away now."

"Sweetheart, the opening to this valley is hard to find even when you know exactly where it is. Unless he's guided in he'll never find it."

"You've got to stop counting on that. If Father needs a guide, he'll get one, one way or another." She clutched his shirt. *"My father always wins."*

Chama took her hands. Enfolding them within his own, he peered deeply into her eyes. "Even if everything you say is true, finding an informer, gathering a force of men, and arranging for the arms and supplies, that all takes time. But still, to be on the safe side, I've asked Tacate and some of the other Apaches to keep an eye out for trouble. They'll let me know if he gets close."

"But don't you see? We wouldn't have to worry about any of this if we left the territory."

"I can't. The gunrunners will be back here in a couple of months. I have to pull some more holdups between now and then."

Guns? Robberies? She wrenched away and stepped back. Tears burned the backs of her eyes. "You don't really care about me at all, do you? Just robbing and killing for all those damned Indians of yours."

He stepped into the empty space between them. "Please try to understand. The soldiers have to be stopped. They're taking everything. Destroying everywhere they touch. If they have their way, there won't be a free Indian left in the whole damned country soon."

Understanding his pain took the sting out of her anger. She lowered her voice. "I know. But no matter how much you care or how hard you try, it's still going to happen. The army has their orders. They can't be stopped."

"Do you know what first attracted me to you?"

"Please don't change the subject. We must settle this."

"It was because you reminded me so much of my mother. You became her in spirit with that same uncomplaining Kiowa bravery. I could never have turned my back on your need. Your face would have haunted me ever more as Spotted Fawn's still does after all these years. But when she needed me I was too young. I couldn't save her when a sergeant by the name of Sweeny got drunk one night and beat her to death. You see," he continued in a rough, grating voice, his eyes sharpening to brittle shards, "my mother belonged to the soldiers. I guess you could say she was luckier than most. She survived eight years with them. On the day of her death I vowed to avenge her . . . and all the other Indian women those merciless white devils kept at the fort."

"I'm so sorry. I didn't know." She took his hand, but he didn't seem to notice.

He chuckled bitterly. "I guess the army was scared of what a seven-year-old boy might do to them, because they shipped me out of Colorado and down to a mission near Santa Fe. But nowhere would have been far enough. I've been killing bluecoats any chance I got ever since. Three years ago when I hit upon the idea of supplying rifles to the renegades, I knew it was by far the best way to avenge Spotted Fawn and all her people. *My* people. So you see, I can't leave here, not even for you."

"Do you think your mother would want you to dedicate your whole life to revenge, even for her? If I had a son, I'd want to think he was living a happy life, with a wife, children. I know it's natural for you to want to pay the soldiers back for the terrible things they did to your mother's people, but when will it be enough? How much blood do you have to spill before you're free to go on with your own life?"

As she waited for his reply, a large raindrop plopped on her head, then another splattered on her cheek.

Chama wiped the second one away with his thumb. "Time to leave," he whispered, then wheeling around, he strode off to fetch the horses . . . strode away, leaving the air thick with unanswered questions.

Watching him go, Carrie sighed from the depths of her defeat. His silence was his answer. They had only now, today. Nothing but a violent end awaited them.

❧ 18 ❧

WHEN TWO WEEKS had passed without any sign of trouble from the *rancheria,* Chama began to breathe easier. Even Carrie began to smile again once in a while. So after breakfast Chama decided to chance a visit to the Comanchero camp, check for himself if all was forgotten.

Nearing the trees across the clearing, he already knew to expect a depleted population. Every day since the gunrunners left, he'd seen men ride out. Looking about, he counted the number of horses grazing in the meadow and those in the corral and figured no more than thirty men remained, along with a few women and children.

Chama headed for the most likely place to glean information—the store. As usual, several men sat on the porch, engrossed in conversation.

One of them noticed him, a towheaded gunslinger called Whitey. "Here's the breed now," he said to the others, then beckoned to Chama with a rawboned finger. "Hey, breed, come on over." He waited until Chama reached the steps to continue. "There's a payroll coming from El Paso up to Fort Bayard and then goin' on to Fort Sumner. Them soldiers ain't been paid for over three months, so there'll be a bushel of greenbacks. You know this country like the back of your hand. Where do you think's the best place to ambush 'em?"

Relishing the prospect, Chama leaned against a porch post, and forgetting all else, was soon absorbed in the planning of his favorite kind of job—robbing bluecoats. And if they had to shoot a few of them to do it, all the better.

Once the plan was set, Chama returned to his reason for coming and inquired in as casual a drawl as possible, "I been kept real busy lately. Haven't been around. Anything I should know about?"

Kelso, a drifter who was given to smiling his way out of trouble, snickered. "Naw. Ain't seen a new face around here since the gunrunners come in with all that scare-talk."

"Aye," English Jack agreed, his accent thick. A grin creased his weather-reddened cheeks. "A body would've thought the entire United States Cavalry was about to ride down on us in a twinklin' of the eye."

"Yeah," another said. "And now we know who's got yellow bellies. 'Cuz we seen 'em slitherin' outta here on 'em real fast. Ain't that right, boys?"

The others burst into laughter at the sport-making. The Englishman slapped his knee while some of the others stomped their boots on the hollow floor.

"Old women," Kelso hooted, enjoying the fun he'd started.

Observing how the men had sidestepped the issue of Carrie, Chama was pleased. Their silence about the matter assured him they accepted his ownership of her. He remained on the porch listening to them deride the departing outlaws until it seemed natural for him to drift on. No way did he ever want them to think he was anxious about his situation.

With a casual nod, he stepped off the porch and started wandering among the huts and wickiups clustered behind the store. He paused along the way, chatting with each person he encountered in the language with which they were most comfortable. Again, the topic of the woman was conspicuously unmentioned, and wherever he meandered he was treated in a casual, offhanded manner. Beginning to truly relax for the first time, he passed Bull Dolan's woman.

Nell stood near her hut, stirring a large kettle of boiling clothes. Seeing him, she swung around, stir stick in hand. "Hey. You. Chamasay."

He stopped and eyed the leathery-skinned woman who went on raids with her man often as not. "Yes? Is there something you want?"

"You're damned right there is," she railed, shaking the dripping stick at him. "Who do you think you are? Puttin' us all in danger, jest 'cuz you want to keep some simperin' plaything."

"Where's Bull?" Chama asked, looking past her for the man who'd been one of Quantrill's Raiders during the Civil War and now unleashed the same terror on the little Mexican villages along the border, looting and killing wherever he and his gang rode.

"Him and some of the boys," she spat as if it were a challenge, "is takin' a little run down into Chihuahua." Standing with her legs apart and that piece of hardwood clutched tight in her hand, she looked ready to do battle this minute.

"Well, when Dolan comes back, if you're still of a mind to meddle in my business, have him look me up."

Either his own fierce expression or his words must have put her in her place, because she clamped her mouth shut and returned to swishing her wash around, but with angry vigor.

Leaving the woman behind, Chama strode directly to the back of the camp where Karl's cabin stood at the edge the woods.

Karl, a late riser, sat at the table, slurping his first cup of brew when Chama entered. His hands shook noticeably. "Have some coffee," he said, pointing to the soot-blackened pot on the table.

After grabbing a cup off the shelf, Chama poured himself some and joined his friend. "Where's the little woman?"

Karl looked around as if he might find her in the small room. "I dunno. Probably out gettin' water or something. And you know how women talk when they get together."

"Well, I know how one woman talks," Chama said, a grin pulling at the corners of his mouth. "Bull Dolan's woman just come flying at me, mad as a wet hen. For a minute I thought she was going to crown me with her wash stick."

Karl chuckled hoarsely, then cleared his throat. "You're lucky she didn't. She could probably whip you and me put together. One night down in Socorro I seen her nearly kill another whore. It took four men to pull her off. And when they did, she come up with a punch that knocked some cowboy's two front teeth out."

"She's a rough one, all right."

"Yeah. I hear she was even too tough for the Apaches. Mangas got hold of her once, and it wasn't no time before I heard he'd traded her off to Cochise, who, in turn, handed her over to the army for a peace offering. Some peace offering. No wonder the Cañada Alamoso Treaty blew all to hell."

"Well," Chama said, stretching his legs out before him, "this time she's put out 'cause I didn't send Carrie back to her father. Everyone else I talked to acted real friendly, so I thought things had cooled off. That is, till Nell come at me."

"Things have cooled off." Karl downed the last of his coffee and wiped his mouth on his sleeve while Chama waited for him to continue. "It was real hot around here for a couple of days. But then Jack Potfeld—I never knew you an' him was buddies."

"We're not."

"Well, he flat stood up for you when Three-Fingered Mike and his bunch was workin' up their nerve to go get Miss Carrie from you. Jack told 'em that every time someone runnin' from the law come up here, this place was put in danger. Then he said, if we start pickin' and choosin' who can stay and who can't, then we don't need no law to come wipe us out, 'cuz we'll end up doin' it to ourselves. I can't remember everything he said, but it was a real fine speech. The man oughtta run for office. Anyway, he rallied most of the boys around, and to them that was still grumblin', he said they should leave till they felt it was safe to come back. And guess what?" Karl's eyes sparked with merriment, and he slapped the table, setting the coffeepot lid to rattling. "That whole damned gang rode out the same day, along with Montez and his *bandoleros*. Good riddance, I say."

"If that's how it was settled, how come Nell's carrying on like she is?"

"Oh, you know women. Her man ain't around to protect her just now, so she's actin' real jumpy."

"Yeah, guess you're right." Chama picked up his tin cup, then, remembering the proposed robbery, put it down. "Kelso,

Black, and some others are planning to hold up an army payroll on its way to Fort Bayard. You want to come along?"

"I can't. Esperanza's due any day now. I don't want to leave her alone." Karl lowered his gaze to his hands and added, "And, well, I guess I won't be going on any more jobs anyway. You see, I sorta promised I wouldn't."

"Sure, Karl, I understand," Chama said with almost a straight face. "You being a family man now, you've got responsibilities to think about."

The sound of the door squeaking open drew Chama's attention.

Esperanza stepped into the room, toting a bucket of water. Upon seeing Chama, she greeted him with a lilting smile. "Señor José!" She glanced around the room. "Señora Jackson, you bring her, no?"

"I left her at home," Chama said, amused that she'd referred to Carrie as a married woman.

"You know," she said, scooting the bucket onto the table, "I say to her, my oven she is her oven if she want to bake bread. But she no come."

"We've been kinda busy the last couple of weeks."

Esperanza pointed her finger only inches from Chama's face. "You tell her I fire up the oven this afternoon. You bring her today. *Comprende?*"

"Yes, ma'am." Chama rose, chuckling. "Guess I'd better get on back, then. See you later."

On his way out, he heard an equal share of amusement in Karl's voice as his friend called after him. "Yeah, Chama. You'd best be gettin' on back to the little woman, now."

Walking home, Chama reminded himself for perhaps the hundredth time that he needed to start keeping Carrie at a safer distance. If he didn't, she'd be running him the way Esperanza did Karl—a man easily three times her size. And, unlike Karl, Carrie wanted something from him that he couldn't give. Wouldn't. He refused to turn his back on his people, even for her.

But despite his repeated warnings to himself, his feet of their own volition picked up the pace the closer he got to the cabin, and he was almost running by the time he burst through the door . . . startling Carrie.

Dropping a handful of dried apple slices, she whirled around. As she recognized him, a hand flew to her breast and she laughed nervously.

"Sorry." Feeling a twinge of guilt, he stooped to help her pick up the spilled fruit. His holster dug into his side. After laying the pieces on the counter, he strode across the room and unbuckled it.

As he hung it over a wall peg, Carrie asked, "Well?"

He turned around and, seeing the anxiety in her eyes, smiled reassuringly. "Everything's all right. Nobody's heard or seen anything about your father coming into the mountains yet. And anyone who was afraid to stay because of him left. For now, anyway, the trouble's over."

"What?" she cried, a great smile lighting her face. "We've been given more time? Days? Maybe weeks?" In a running leap, she threw herself on him, almost knocking him over. Laughing joyously, she mussed his hair and scattered kisses on his cheeks, his nose, his lips.

Infected with her change of spirit, he growled playfully and swung her around. Capturing her mouth with his own, he delighted in her eager response as her lips careened across his.

Unable to contain his amusement at her ravenous assault, he pulled her off of him and grinned. "Why, you're nothing but a shameless hussy, trying to seduce me. And here it is, the middle of the day. But of course, me being the weak man I am," he said, running his fingers through his mussed hair, "I'm sorely tempted, sorely, but . . ."

"But what?" she said with a seductive pout as she started unbuttoning her shirt.

"But," he stalled as he watched her fingers slowly do their work. "I've been given orders by Esperanza to bring Señora Jackson, *Mrs. Jackson,* to her house after nooning to bake bread."

Those danged fingers stopped between the second and third buttons, and the wanton expression on Carrie's face changed into one of propriety. "Oh, really?"

"Yes," he groaned as he watched her restore order to her clothes. "Isn't it amazing how with one little 'señora,' Esperanza's magically turned you into a straight-laced lady." He took her face in his hands and gave her a quick peck on the lips. "Esperanza does have a way of simplifying life. Don't you wish it was really so clear and easy?"

Sitting across from Carrie during the noon meal, Chama noticed that her happy mood had disappeared. She sat brooding, merely toying with her food.

"Sunshine?"

She looked up, startled, as if she'd been caught doing something naughty.

"I thought you liked Esperanza and wanted to visit her."

"Oh, I do."

"Well, you sure don't act like it. Does it offend you, her pretending you're married?"

"It's not that. I was just wondering—will we be seeing any tortured bodies hanging in the trees on our way to the Shipsteads'?"

"No!" he answered with force. "The body you saw when we first arrived was taken down a couple days later. That particular man sold some Chiricahuas a barrel of bad whiskey. It made 'em so sick, three of 'em died. When the rest of 'em got back on their feet, they tracked him down here and put an end to his whiskey-trading days forever."

"I see," she mumbled. Apparently satisfied with his explanation, she spooned in a mouthful of beans.

"You've got nothing to fret about as long as you're with me. Remember, though, keep yourself covered. I'd just as soon not have to shoot any of the scum over there for panting after you."

Carrie's insides knotted at the idea of stepping foot in the evil place as she and Chama started across the meadow. Although she did her best to concentrate on the soft pastels of the long-stemmed flowers springing up among the grass blades, she couldn't help making certain her shirt was bloused out enough, or checking for opened buttons and feeling for any loose strands that might have escaped her bonnet.

Chama must've noticed her anxiety. He shifted the bag of fresh venison he toted into the hand with the flour sack, and wrapped his free arm around her shoulders. "It's a good day for baking bread. Don't you think? Not too hot."

Nodding, she leaned into his side, drawing his warmth, his strength. She matched her steps to his and, nearing the first huts, gave him her bravest smile. They'd been given more time. She wanted to make the most of it.

Chama steered her away from the store, taking her through a haphazard row of huts and wickiups. She had to lift her skirt as they picked their way past human waste and carelessly scattered garbage. The stench floated up in waves, smothering the fresh scents of the forest. Carrie had always been told crime didn't pay. Now she saw the truth in those words firsthand.

As they passed a rude shack, a woman came outside, slapping absently at flies that buzzed about her. She appeared underfed and work-worn in faded, frayed clothes, and her hair looked like it hadn't had a good brushing in days.

Carrie caught a flash of movement behind the woman's drab skirt and saw a small child clinging to her, his face and hands as dirty as his clothes.

"Mornin', ma'am," Chama said as if nothing were amiss.

The barest smile flickered at the woman's lips as she mumbled something in return. But what tugged at Carrie's heart the most were her eyes. They held nothing but a vacant look of hopelessness.

Traveling on, a staggering revelation struck Carrie. She, herself, must have looked just as vacant and hopeless these past years, and still would if not for Chama.

She glanced back, but the woman had disappeared inside. Turning forward again, she noticed another woman farther on crouched before a flat stone, making tortillas. Her clothes appeared tidier, but when she looked up, the expression in her eyes also lacked spark.

These women certainly were not where they wanted to be. Were they captives like her or captives of their own poor choices?

Overwhelmed with gratitude for being given these few more precious days of feeling wanted and, yes, loved, Carrie reached up to her shoulder and squeezed Chama's hand, then wrapped her other arm around his waist as she smiled at him.

He must have instinctively understood because, without a word, he paused and ducked beneath the bill of her bonnet to brush his lips across hers.

Reaching a little square surrounded by four cabins, Chama directed Carrie toward one, the Shipsteads'. She was pleased to see no garbage strewn about. She also noticed that the ground around the clay oven and a flat-topped boulder used for meal grinding had been swept smooth. Her admiration for the winsome young Mexican girl grew.

Esperanza saw them as they approached her open door. "Come in, come in," she whispered with an animated smile as she pointed to Ingacita, who napped on a pallet in the back corner. *"Mi casa es su casa."*

"Gracias," Chama said, returning her friendly greeting just as quietly as he and Carrie tiptoed inside. "I brought you some fresh meat. I hope you can use it."

"Oh, *sí*, Señor José. *Muchas gracias*." She took the hefty tote bag from him and set it in a tub beneath the counter.

Chama glanced about. "Where's Karl?"

"The store of Señor Rodriguez. He say you come. Sit with him there."

Chama looked at Carrie, his brows raised questioningly.

She nodded. "Go ahead. We'll be fine here," she said, keeping her own voice hushed.

After he'd gone, Carrie helped Esperanza mix the ingredients and knead the dough. While waiting for it to rise, they walked outside and sat on the top porch step.

As Esperanza chatted about her happy childhood, about being raised in a large, loving family, it brought back Carrie's own memories of Carolina. Her mother, too, had sat outside on sunny afternoons talking to the neighbor ladies. And now having a woman of her own to visit with after all these years felt wonderfully good. Another slice of joy to be savored.

Carrie rested her back against a nearby post and wrapped herself in the warmth of Esperanza's lilting patter as the young girl told her that Karl had promised to take her back to Chihuahua to live as soon as she and the new baby could travel.

"*Mi mamacita*, she be so happy to see me. And when she see *mi* Ingacita!" A joyous tinkling laughter spilled from her as she hugged herself. "Señor José, he promise to guide us home."

"Chama? He's taking you to Old Mexico?" He'd never mentioned that. But, then, why bother? He couldn't very well do it, not with scores of men out there bent on tracking him down.

"You come, too? You meet *mi familia*. We make *la fiesta, muy grande*. You like?"

"Yes," Carrie said, determined to keep the inevitable at bay. Instead, she allowed herself to get caught up in Esperanza's enthusiasm. "I would like that very much. When's your baby due?"

"Soon. Any day."

"If you would like, I could come help you deliver it."

Esperanza took Carrie's hand and looked up at her with that innocent openness. "Oh, *muchas gracias*. I no trust most the womans in this place. But your eyes, they are kind."

"I like you very much, too. So, it's settled. When the baby is coming, you send Karl for me, and I'll hurry straightaway."

By the time the dough was ready, they'd already built a fire in the beehive-shaped oven and fed Ingacita, who'd awakened with sleepy-eyed smiles. As they walked outside, Carrie spotted two unkempt women down on their knees grinding dried corn on the flat boulder pocked with holes.

The women looked up and without smiling nodded in greeting, then immediately returned to their task.

Carrie noticed that Esperanza's returning dip of the chin held no more friendliness than theirs had, reminding Carrie of what Esperanza had said earlier—the girl didn't trust most of them.

Deciding to follow the young Mexican's lead, Carrie tried to ignore the fact that the other two worked only yards away as she and Esperanza shoved the loaf pans onto the floor of the hot oven and closed the door. This time as they sat on the porch step Esperanza remained quiet. Without a doubt, Carrie knew the other women's presence intimidated her.

Taking Esperanza's cue, Carrie concentrated on Ingacita, watching her scamper after a fluffy-tailed squirrel. But before long, she became aware that the two squatted at the stone were now doing a whole lot more whispering than grinding.

The women dropped their mallets, then stood up and walked out of sight between two of the cabins.

Once the women were out of hearing range, Esperanza relaxed and began to chat again. And once again Carrie basked in the sunny music of her lilting voice.

A few feet away Ingacita squealed with delight as she dragged a stick across the fine dirt and watched the scraggly lines that followed.

Yes, Carrie thought as a soft breeze washed the cool fragrances of the forest over her, this was a moment to be treasured. A lazy afternoon. Small talk. The laughter of a child. *Thank God I'm alive again. It feels so good. I feel so good.*

Carrie, too, began to talk idly about her own childhood, about the Christmas parties her family had been famous for.

Then at one point Esperanza expressed the impossible wish. "Maybe this year you and Señor José give a big party. Start your own happy times."

Before Carrie could collect herself enough to reply, the two untidy women returned along with a third.

"Nell," Esperanza breathed in a rushed whisper.

Carrie glanced at Esperanza and saw fear in her eyes.

This Nell person strode with swaggering purpose toward them, exuding strength in her wiry frame. She stopped directly in front of Carrie and stared boldly, her feet apart, her hands on her hips.

The fine hairs on the back of Carrie's neck prickled as Nell's two comrades came up on either side of her.

"So, this here's the sheriff's daughter what don't want to go home to her *daddy*," Nell chided.

Carrie felt her very pregnant friend stiffen, confirming the obvious. Violence was a breath away. Her first concern had to be Esperanza and little Ingacita. Her heart pumped fiercely as she rose, bringing Esperanza up with her. Then, moving away from her vulnerable friend, she stepped off the porch and circled around to the other side of Nell and her cohorts while speaking in the most gracious of tones she could rally. "How do you do? My name is Carrie Jackson. I don't believe I've had the pleasure of an introduction."

"What have we here?" Nell jeered as she swiveled to face her prey. "A fine society lady." The laughter that followed sounded more like a taunt.

The other two snickered nervously as their eyes darted to Nell, then back to Carrie.

Nell reached out with the speed of a striking rattler, tearing loose the ribbons beneath Carrie's chin and ripping away the bonnet.

Carrie's hair fell in a weighty mass down her back.

"This must be the latest thing in hats," Nell sneered and slapped the floppy calico covering on the head of the skinniest of her friends. "It suits you much better, Cora. Don't you think so, Mabel?"

"Oh, yes," the other, who had the rawboned hardness of a farm woman, agreed. "It looks right smart on you, Cora."

"You think so, too, don't you, Miz Jackson," Nell bawled, leaning within inches of Carrie's face.

Carrie had witnessed her father and his deputies torment some poor soul in this same manner on a number of occasions. They always began the ritual by terrorizing him verbally, then they would roughly shove the pleading man back and forth between them before they finally beat him senseless.

Nell bared her teeth in a sneer and looked from one friend to the other.

If Carrie didn't act now, it would be too late.

Replacing her hands on her hips, Nell's stingy dark eyes challenged Carrie. "I said, don't you think it looks better on—"

Carrie silenced her with a rocking blow to the nose.

Nell crashed into Cora, whose hands were at her own throat, tying on the bonnet.

In the next instant Carrie knocked past Mabel and ran for her life.

The woman managed to whirl around and grasp the back of her shirt. Buttons popped and the material began to rip.

Carrie jerked free, leaving behind a piece of cloth and some strands of pulled-out hair. She escaped around the corner of one of the cabins and raced in the direction of the large central buildings as she heard Nell wail.

"She broke my nose. I'll kill the bitch!"

Carrie lifted her skirts, wishing fervently that she had on something other than her brother's oversize boots. Even barefoot she would've had a far better chance. She dodged past huts and wickiups, caring not what messes of refuse she plowed through.

Two men and a child gawked as she rounded a corner. They jumped out of her way.

A few yards farther Carrie slowed, searching for the most direct path to the store, then glanced over her shoulder.

Her three assailants, their skirts hiked up past their knees, barreled after her, rapidly closing the gap.

She prayed desperately that she would reach the store and Chama before they caught her in her blasted farm boots. She lunged forward.

Thank God, the buildings loomed close.

But the screeches of her pursuers raged even closer.

At the ever-louder pounding of feet, Carrie dared not look back. She pressed harder though her legs shook and her lungs felt on fire. Rounding one of the corrals behind the store, she spotted an old ax handle leaning against a fence post. She veered over to it and snatched it up. The women would no doubt catch her before she found Chama.

As Carrie rounded the corner to the front of the store, someone grabbed a handful of her flying hair and jerked her back.

Carrie screamed with pain and swung the club around, catching Cora, the skinny one, hard across the midsection.

The woman crumpled to the ground, clutching her belly and moaning.

Out of the corner of her eye, Carrie saw the other two almost upon her. Spotting a small rise a few feet from her, she ran partway up and spun around to face her enemy, every nerve, every muscle alive and ready.

Nell, blood spraying from her nose with each rasping breath, stopped abruptly, along with her sturdy ally . . . just out of reach of Carrie and her long piece of hardwood.

Between gulps of air, Nell wheezed, "I'm—going—to—get—you!" She gave Mabel a shove, and the two began circling in opposite directions.

Nell jumped forward, then back, feigning attack as Carrie held her ground and watched warily.

Mabel followed her friend's lead and did the same.

Carrie refused to be baited into swinging wildly. She tightened her grip on the bat and waited.

The commotion of screaming women racing through camp had attracted attention. People came running up to watch the spectacle. Laughing and cheering, they formed a ring around Carrie and the two crouched attackers.

"I'll give you two to one on Nell," yelled someone.

Nell and Mabel started to move behind Carrie.

She backed farther up the rise.

"Mabel! Now!" Nell shouted, and they charged simultaneously.

Fearing Nell the most, Carrie swung first at her.

Nell jumped back, narrowly escaping.

Mabel leapt behind Carrie, grabbing her around the neck.

Carrie wrenched sideways and delivered a vicious jab with the butt of the ax handle. She heard Mabel's ribs crack.

The woman staggered back, holding her side, then dropped to her knees.

Nell retreated a few steps, no longer looking quite so confident.

Carrie remained where she was, watching both women until Mabel rolled onto her side and drew up her legs. Dismissing her as a threat, Carrie concentrated on Nell, who now took a couple more steps back into the crowd, quickly glancing from side to side.

Some of the more vocal spectators began to taunt.

"What's the matter, Nell? She too much for you?"

"The queen is dead! Long live the queen!"

"Nell's gone yellow!"

Others shouted encouragements.

"You can take her, Nell!"

One with a gravelly bass voice yelled, "Take that stick away from her an' whoop her with it."

Nell swiped the blood from her nose and gave Carrie a mean, measuring look, and Carrie knew the woman would not back down.

Carrie gripped the ax handle with both hands and crouched.

19

CHAMA WAS FINALIZING the robbery plans in the back room of the store when he and the other men heard the uproar out front. Always attracted to excitement, the others poured out onto the porch. Irritated at their lack of commitment, Chama lagged behind.

By the time he reached the top step, the others had already run down and charged into the shouting circle of people. From Chama's vantage point, he looked to the center . . . *then looked again* before he could believe that his Carrie stood on a small rise in a warlike stance, with an ax handle at the ready. Her hair flew in wild disarray about her gaping shirt that exposed entirely too much of her breasts as she took in great gulps of air. Off to the side, he saw Mabel Spivy hunkered down, holding her side.

Pushing past the others, he jumped off the porch and shoved his way through the crowd. Then he saw the one Carrie watched with such intensity—Nell, Dolan's woman, bloody-faced. Wild-eyed. *Dangerous*.

He started for Nell just as she reached for a bystander's hunting knife.

She saw him and turned his way on wary feet.

Keeping track of Dolan's woman out of the corner of his eye, Chama faced Carrie and yelled the only thing he could think of that might bring an end to the confrontation. "Woman! Have you no shame? Look at you."

Carrie's eyes widened at the sound of his voice. She found him, and her expression collapsed with relief. An instant later his words must've sunk in because she looked down and saw herself, her ripe breasts displayed for all to see as her tattered shirt billowed with the breeze. Letting go of the bat with one hand, she tried to pull the remnants across her bosom.

"Get home, now!" Chama commanded. "Before I take a whip to you!"

Carrie glared at him, her turquoise eyes glittering with rage.

Nell, on the other hand, relaxed her stance and folded her arms across her chest, smiling triumphantly—a good sign that Chama had managed to defuse the situation before it grew any worse.

Then, without warning, Carrie flung the ax handle. In a whir, it flew end over end straight at him.

Chama and everyone else within ten feet dodged out of the way. By the time he looked back at her, she'd already spun around and was charging through the jeering crowd, heading toward their cabin across the meadow.

"Hey, breed, I thought you said the sheriff's daughter was *real* ugly," someone brayed from behind.

"Yeah, ugly as homemade soap," another hollered.

Turning toward the last voice, he recognized Waco Bob. "Well," he countered, forcing a grin, "at least it kept the wolves from the door."

"That it did, that it did," laughed a newcomer through his wiry beard.

Barney Kelso, a notorious womanizer, slackened his mouth into one of his practiced grins. "That's a real fine-looking woman you got there, Chama."

"Just don't you forget she's *my* fine-looking woman."

More laughter, along with whistles and catcalls, followed on the heels of Chama's statement.

Nell, who'd been gingerly dabbing her dripping nose, dropped the hem of her skirt and spun toward the loudest ones. "You men can all stop your droolin', 'cuz when I'm finished with her, even the dogs won't want her."

"What's the matter, Nell?" Waco Bob baited as he pushed back his felt hat. "Did she whoop up on you and your girls?"

"Yeah, you shoulda knowed better than to tangle with any kin of Sheriff Jackson," another hooted.

"She's dead, ya hear? *Dead*," Nell railed.

"No. You are dead, woman," Chama said, clearly emphasizing each word. Then he raised his voice to include the others. "And that goes for anyone else who so much as touches another hair on her head."

Nell pulled herself up like some strutting rooster and took a step closer. "You won't be talkin' so brave when Bull gets back. He'll skin that greasy hide right off your Injun back."

"Like I said before, when he returns, just send him on over."

Fists clenched, Nell opened her mouth as if to speak, then, instead, stalked away in a haughty retreat. Ignoring a chorus of taunts, she yelled back to her cohort. "Mabel. Pick your lazy ass up and come on. I'm finished here. *For now.*"

Still disguising his smoldering anger, Chama spread his lips in what he hoped was a disarming smile. "Well, I best be getting on home to the little woman."

"You sure you won't be needin' some help?" Kelso offered with mock seriousness. "Looks like she's more'n one man can handle."

"If I need any, you'll be the first I call on, Barn," Chama quipped, turning toward home as the men on the other side of the circle stepped aside, making a pathway.

Kelso's big-mouthed words followed after. "Don't you be forgettin' now."

Upon slamming into the door of the cabin, Carrie ripped the remnants of the shirt from her body, wishing the torn thing were those ghastly women. Or Chama. Hands trembling with rage, she wet a cloth and dabbed at her cheeks, trying to cool them.

After several moments, her breathing slowed and she began to calm enough to clean up. She soaked the cloth again and, standing before the mirror, swiped at the sweat and grime. As she did, she spied several nail gouges on her neck.

"When was I clawed?" Continuing to wipe, she found another scratch running down her back. Oh, yes, the big one had snatched at her when she first escaped. And again in front of the store. She exhaled a ragged sigh. But she was here now.

Safe. As unbelievable as it seemed. She looked around the little room, taking in every splintery board, every dented cup, and thanked God they now surrounded her.

After a quick spit bath she began to brush the tangles out of her hair, taking care not to pull on a tender spot at the back of her head. While brushing, Chama's words, those shaming words, came hurling at her again.

Her face burned anew, and she began to thrash at her hair with a vengeance, jerking through the tangles, ignoring the pain.

At that moment Chama walked through the door.

She whirled on him. "How dare you!" With all her might, she threw the brush at him.

Chama ducked and deflected it with his arm. "What's the matter? I saved you, didn't I?"

"What's the matter?" The insufferably innocent expression on his face infuriated her even further. Flying at him, she pummeled him with her fists.

Ducking her blows, he captured her wrists.

Undaunted, she kicked at his shins with her boots.

He tried to dodge, but in vain. He released her.

She took another swing, but her fist caught only air as he swooped her into his arms. She flailed at him, slapping at his face and shoulders until she found herself sailing through the air. She landed on the bed.

He flung himself on top of her, recapturing her wrists as he did.

Beneath him, Carrie's anger and frustration mounted as she struggled to free her hands.

"You're nothing but a little she-cat," Chama said between chuckles, and Carrie suddenly realized he was enjoying their battle. Her rage redoubled.

He lowered his face to hers.

She bucked against him and thrashed her head back and forth, dodging the lips that tried to claim hers.

He drew her hands together above her head, then pinned both of them with one of his, freeing the other to catch her chin. He trapped her face and began dropping kisses on her.

After more futile moments of struggling, all Carrie's pent-up energy abandoned her, leaving her limp. She lost her will to fight and fell still.

Chama's lips curled at the edges. "That's more like it."

Her rage unraveled into self-pity, and sobs from deep within broke free as tears welled up and spilled over. Utterly defeated, she didn't know if she hated him more for making her cry or herself for being so weak.

Even through a blur of tears, she could not miss the way his expression changed to one of confusion, then dissolved into pity.

It only made her cry harder, knowing she deserved and needed every bit of his compassion.

"Please don't cry." Lifting his weight off her, he rolled to one side and gathered her into his arms. "Don't you know how proud I am of you? My brave and beautiful Woman From The Sky."

The following morning Chama looked up from splitting logs to see the Shipstead family coming across the meadow. He dropped his ax and walked to the open door of the cabin. "Carrie," he called. "Company's coming. Karl and Esperanza."

She whirled around and surprised him as she often did with her beauty. The feminine curve of her neck and shoulders, the upper swell of her breasts now edged by the lace-trimmed bodice of a peasant blouse, rivaled her trim ankles and calves below an enticingly too short red calico skirt. And her feet looked incredibly more delicate in a pair of deerskin moccasins.

Earlier, when he'd risen, Chama had pulled the clothing from the trunk of women's things and offered them wordlessly to her before going out to do the chores. Not being overly experienced in the ways of women, he'd felt it would be better to say nothing than to risk a repeat of the previous afternoon's hysteria.

Now, filling his eyes with her, he rested his hands on the doorjambs and whistled his approval. "You have got to be the finest-looking woman this side of the Mississippi."

The color in her cheeks heightened, and she looked shyly off to the side as a fleeting smile crossed her lips, a sign that she hadn't fully recovered from yesterday's trauma.

As she came forward, he stepped back to make a path for her, but more, to watch the way her hips sent the generously gathered skirt to swaying. The single braid trailing down her back swished back and forth, keeping time. He wished his hands were making the same trip as that rope of hair, but he knew he'd have to give her a little more time to recover. He followed her to the edge of the rise to wait for the Shipsteads.

"Santa Maria!" gushed the out-of-breath expectant mother when she reached the top with Karl and their tot. "Yesterday I am *mucho* worried. *Mucho*." She took Carrie by the arms. "I think them bad womans, they kill you. My belly, she is too big. I no can help."

"I know," Carrie said with a reassuring smile. "I'm just glad I was able to get them away from you and little Ingacita. I would never have forgiven myself if anything had happened to either of you because of me."

"You no worry about us. Baby Jésús, he watch over *mi familia*. But I am *mucho* worry for you yesterday. Over and over I ask Jésús to make the miracle for you, like when Ingacita is *enfirma*. And he did! When Karl come running home—" She swung her big eyes up to the Swede who toted Ingacita. "*Mi* Karl, he is *muy* afraid. No?"

Wearing a smile that didn't reach his worried expression, Karl nodded.

"He think something bad happen to us when he see you at the store. When he tell me, I know it is big miracle. Your heart, it is full, too, no?"

"Yes," Carrie said, laughing lightly. "It was a miracle, and so are you." She gave Esperanza a resounding hug, then stepped back. "Would you like to help me fetch coffee for the men?"

"*Sí*. And here." Esperanza handed her a towel-wrapped loaf of bread. "You go home without it."

After they'd served the men and gone inside with their own full cups, Chama continued to stare at them, speechless.

Karl lumbered over and dropped a heavy arm across his shoulders. "It's hard to get used to, ain't it?"

"What is?"

"Livin' with a *good* woman."

Chama chuckled low. "It's different, that's for sure." He pointed to the location where the woman had embraced a few moments before. "They just stood there talking about Carrie sacrificing herself to save Esperanza, and how Esperanza prayed up a miracle to save her in return. Then they sashayed into the cabin as if miracles like that happen every day."

"You'll get used to it. And if you don't watch out, it'll start to rub off on you," he finished with his own nervous laugh.

"I know you may think I'm trying to pass some Indian superstition off on you, but I think Carrie's eyes are her protection. I've never seen a purer color of turquoise."

Karl shrugged. "Could be. Who am I to say it ain't so?"

With their steaming cups of brew in hand, the men drifted toward one of the logs where Ingacita already crouched on all fours, trying to balance herself. As Chama sat down, he gently pinched her protruding bottom, causing the fluffy-haired imp to jump and giggle.

She clambered over him and crowded down between the two grown-ups. Then, snuggling against her daddy, she amused herself by pulling at the blond hairs on his arm.

"Bobby Crocker rode in last night with some news," Karl drawled.

"Who's he?"

"One of Bull Dolan's boys. Seems as though Dolan and his whole gang was all either killed or captured. A troop of cavalry out of Fort Hancock was down patrollin' the border and caught 'em red-handed sneakin' back from Old Mexico. Crocker's horse had come up lame and couldn't keep up or he would've been taken, too."

"Did the bluecoats take 'em back to the fort?"

"No. They turned 'em over to the law in El Paso. One cheerful thing has come out of it, though."

"What's that?" Chama asked, though as far as he was concerned, having Dolan and his cutthroat bunch locked away was cheery news in itself.

"Dolan was one of the men they took alive. So Nell has talked Bobby into takin' her and her camp-following buddies down to El Paso to see if they can break him out. Mabel is favorin' her left side real good where Carrie jabbed her, but she's hell-bent on goin' along."

"When are they leaving?"

"They was about loaded up when we passed 'em a while back."

"That *is* good news. You know, Nell's not the sort to take being made a fool of without wanting to get even. Even if you don't consider the fact Carrie bashed her nose with the ax handle."

"It wasn't the ax." Karl's chest rumbled with a chortle. "Carrie broke Nell's nose with her fist. She come up with a real whopper from what Esperanza said."

"All the more reason to get Nell's dander up. But you say they're leaving. Well, let's not tell the women. Or they'll sure enough have us down to the church in Socorro or some such place, saying a bunch of Hail Marys."

Chama finished his coffee, then concentrated on Ingacita for a few minutes. He tossed her up in the air several times, delighting in the sound of her gurgling laughter, the fragile softness of her tiny body. Someday, he mused, someday, after the soldiers were run out, there'd be time for lots of little ones of his own.

After a spell, he set her down, and it suddenly occurred to him that Bert could very well have been in the crowd yesterday. He was sure to have gotten an eyeful of Carrie. "I wouldn't be surprised if Wormely shows up here today, too, asking for more money for his share of Carrie . . . at the very least."

"Guess you haven't heard." Karl's bushy brows shot up, accompanying a devilish smirk. "He skedaddled outta here two weeks ago when them others did. He's so scared of Jackson and that knife of his, he took off, draggin' that sloppy whore with him. Hangin' on to her with one hand and his balls with the other."

Chama exploded into laughter, along with Karl.

They laughed so long and loud, Carrie came to the door and looked out. She glanced back and forth between them, a questioning expression lining her forehead. Their unbridled merriment must've rubbed off on her, though. By the time she turned back, she wore a beaming smile.

"*Qué paso?*" Chama heard Esperanza call from inside.

"Oh," Carrie answered, walking inside. "They're just out there acting like a couple of fools. Dear sweet fools."

≈ 20 ≈

CARRIE STOOD IN the door frame of her home and watched the Shipsteads until they'd disappeared from sight. Then, checking on Chama, she saw he still sat by the smoldering fire. He held a chunk of wood and a knife. His head bent, his concentration centered on whittling.

Curious, she walked out across ground strewn with pine needles and sat down beside him. Stretching her now comfortably moccasin-ensconced feet toward the fire, she crossed her ankles. "What are you carving?"

"I'm making a doll for Ingacita. When I'm finished, would you make it a dress?"

"Oh, yes. I'd love to." She glanced at his strong, dangerous-looking profile and smiled, knowing what a gentle man he really was. "She's at such a cute age, isn't she? It's a joy just to watch her. Everything she sees is so new and exciting."

"Yeah, she's a real corker, all right."

Carrie breathed in the scent of fresh-cut wood while watching the intricate patterns of smoke created by dying embers. While the time passed lazily, her thoughts drifted, as they did quite often these days, to her childhood in South Carolina and what it would be like to have that kind of a family life again. She glanced over to the doll taking shape and knew in her heart that Chama wanted the same thing, no matter what he'd said before. Gathering her courage, she ventured, "Wouldn't it be wonderful if we lived someplace and had the Shipsteads or people like them for neighbors? It's been so long since I've had friends just drop by to visit, I can hardly remember."

"The Shipsteads *are* our neighbors," he said without looking up from his whittling, "and they did just drop by."

"It's not the same, and you know it. Tomorrow they could be gone—or we could. You said so yourself just the other day. Remember? This valley is just a rendezvous."

"That's true. But even when we leave for the winter, we'll still be seeing them." He lifted the doll closer and rubbed his thumb over its head. "Karl and me, we've become good friends."

At the mention of leaving, Carrie's ever-nagging sense of urgency came to the fore. "But, Chama, none of you is going to be alive to stay or go or anything else soon. I've told you and told you, but you simply won't listen. My father is coming. He's going to find this place, and when he does, he'll tear it asunder. He will. He always wins in the end."

Chama laid his work in his lap and eyed her. "Carrie, you talk as if your father has unearthly powers. Did he ever live with the Apaches? Does he understand the ways of the spirits?"

"What? No. He doesn't believe in any of your Indian gods. But you can bet he's made a deal with the devil."

"Look, my beautiful Sunshine," he said, covering her hand with his. "There's nothing for you to worry about."

"He'll find this valley. Mark my words."

"Even if he does, the guards above the pass will warn us in plenty of time. I'll see to it you're kept safe."

"And what about you? Are you going to be safe, too? If you try to pit your power against Father's, you'll lose. He always makes sure the odds are on his side before he ever starts out." She placed her fingers over his. "Please, listen to me. We must leave here. Get away, far away."

Chama's expression hardened. "Next month. We'll go for a while then. I can't right now. Me and some other men are leaving in a couple of days to go take an army payroll. I'll be back in eight or ten days. Then as soon as Esperanza and her new baby are strong enough to travel, we'll leave. I promised Karl I'd take them to Esperanza's people down Chihuahua way."

Carrie lunged up and swung to face him. "You mean you're leaving me here, alone, in this place while you go gallivanting off with some worthless thieves?"

"I'm not going to leave you here *alone*. You'll be staying with the Shipsteads."

"Esperanza said Karl drinks every night. How much protection is he going to be when he's passed out drunk? Do you think his snoring will scare anyone off?"

Chama reached around her waist and pulled her between his legs, then treated her to an infuriatingly charming grin. "If his snoring doesn't scare 'em off, then the thought of what he'd do when he woke up should keep the wolves away. Of course, when I get back you won't be the least bit safe. After nine or ten days living like a padre, I'll be showing you the fullest meaning of rape and pillage." Hugging her closer, he nuzzled between her breasts and nibbled at them through the thin cotton blouse.

Her tension began to melt away as it always did when he started caressing her. She pressed him to her bosom and kissed the top of his head. Then, coming to her senses, she broke free, retreating from his reach and spoke in a quiet, measured voice. "I love you very much, Chamasay."

His heart lurched. She'd never said the words before.

"Don't lose us," she added. Then, whirling around, she ran into the cabin.

Chama stared at the closed door long after she'd gone inside. His Woman From The Sky had just said she loved him. Him, a half-breed Comanchero outlaw. Waves of exhilaration surged through him . . . then spilled away as her last words sank in. Why couldn't she have just told him she loved him? Why'd she have to follow those treasured words with the condemning ones?

It was very possible she didn't love him at all. She may have said the words just to get him to take her away.

His chest tightened, causing his laboring heart to ache. He started to get up, to go have it out with her, then reason cleared his thoughts. She did love him. She was just scared.

Settling back, he felt pain in his hand. He looked down and saw he had a stranglehold on the piece of wood. He slackened his grip, and began carving again, shaping the tiny nose. As he did, a curious thought came to him. Had Carrie's father ever taken the time to whittle his daughter a doll? If so, how could he have kept her hidden out on that broken-down ranch long past her marrying years, deliberately wasting such a beautiful young woman?

Chama blew away wood shavings from around the now-fashioned nose, then, with the point of the knife, outlined two large eyes the same shape as Ingacita's as his concentration returned to Carrie. He knew instinctively that the sheriff had never fashioned a doll for her.

But if he had, the eyes would've been set with the purest turquoise, nothing else would've done her justice. Yes, with eyes as beautiful as hers, Jackson could've married her off to a land baron or one of those rich mine owners over in Silver City.

But the sheriff must not be interested in money or family. Power. He craved power. From what Carrie said, he controlled everything and everyone around him. "And like the damned fools we were," he said out loud, "we not only swooped down and stole off with his town's money, we took his own personal slave."

Chama swung in the direction of the valley entrance. He'd been so wrapped up in his war with the army that he hadn't given the sheriff his due. Chama set the knife and piece of wood on the log beside him. Maybe he'd better go talk to Rodriguez. Have the trader post a couple more guards farther out.

He stood up. When he did, he heard someone call to him from the direction of the *rancheria*. He turned and saw three men approaching.

The tallest waved.

As they strode closer, Chama recognized them: Barney Kelso, Augie Stockman, a fast-talking Scotsman, and, to his surprise, Jack Potfeld.

"Come on up and sit a spell," Chama invited as they climbed the knoll, although he would've preferred to meet with them at the camp. "What brings you out here?"

Lanky, tousle-haired Kelso reached him first and extended a hand.

Chama shook it, concealing his displeasure over the intrusion.

Kelso flashed his crooked-toothed grin that always seemed to have a double meaning. "Augie, here, is back with the information we needed. He knows when the army is moving the payroll and what route they're taking."

"Good. Have a seat." Chama turned to the Scot, a compact man with fair skin smoothed across a square face and framed by a shock of curly red hair.

"If me friend is right," Augie said, his tongue rolling across the r's, "and he never been wrong afore. The payroll weel be passin' through Arroyo Blanco in five days time."

"That soon?" Chama said, watching the others move to sit around the dying campfire. "It's a hard three days ride from here. So to be on the safe side, we'd better leave tomorrow."

"That's how we figured it." Kelso shoved back his hat and eased down.

Jack Potfeld noticed the unfinished carving beside where he sat on a log. He picked it up. "Appears to be a fine doll you're whittling."

"Yeah." Chama looked down at him, a touch embarrassed. "I'm making it for the Swede's youngun."

Putting it aside, Potfeld chuckled. "She sure is a cute little tyke, just like her ma."

"So, you reckon we should be leavin' tomorra," Augie said, getting back to business. "What time?"

"Soon as we can after breakfast," Chama said. "Is that all right with you, Potfeld?"

"Sure. Is Shipstead going?"

"No. His woman's expecting anytime now, and he doesn't want to leave her for that long."

"Speakin' of women," Barney interjected, "I don't see yours anywheres about."

"She's in the cabin," Chama said with measured calm. He had planned to sit down, but changed his mind.

"I'm plumb parched." Barney sprang to his feet again. "Think I'll see if she'd mind pourin' me a cool drink of water or maybe a cup of coffee."

"No need to bother yourself," Chama said, deftly blocking the taller man's path. "Sit back down. I'll have her get it for you. Stockman? Potfeld? Would either of you like some coffee?"

"I'd be fiercely grateful," the Scotsman replied. "Besides, I ain't as yet seen the legendary lady. Barney says she's more bonny than the one in the picture hangin' in Roddy's Saloon down in El Paso."

Chama narrowed his gaze onto Kelso. "You mean the painting of the naked woman lying on a red satin sheet?"

"Meanin' no disrespect," Kelso blurted. "What I said was, her *face* is prettier than the *face* of the woman in that picture. Ain't that right, Stockman?"

"I could use some coffee, now," Potfeld broke in. "If your woman wouldn't mind fetching it."

Chama uncoiled his muscles only slightly before he strode inside to Carrie, who was busy slicing vegetables. "There are three men outside." Recalling the confession of love she made just a few minutes prior, he gentled the tone of his voice. "They're here to discuss some business, and they'd like some coffee. I'd get it myself, but they're chomping at the bit to get a close look at you. So, go ahead and pour it for 'em. Then I want you to come straight back inside."

Her own gaze faltering, Carrie put down the knife and plucked three tin cups from the shelf above her. "Do you want some, too?"

"No. They won't be staying that long."

Chama held the door open for Carrie as she took a deep breath and stepped out to the eagerly awaiting men.

Augie gasped, and Jack's mouth dropped open upon seeing her.

"See? What did I tell you? Ain't she a beauty?" Kelso bragged.

"You most certainly are, ma'am." Augie sprang to his feet and doffed his sweat-stained hat.

The other two followed Augie's lead.

"Please, be seated," Carrie ordered softly as she neared the campfire. Lifting the coffeepot off the flat rock next to the fire, she poured a cup and handed it to the Scot.

"I thank ye, most kindly," he said, taking it as his small blue eyes followed her with longing.

She then poured another and handed it to Jack Potfeld.

He took it with a polite smile. Then, turning to Chama, he thrust it forward in a silent toast.

After filling the last one for Barney, she moved toward him.

Nothing was hidden in the way the man watched her. Hungry lust, mixed with all the grinning charm he could muster, lit his face. When she held out his drink, he slid his bony fingers over hers.

Chama tensed.

Carrie shoved the cup at Kelso, then whirled away and practically ran back to the cabin, her braid bouncing with her long strides.

Kelso called after her in an insolent drawl. "Thank you kindly, ma'am."

Chama started for him, itching to rearrange some of the bastard's teeth.

"Kelso. Chama." Potfeld spoke with harsh authority.

Chama swung toward him.

Potfeld looked sternly from Chama to Barney and back. "Sit down. We have a heavily guarded shipment to rob, and I want to finish up with the plans. I have my own woman to get back to."

Barney, pretending he'd done nothing wrong, looked at Jack with a blank expression of innocence and sat down.

"Chama. Do you think fourteen men will be enough?" Jack asked pointedly.

Although Chama would've liked nothing better than to take care of Kelso here and now, he knew Potfeld was right. Attacking a heavily guarded army transport would be dangerous enough without stirring up trouble beforehand. Kelso would have to wait. Chama strode to the vacant log and propped a foot on it. "Fourteen. Is that counting us?"

21

"I DON'T WANT to go there. At least not before I have to." Carrie looked up at Chama astride his beautifully marked pony. Looking very much the deadly renegade, he wore the same rawhide vest, turquoise and leather neck thong, and pair of sturdy denims he'd worn the first time she'd ever seen him. Packed and ready to go, his saddlebags bulged.

He exhaled impatiently. "I guess you'll be safe here for a few hours. When I ride out most of the men will be going with me. I'll go by and tell Karl not to come for you until later this afternoon. I left a rifle behind. It's loaded. Take care to keep your eyes and ears open."

"No. You be careful. If you won't let me talk you out of this reckless lawlessness, don't you dare get yourself killed."

He had the audacity to chuckle as if she'd said something funny. "Don't worry. I'll be back in eight days, nine at the most. Stick close to the Shipsteads."

He was really leaving. Her eyes began to flood.

Chama leaned down and, taking her chin, kissed her one last time with such tenderness she barely felt the loss of his lips when they left hers. "I *will* be back. I promise." Then, releasing her, he spurred the paint into a gallop and bounded off the hill for the Comanchero camp.

Watching him go, Carrie had never felt so abandoned in her life. How could he take such a chance? Place himself in such danger and her as well? And after she'd told him she loved him. If she ever needed proof, this was it. He couldn't possibly care for her the way she did him.

When Chama disappeared behind some buildings across the clearing, Carrie turned away, bitter disappointment weighting her every step toward the cabin. And tonight she wouldn't even be able to sleep in her own bed. She swiped at the tears spiking her lashes. Then, not knowing what else to do with her hands, she let them fall limply to her sides. They felt as useless and empty as the rest of her.

She took a shaky breath, dreading the many days she'd be crowding in on Karl and Esperanza and little Ingacita. At the picture of the darling wispy-haired tot, she spotted the doll Chama had all but finished, lying on the table. It looked just as abandoned as she felt. Picking it up, she hugged it to her bosom. Maybe making the clothes for the wooden figure would keep her mind occupied for a while. Yes, clothes, shoes, a hat. A whole wardrobe.

After Chama arranged with Shipstead to fetch Carrie, he trotted Eagle Wings past the clusters of rude dwellings toward the store. The guilt caused by leaving her rode with him. Time and again he had to remind himself of the vow that had taken him along this path his entire life. A just path. A righteous one. He couldn't forsake it now because of this woman no matter how much he cared for her. No matter how much those beautiful eyes pleaded.

Chama's fingers went to his throat where his turquoise stone now rested for the first time in weeks. As long as he'd had her eyes to behold, he hadn't felt the need for it. But now . . .

Rounding the corrals to the main building, he found the group gathering. Most had already arrived, but a few were still missing.

In the next instant, two men came tramping down the steps of the store with stuffed and cinched tote bags. They mounted up to join the rest.

"Ready to go," yelled one, the eagerness in his thin voice as evident as the nervously prancing horses.

Chama looked around him, counting. "Everyone's not here. I see only thirteen."

"Thirteen! Es numero malo!" Paco Gonzales said. The superstitious Mexican was one of Jack Potfeld's men.

"Shut yer yella mouth," Augie spat and grabbed the bridle of the *bandido*'s horse, reining Gonzales close to him. "I make me own luck. Ye hear?"

"Kelso's missing," Chama said. "Where is he?"

"He can't make it," drawled Waco Bob with an amused grin. "He spent all last night runnin' to the outhouse. And this mornin', every time he tried to pack his poke, he'd be chargin' off to take another crap. He must've eaten somethin' rancid."

"Yeah," Potfeld said with a chortle. "He acts like he's practicing up for a Fourth of July footrace."

"Since Barney was in on the plannin' from the start," Bob added, "he figures he should be in on the cut. Not so much, but he reckons somethin' is due him."

The Mexican spat off to the side, expressing his disdain. "Talk, she is cheap. He want a cut? He take the chance like the rest of us."

"We can discuss that later." Chama spurred his pony into the lead while the others scrambled for position behind. As they galloped out onto the meadow, Chama glanced across to his cabin, hoping for one last look at Carrie. But she'd gone inside. His disappointment angered him. The woman had to stop stealing his every thought.

Maintaining the lead of the small army, Chama took them on the straightest route through the woods to the steep trail out of the valley, not slowing until they reached it. Then they fell into a line behind him and clambered up the precarious, rock-strewn path that zigzagged to the top of the cliff.

When they'd reached the narrow slit in the mountain and rode beneath the first lookout position high above them, Chama belatedly remembered he hadn't asked Rodriguez to add more guards. He'd forgotten about the possible threat of the sheriff. Then, peering into the deep, dark passage, Chama wagged his head, feeling again like the foolish old woman Carrie would turn him into if given half the chance. No one could find this one narrow little crack in these hundreds of square miles of mountains on his own. And he knew the Apaches would never betray its location any more than the handful of white men who guided the others in. They all knew anyone trying to bring down the law would be shot on the spot by the guards posted above. He settled back in the saddle and patted his horse's withers. Carrie was perfectly safe. She'd be fine till he got back.

By unspoken agreement Chama and the other men continued in silence as they picked their way through the deep canyon. Emerging at the other end, the last man obscured the entrance with a tumble of brush, then they traveled another couple of miles before the group, whispering at first, paired off to chat. Jack Potfeld fell in beside Chama, surprising him only a little. The two of them hadn't reached a point of liking one another, and maybe they never would, but they were developing a trust that was unusual in this company of men.

"If we make a decent haul, this will be my last job," Potfeld, a normally very private man, said. "I'm taking my woman as far out of this territory as I can get. Maybe even as far as Canada. I'm tired of living from hand to mouth, looking over my shoulder all the time."

"I hear Canada's mighty cold in the winter."

"Not as cold as Denver or Kansas City would be if I tried to settle down there with an Acoma woman. I hear tell, in Canada a man isn't looked down on so much for taking an Indian wife."

"Could be. I haven't heard that much about the place, except how it's under ten feet of snow nine months a year."

"That sounds like some old coot's tall tale, if you ask me. And if you plan on keeping that woman of yours, it wouldn't be a bad idea for you to be thinkin' about moving on yourself. You being a breed and all. Then, of course, there *is* her father."

Chama grunted noncommittally and nudged Eagle Wings into a faster pace. Potfeld was beginning to pry.

A couple of hours later, Chama led the group along the steep spine of a high rocky ridge scattered with only a few gnarled and stunted pines, avoiding all trails as they traveled southeast. Reaching the highest point, he halted his horse and looked about him. Row beyond row of rugged ridges spread to the horizon on either side—an exhilarating view of this land of enchantment. He glanced longingly down at his pony. If only, he thought, the horse did have the wings of an eagle and could soar him out over the endless expanse. What a feast for the eyes that would be, as well as every other sense. He could feel the weightlessness of flight, the speed of the cool wind washing over him, the freedom . . .

"Quite a sight, ain't it?" Jack said, breaking into Chama's almost trancelike state.

"Yeah," he mused. "From up here, it's like nothing in the world could touch you. It's just you and all you survey." Taking one last look, he heeled his pony forward again.

"Yeah," Jack agreed, doing the same. Then his horse's hoof clanged over a rock and it almost lost its footing. Jack dug his feet into his stirrups and hung on until the sorrel steadied itself. When he'd caught up again, he asked, "Whereabouts is Arroyo Blanco from here?"

Chama pointed to a lower, more desertlike range to the south. "See those twin buttes?"

"Yeah."

"We should reach them by tomorrow afternoon. A pass runs between 'em. Once we're through it, we'll be able to see the canyon down off to the left. You can't miss those chalk-white walls."

Reaching a sharp drop-off, Chama scanned the panorama once more before starting down. Then, feeling as if he were being watched, he looked back to the dense forest from whence they'd come. A sudden wind rushed from out of the shadows. It whispered a name. *Kelso*. Foreboding spilled icy fear through his veins. *Kelso was coming for Carrie*.

Wheeling Eagle Wings around, he slammed his heels into the animal's flanks. "I have to go back! Go on without me!"

He raced past the men, who all stared, their mouths agape. Several shouted out, amazed.

"What the hell?"

"Who put a burr under his saddle?"

"What's he running from?" another yelled in a panicked voice.

"It's all right," he heard Jack call. "He must've remembered something real important. Got a real queer look on his face and said he had to go back."

Chama steered the pony to the edge overlooking a steep landslide.

The horse balked.

Chama slapped the reins back and forth across the animal's neck, and Eagle Wings leapt forward.

"I don't want to go to that awful place," Carrie muttered to herself for the hundredth time as she gathered the things she would take to Esperanza's. If only she'd thought to have Chama ask the Shipsteads to come here to their cabin instead.

They wouldn't do that, she knew. They had Ingacita to think about, and everything at their place was ready for the new baby's arrival. They wouldn't uproot three of them just for her selfish whim.

She stuffed her clothes into a tote bag. Then again, she argued, maybe Esperanza would jump at the chance to stay out here, away from the camp. A smile tugged at the corners of her mouth. Yes, that could be quite possible. She'd drop a couple of hints when she arrived at the Shipsteads' and see what happened.

As Carrie filled another tote with food, not wanting to be an extra burden, she looked out the stick-propped shutter. The afternoon sun had already dipped behind the rim of the western wall, a sign that Karl would arrive soon to get her. She'd better go saddle Hickory.

As Carrie walked into the stable, the horse rumbled a soft greeting through his rubbery lips.

"And a good evening to you, too," she said with a light laugh. She threw a horse blanket onto the bay's back. "At least *you* won't be lonely while Eagle Wings is gone. You'll have lots of other horses to visit with in the corrals. Anyway, I suppose that's where Karl will put you."

Picking the bay's bridle off a hook, she slipped it over his head. As she did, she whispered playfully into his ear. "Who knows, while you're there, maybe you'll meet a frisky little filly. Whoops, I forgot. You're a gelding, you poor thing. Well, try and have a good time anyway."

When she'd finished saddling the horse, she led him outside and tied him to a tree, then returned to the cabin to fetch the two bags. After looping them over the pommel, she checked the area around the dwelling. All that remained in need of attending was the campfire.

Once she'd shoveled dirt onto it, she returned inside and poured herself a cool drink of water from a clay jug, then sat down to wait for Karl. She took a generous mouthful and surveyed the room, already missing it. It was hard to believe how attached she'd become to the dark, crudely built hut. She would yearn for it, she knew, almost as much as she already longed for Chama. *And* feared for him.

She sighed and looked heavenward. "Keep him safe. I know he doesn't think what he's doing is wrong. So please don't judge him too harshly. Send him back to me. I need him."

It had been so long since she'd prayed, it seemed strange to start trusting enough to petition God again. But after seeing Esperanza's simple yet unwavering faith even after all the horror that had befallen her, Carrie felt an encouragement she hadn't trusted since her mother had given up all hope.

A knock resounded at the door.

Carrie jumped, startled by the sudden banging; then, realizing Karl had arrived, she went to answer.

Barney Kelso, the man who'd been there the day before, stood before her.

Her heart thudded a warning. "Yes?" Ready to slam the door at the slightest wrong move, she watched the lanky, fresh-faced man.

He doffed his hat and flashed a boyish grin. "Howdy, ma'am. I wasn't able to go with the boys today—I been feelin' poorly. So the breed asked me to look in on you. Make sure you was all right."

"I'm sorry to hear you're not feeling well," she said politely, not fooled for one minute.

Nonetheless, she must've dropped her guard because he pushed past her before she could stop him. "I got a powerful thirst. I could sure use a drink."

"It's nice of you to drop by," she lied smoothly, trying to conceal her apprehension. "But I was just leaving for the Shipsteads'. They're expecting me, and I'm late now."

"Oh, they wouldn't mind waiting just a few minutes longer whilst you get a poor sick fella a drink." The lopsided smile widened hopefully.

His innocent-looking expression didn't ease her apprehension in the least. "I'm sorry, but I promised the *big* Swede I'd be there before the sun disappeared. I'm really late. I'm sure he's on his way here right now." Which he probably was, she reassured herself silently.

"Probably so." Yet his confident grin didn't diminish one iota. "Could I have that drink now?"

Relenting, Carrie turned to get a cup. After all, no one would be fool enough to try something with Karl on his way. She reached for the jug.

He lunged. Caught her hand and her against the sideboard.

Trapped, panic rising, Carrie tried to swivel away.

He shoved harder against her back.

She slammed the tin cup alongside his head.

Unfazed, he caught her free wrist and shook the cup from it.

She bucked against him.

"Oh, yeah," he chuckled. "Do it again."

Feeling the evidence of his lust bulging and smashing against her rear, she froze, not wishing to incite him any further.

It didn't slow him as he forced her wrists together and clamped a hand around both.

Straining against his hold, she tried to jerk away to no avail—his strength far outmatched hers. Trying a new tactic, she swiveled to bite his arm.

"You don't want to do that," he drawled as he jerked her head up by the hair, then shot his hand over her shoulder, diving it into her string-held bodice, across a breast.

She screamed her terror and outrage.

Undaunted, he cupped it. "Oh, yeah," he sighed and squeezed.

In shock, she gasped, but for only the briefest second before fear and rage sent fiery strength to her limbs. She butted and twisted with everything in her.

His strength, too, seemed to multiply as did his bulge gyrating against her, causing her pelvis to grind painfully against the counter.

"No!" she screamed. "Stop it! Stop it!"

"Now, honey, don't be like that," he crooned into her ear between rushed breaths as he pawed her breast, rubbing in a fevered circle. "Relax. I ain't gonna hurt you. But you gotta understand—I have to have you. I ain't thought of nothin' else since I first saw you standin' there with that club in your hand and these big tits winkin' at me past that ripped shirt."

"Karl's on his way," she hissed. "He'll kill you."

"I don't think so. Not after all the money I just paid out on whiskey to fill up that tub of guts."

Hope fast disappearing, Carrie tried to take her mind off of his pillaging hand while searching for something else that would discourage him. "If you leave right now, I promise I won't tell Karl or Chama you were here."

"Well, now," he drawled while his fingers clawed across to her other breast, "we ain't gonna be seein' hide nor hair of them no more. You and me is leavin' this place . . . soon as I'm through pleasurin' myself."

His words infused her with renewed determination, and she wrenched her hands up.

His grip slipped, then tightened as he slammed her against the sideboard again.

Pain shot across her pelvic bones, slowing her struggle, but for a mere instant. Twisting and shoving, she stretched out her fingers to claw him. "They'll track you down," she screamed, then finding skin, dug in.

He yowled and dropped her wrists. "You wildcat!"

She jerked to the side, throwing him off balance.

Losing his grip, he snatched at her blouse.

It ripped away in his hand as she hurled herself toward the entrance.

She yanked on the latch.

He crashed across her, slamming the door shut, then snagged her around the waist and dragged her across the room to the bed. Throwing her onto it, he dove on top of her, his lust-crazed eyes devouring her.

Hysterical, she flailed and kicked, scratched and bit. Animallike growls rasped from her throat.

He grappled with her, trying to recapture her hands. Then with a frustrated growl, he stopped. Straddling her, he sat up. "You asked for it, bitch." He doubled his fist and drew it back.

Carrie saw it coming . . . too late.

❧ 22 ❧

THE CABIN CAME into view. It lay in an eerie hush. Nothing moved. Nothing stirred.

Except Hickory.

Chama's worst fear was confirmed as he eyed the saddled and packed bay meandering untethered in the meadow below, idly cropping grass.

He slammed his heels into Eagle Wings, demanding more speed from the spent and winded animal.

The pony stretched into a lumbering gallop as they crossed the meadow. Reaching the rise and starting up, he slowed again to pathetic, staggering leaps.

Chama vaulted off the stallion's back, hitting the ground at a run, his own lungs on fire. He charged up to the cabin and crashed through the door.

The light shafting from the entrance caught Kelso's expression. Wild with amazement, he turned to gape. And in that instant Chama saw it all: the son of a bitch crouched over a lifeless Carrie, his engorged penis in hand, poised to enter her.

Chama charged past the table.

Kelso rose to his knees and threw up his arms.

Chama smashed through the feeble protection. In a steellike grip, he grabbed a clump of hair and wrenched the bastard off Carrie, flinging him across the room.

A shriek tore from Kelso as he skidded across the floor into a bench.

Chama delivered a crushing kick to the man's groin.

The bastard wailed again and grabbed himself. His impatient seed spewed between his fingers.

At the sight, fury almost blinded Chama. He savagely slammed his boot into Kelso again, then jerked him up and threw him out the door.

Kelso tried desperately to come to his feet, but the britches bunched at his ankles tripped him, and he sprawled in the dirt again. His naked butt shining, he started crawling at a frantic pace.

Chama lunged after him. Raising a foot, he booted the bastard over while he drew his revolver.

Kelso looked up through crazed, tear-blurred eyes and clawed at the air. "No! Please!"

Chama vaguely heard, but nothing the man could have said would have saved him. Chama fired. Again and again. He fired until the twisted, lusting face had turned to a red pulp. He fired until he realized the gun was empty and now made only clicking sounds.

A wildfire still sweeping through his veins, Chama tossed the revolver aside and battered the half-naked body with two more vicious kicks before he hoisted up the carcass and flung it off his knoll.

He glared down, fists clenched, chest heaving until slowly, gradually, the fiery haze clouding his thoughts began to clear.

Carrie.

Spinning around, he raced back up the incline and into the cabin where she lay still as death, her skirt pushed up to her waist, her blouse ripped down. Quickly, he spread them over her, then dropped down beside the bed. He placed a hand at the side of her throat, but his heart sledgehammered so, it took a moment before he could separate her pulse from his or see the faint rise and fall of her chest. When he did, his relief was so profound, his whole body lost strength, his head sank onto the pillow beside her. He moved closer and pressed his brow to her cheek, breathing in her scent.

After a time he regained something of himself. Rising up, he saw a trickle of blood at the corner of her swollen and discolored lower lip. She'd been knocked unconscious.

Another rush of fury claimed him. Dragging in a controlling breath, he got up and went to fetch a cloth, then wet it. Returning, he gently wiped away the blood, then pressed it to her cheeks and the puffy lip to cool them.

Carrie's eyelids began to flutter, then gradually open. Her groggy expression finally focused on him, and she started to smile, then winced. She touched her jaw, and her eyes widened. She lurched upward.

Chama caught her shoulders and pressed her down again. "It's all right. You're safe now. He won't ever touch you again. No one will."

Her eyes filled with unspilled tears.

The sight tugged painfully at his heart. "I'm here," he whispered and crawled onto the bed beside her, gathering her into his arms.

She clutched at his vest, her whole body going rigid.

"I have you now. You're safe." He pulled her closer and began to rock her, to stroke her hair.

A shudder traveled her length.

He tightened his grip and feathered the top of her head with kisses and more whispered assurances.

Considerable time drifted by—he didn't know how much—before all the tension in her body drained away, and she fell into an exhausted sleep. Careful not to disturb her, he rose and pulled a blanket over her. When he did, he noticed his own muscles were stiff and sore beyond anything he could remember.

The ride back.

It had been a bone-jarring, horse-punishing race against the nightmare. Panic, like a tightened cinch, had squeezed at his heart and lungs. His blood had throbbed into his head with ever-increasing force as fear rode him all the way back. Each mile up the mountain had stretched unending as his tense, sweating hands slicked the reins he'd used to thrash his stallion to greater speed. Never in his life had he felt so powerless, so helpless.

Completely drained and feeling nauseous, Chama walked outside for some fresh air. His gaze gravitated to the pinks and corals of the wispy clouds above the western wall, and to his astonishment he realized darkness had yet to shroud the valley. How could that be? Hadn't the nightmare been going on forever?

Rasping wheezes slowly penetrated Chama's consciousness. He turned toward the sound.

Eagle Wings.

"My God."

The pony's head hung limp, his legs trembled, and his bloodshot eyes were glazed over as his sweat-foamed body struggled for each breath.

Chama stared hopelessly at the cruel ruin of his once-proud stallion. He had destroyed this trusting, obedient animal. A weary sadness reached into Chama's bones as he moved to the wind-broken animal and pulled his Winchester out of its scabbard. He raised and pointed it at the horse's head. "Funny how heavy it feels," he murmured. He hesitated.

The wheezing grew louder. It seemed to virtually thunder in his ears.

He pulled the trigger.

The animal crumpled to the ground.

Uncaring that the rifle dropped into the dirt, Chama turned away and trudged to one of the fallen logs and slumped down, sitting in a limp daze as the daylight faded away . . . until he heard a sound from the direction of the clearing. Looking up, he saw the shadowy figure of Karl lumbering unsteadily across the meadow.

The drunken man didn't try to jump the stream, but plowed through it and staggered on up the small bank. Then he jerked to a halt. "Good God A'mighty!" He gawked at the faceless corpse as he skirted it. Then, abruptly, he halted. His face hardened, and he drew his revolver and charged up the hill in a heavy-footed run.

Chama stood up, catching Shipstead's attention. "It's all right. Carrie's safe now. She's in the cabin asleep."

"What are you doin' here?" Karl asked while aimlessly waving his gun in the air. "What happened? Whose body is that down there?" Then Karl spotted the dead pony. He took a step toward it. "My God, man, what happened to your horse?"

* * *

When Carrie awakened the next morning, from the brightness of the light coming through the cracks, she knew the sun had already topped the ridge. Chama must have risen hours ago. Feeling the sluggishness of too much sleep, she rolled out of bed and came to her feet. When she did, a rush of pain exploded near her chin, and she remembered the cause. Gingerly, she touched it and felt puffy flesh.

Choosing not to ponder the events that precipitated the injury, she sidled up to the mirror. To her horror she found a purple, lopsided jaw. It would be an ever-present reminder for days. Sighing, she felt in need of a strong cup of coffee. She changed into a fresh blouse and another short but swingy calico skirt and went outside.

Although the morning had yet to lose its chill, no flames burned in the campfire. And after reaching for the blackened pot, she found it not only cold, but empty. It must be much later than she thought. But when she glanced up at the sun, she judged the time to be no more than eight. She looked about her for Chama, but neither saw nor heard any sign of him. Strange. He'd never left the hill before without telling her. An uneasy shiver traveled up her back, but she refused to give it credence.

Nonetheless, she gravitated to the edge of the knoll and looked across to the *rancheria*. From that distance, the only movement she could see was a few lines of ascending smoke. Maybe she'd only dreamed he'd returned. It was probably Karl who'd actually saved her.

Turning back, she spotted a blanket-covered body. It lay alongside the cabin. Surely Karl hadn't killed that awful rapist and left the body there.

Her hands clenched tightly together, she approached. Then, to her immense relief, she saw Chama's thick black hair peeking out at the far end of the bedroll. He had returned. Letting out a whoosh of air, she realized she'd been holding her breath.

Then it came to her—why on earth was Chama sleeping outside, and so late, at that? She reached down and nudged his shoulder. "Chama?"

Groaning, he twisted around to face her. Warmth flickered in his eyes, but quickly disappeared. He stared up stony-faced for another moment, then rolled back toward the wall. "Leave me alone. I need more sleep."

Carrie gaped, rooted to the spot.

Moments passed before she managed to convince herself there had to be some reasonable, logical explanation for his strange behavior. She walked away telling herself not to be so sensitive. But still . . . She glanced over her shoulder at him once more, a sick feeling in the pit of her stomach, before she went to start a fire.

Near noon, Chama finally got up. He rejected her offer of breakfast, and after ignoring her questions concerning his aborted trip, he left for the Comanchero camp without a word, not even so much as a good-bye. As she watched him walk away with wooden stiffness, she could no longer ignore the uneasiness that had nagged at her all morning.

Although she'd avoided all recollections of the day before, she knew she would have to re-create it, remember what led to the shocking events. Considering that she'd begged Chama to let her stay at the cabin until evening, perhaps he thought she'd brought the whole calamity upon herself. *She had let the wolf in.*

Her palms turned clammy. "Or maybe," she said aloud as she rushed to the widest opening in the trees to scan the *ranchería*, "maybe he's gone to the camp to have it out with Kelso." As she wiped her hands on her skirt, the marauder's face grinned at her with vivid clarity. Clenching her fists with avenging fury, she hoped Chama did confront him. Knocked every one of those sneering teeth down the pig's throat.

Yes. Once Chama dealt with Kelso, he'd be fine again. Everything would be just fine.

Fear for Chama's safety gripped her as she waited, her back against a tree trunk. Every second she expected to hear gunshots or some kind of commotion. But all seemed peaceful and quiet. Unusually so.

Long minutes later, she saw someone walk out of the trees

on the other side and head her way. Chama! Thrilled that he was safe, she almost laughed out loud for joy.

As he came closer, she noticed he carried something. A bottle. It looked like whiskey. By the time he leapt across the stream, she was certain. *A bottle of cheap whiskey.*

He climbed the rise and brushed by her as if she didn't exist, then walked past the cabin to the shed and slid down to sit against the side wall. Pulling the cork, he raised the bottle to his lips.

Throughout the rest of the day he remained there, drinking. And if she came within twenty feet of him, he shot her a dark, deadly glare that kept her at an uneasy distance. Mostly she stayed inside. She didn't even bother to cook—she couldn't have forced anything down if she had.

Near nightfall, he staggered to his feet.

At last, she thought as she heard him stumbling about. The interminable waiting had come to an end. She went to the door.

But he merely trudged to his bedroll beside the cabin. Collapsing onto it with a grunt, he covered himself with fumbly fingers and rolled to face the wall again.

Carrie sat late into the night, her mind in a whirl. Why was Chama rejecting her so totally? If he no longer wanted her, why didn't he simply tell her to leave instead of sitting there all day getting himself stinking drunk? Something else must have happened yesterday. But what?

Slumping dejectedly at the table, she rubbed her tender chin. What did happen? She was fairly certain she hadn't actually been raped. Had Karl scared him off just in time? Or killed him? Or was it Chama? Or, she thought, sipping her cold coffee, maybe Kelso *had* raped her, and Chama thought she was now too dirty. *Too tainted for him.*

She straightened in her seat. That was a laugh. The more the idea ate at her, the angrier she became. How dare he think she wasn't worthy to be in his *saintly* company any longer. Eyeing the wall that separated him from her, she had the strongest urge to throw her bench at the spot where she guessed his head must lie.

Not quite brave enough to actually do it, she took another gulp of coffee, all the while wishing it was some of that rotgut he'd been swilling down all day. He wasn't the only one who needed a little pick-me-up. "Who does he think he is?" she spat. "Judging me unfit to live with a Comanchero half-breed? In this hellhole? Ha! If anyone should be looking down her nose at someone, it's me. At least I'm not a thieving, killing son of a whoring soldier."

≈ 23 ≈

THE FOLLOWING MORNING Carrie fed the one horse and ate her breakfast. Then she'd sat outside drinking coffee and watching the sun's shadows steadily shrink for a good two hours before she finally heard Chama stir. She tapped her fingernails impatiently against the tin cup, waiting for him to show his face. Today she would have some answers or else. This morning she'd even noticed Eagle Wings was missing, for heaven's sake.

When Chama finally ambled around the cabin corner in rumpled, slept-in clothes, he shuffled on unsteady feet, his head drooping. As he passed through a patch of sunshine, he flinched and squinted.

And he smelled just as bad as he looked. "Coffee?" she asked in a deliberately loud, sharp voice, taking pleasure in watching the hungover man recoil at the blast.

He nodded and mumbled something unintelligible as he eased ever so slowly onto the other log . . . a safe distance away.

Rising, she picked up the cup she'd had waiting for him on one of the brim stones. Seeing a fir twig lying at the bottom, she was tempted to leave it. Dumping it out, she poured in some misty-hot brew and offered it to him.

Without looking up, he took the handle in fingers that trembled even worse than Karl's had that second morning on the trail.

Carrie sat down again while allowing him to take a couple of sips. But only a couple. She hiked up her chin. "I *will* have some answers from you this morning. I have done nothing to warrant this kind of treatment. When I opened the door to

Kelso, I assumed it was Karl. He was already overdue."

Chama swatted at a gnat as if she'd never spoken and took another sip of his coffee.

Carrie's irritation doubled. She sprang to her feet. "The brute barged past me. And it's not as if I didn't try to stop him. How else do you think I got this fat lip?"

Again she received not the slightest response from him.

She let out a huff. "Fine! If you won't talk about me, then what about the horse? Where's Eagle Wings?"

This time, at least, he tipped his head slightly and squinted at her through horribly bloodshot eyes. For a second she thought he would speak. But he didn't. Sighing heavily, he closed his eyes and took another drink.

Carrie couldn't have been more furious if he'd slapped her in the face. "So that's the way you want it. Well, you've come to the right person. I've had plenty of experience with cold silences. My father was a master at it. So you needn't worry, I won't be bothering you with my useless prattle ever again." Whirling around she grabbed the half-empty bucket and strode down the hill to fetch some water. And maybe splash some on her overheated face while she was at it.

As the day wore on, Chama spent most of his time in the stable, cleaning it and brushing the long-legged bay until not a trace of its winter hair remained. He worked on the horse so long that the usually drab-looking animal's coat shone like a pair of spit-polished boots.

Carrie whiled away her day mostly inside, avoiding him as stubbornly as he did her. She finished the doll's clothes. Searching for something else to do to keep her mind occupied, she added several inches to the lengths of three skirts from the material of another. After that she mended the rip in her blouse, then resewed every button on Chama's store-bought shirts. Too soon, she ran out of chores. As she idly sat, nothing remaining to distract her from her predicament, her thoughts jumped without fail to the wretched state she again found herself in.

She bitterly regretted her rash vow of silence and, more, resented Chama for triggering it. Just the thought of again living a wasted hate-filled existence twisted her insides into knots. How could Chama do this to her? How could he shun her when his own mother had suffered at the hands of brutish men the same as she had, had even died from it?

By the time she'd retired for the night—*alone again*—she'd convinced herself there had to be more to his rejection of her. Something more must've happened that was so terrible he couldn't speak the words. And if he wouldn't tell her, she knew who would.

At the first faint light of dawn, Carrie quickly rose and dressed. In her haste, she merely brushed, then caught her weighty mane at the nape of her neck with a leather thong. Then, quietly closing the door behind her, she stole down the hill. At the bottom she glanced back once to assure herself Chama still lay asleep beside the cabin. Satisfied, she stretched her legs into long strides. As the newly attached yellow ruffle on her blue print skirt brushed across her ankles, she felt slightly better, knowing she was now more decently covered.

Reaching the trees edging the *rancheria*, she was especially grateful for her quiet moccasins as she picked up the pace, hoping to traverse the slumbering village unnoticed. Although she couldn't help thinking eyes followed her from behind every tree, she reached Esperanza's unscathed just as the rim of the eastern wall was trimmed with light.

Stepping up on the porch, she hesitated. To call on anyone at this hour was wholly unacceptable. But, she argued with herself, her need for answers far outweighed her lack of manners.

She knocked, waited, then knocked again before she heard Esperanza's groggy yet wary voice. *"Que está?"*

"It's me, Carrie. Please let me in."

While she waited for Esperanza to shuffle to the entrance and lift the wooden bar, Carrie looked both ways, still edgy about being in the camp unescorted.

A thud resounded on the other side, then Esperanza swung open the door with a puzzled frown.

Upon stepping within, Carrie spotted Karl and Ingacita snuggled in their beds at the far end of the room. "Sorry to bother you," she apologized in a whisper. "I know it's much

210 / Elaine Crawford

too early to accept callers, but I just—"

Esperanza placed a silencing finger to Carrie's lips and motioned for her to be seated at the table while Esperanza moved to the corner and modestly turned her back to change into her day clothes.

While Carrie waited for the pregnant girl, she could've kicked herself for being so tactless, but only in the stillness of dawn would she have braved crossing the camp.

Once dressed, Esperanza picked up some cups and a sack of coffee, then beckoned for Carrie to follow as she walked outside to start a fire within a circle of blackened rocks.

Carrie swept the ashes from the banked coals and began adding dried pine needles as her dark-eyed friend brought several splintery sticks to nurse into flame.

After they had a small blaze licking up through the loose jumble, Esperanza straightened, one hand going to her back, the other to her swollen belly. "Why you come so early? Why Señor José no come with you?"

"I needed to speak to you alone. Chama won't talk to me. He's completely ignoring me. I was hoping Karl had mentioned something to you."

"You mean about the bad thing that happen at *su casa*? You are there. How you not know?"

Carrie pointed to her bruised jaw. "One of those filthy Comancheros barged in three days ago. I tried to fight him off, but he knocked me out. Chama was supposed to be gone for a week, but when I woke up, Kelso was gone and Chama was there. And he was being so sweet to me. You know, holding me and telling me I was safe and that everything was fine. But the next morning when I woke up, I found him sleeping outside next to the house."

"He was standing guard, no?"

"No. He just moved out there, out of our bed. And that first day he got as drunk as an old sot."

"Señor José, he get drunk? I never see him do that."

Carrie shrugged helplessly. "And now he acts like I'm not even there. It's driving me crazy. Please, if you know anything, anything at all, tell me."

"All I know is Karl, he go to *su casa,* and he see a dead man. The man, he has no face. But Karl say it is this man Kelso. My Karl, he say, *qué pasó*. But your man, he no speak. Karl thinks this Kelso shoot Eagle Wings and Señor José shoot him."

"Eagle Wings is dead?"

"*Sí.* Karl help to bury him. He ask where you are? Señor José say you are sleeping. That is all. He not say to Karl, either, why he come back."

"Well, that clears it up somewhat. Chama has killed Barney Kelso. Maybe they were good friends, and Chama is upset over it."

"*Es posible.*"

"Kelso must've heard Chama coming and took a shot at him, but missed and killed the pony instead."

"*Sí,*" Esperanza said, nodding in agreement as she tossed more wood on the fire.

"Yes. But like Karl, I don't understand why Chama returned. For two days I tried to talk him out of going, but nothing I said would sway him. When killing soldiers is involved, he's like a rock. But now, not only is he not listening to me," she said, filling the coffeepot from a water bucket, "he won't speak. Not a word."

"This thing between you, she will pass." Esperanza dropped a handful of grounds into the smudge-blackened pot and hung it over the fire. Turning back, she took Carrie's hand and led her to a nearby stump to sit. "I pray for you. Baby Jésus, he make the heart of your man soft for you. He talk to you again. You see."

Carrie took comfort in the easy manner in which the words "your man" rolled off Esperanza's tongue. But the girl was such an innocent. And, Carrie noted, she always talked about the future as if nothing threatened it. Yet, considering her delicate condition, Carrie supposed that was best. "Thank you, dear friend, for the uplifting words. But enough about me. How are you doing?"

"Oh," she laughed lightly and cradled her huge belly. "My baby is *muy grande*. I think he come *muy pronto*."

Carrie couldn't help smiling at Esperanza's impish expression. "So, you think it's going to be a boy."

"*Sí.* Yes. This baby, he is too big for girl."

She gave a playful tug to one of Esperanza's pigtails. "I see. Well, we'll know for sure pretty soon, won't we?"

Carrie was unwilling to leave her guileless friend's congenial company to go home to Chama and his wall of silence, so she remained, warming herself in its glow and that of the blazing campfire.

Over cups of the rich brew, Esperanza chatted about various members of her large family in Chihuahua until Ingacita bounded out to them and filled the air with her childish chatter. Later Carrie helped Esperanza prepare breakfast that she shared with the two of them at the table inside, even while Karl lay snoring.

As she finished her bowl of corn mush, three hard rapid knocks sounded at the door.

Esperanza hurried to open it.

"*Buenos dias. Perdone,* Señora Shipstead. *Pero*—" Chama stopped midsentence as he spotted Carrie. He brushed past Esperanza, his flaring brows dipped into a glowering vee.

Carrie shot to her feet, her last bite lumped in her rapidly closing throat.

He grabbed her arm. *"You are here."*

Her own ire sparked, she jerked away and hissed, "Come outside. You'll wake Karl."

His jaw muscles knotting, he followed her out. Once they were down the steps he caught her shoulder and whirled her to face him. "Don't you ever walk away from the cabin again without telling me."

His audacity infuriated her. She bristled. "I will go when and where it pleases me. I'm not your wife—you don't own me."

"The hell I don't!" Snatching her hand, he yanked her across the dirt square and back through the *rancheria* at such breakneck speed, she had to run to keep up. And all the way home not another word spewed from his mouth.

For once she was glad. Until he apologized for his ruthless behavior and for shaming her in front of Esperanza and all those now up and gawking at them as they passed through the camp, she didn't want to hear anything he had to say.

She needn't have worried. During the following week the silence between them stretched out as thick and cold as a foot of snow, with Chama never stepping off the place, not to go to the store or even to deliver Ingacita's finished doll.

Using the cracked door for a shield, Carrie peeked out, knowing without a doubt where he'd be. He sat in that same spot on that same log, whittling, as he'd done every day. But now he worked on a horse. Probably in remembrance of Eagle Wings, she thought, her hostility deepening. He obviously had cared more for the pony than he did her.

Carrie stalked back to the sideboard where she'd been peeling potatoes. Gathering up the knife, she caught a flash of movement out the propped-open window.

Someone was walking across the meadow.

She strained to make out the man's features beneath his hat, but he was still too far away. This would be the first person to venture over here since the incident. But she had no problem understanding why they'd all stayed away, considering the killing and then Chama's deplorable behavior the day he dragged her through the *rancheria* at the exact moment everyone sat outside having breakfast.

Carrie savagely sliced the knife across the potato. If she had a choice, she wouldn't be here either. She'd been such a fool to trust him. And worse, she recalled with a cringe, she'd told him she loved him. Well, he couldn't keep his eye on her day and night forever. The next time he left to go rob some poor soul, she'd escape. She'd rather take her chances against the Comancheros and Indians than live like this.

Her gaze slid to the bed that had been so unbearably lonely these past nights and a hungry ache gnawed at her intimate reaches. Her frustration stiffened into anger. And how dare he awaken her body, do things to make it constantly crave him, then discard her as if she were just so much trash?

Paring knife in hand, she edged to the doorway and looked out at Chama again. Watching him sit there, absorbed in his carving, she couldn't deny her attraction to him; even the sight of his hands as they smoothed shavings from the piece made her breasts harden for the want of their touch. But beneath all that enticing maleness hid a replica of her father. If she hadn't let her own urges blind her, she would've seen it. He was hard. Stubborn. And now he was showing her how cruel he could also be. And the worst kind of deceiver. Just like Father. Father had sweet-talked Mama at first, too. Got her to love and trust him, then turned on her, treating her worse than a dog. Mama hadn't started the Civil War. None of it had been her fault, no more than Barney Kelso had been Carrie's.

Chama glanced up from his whittling.

Carrie shrank deeper into the shadows.

He looked toward the meadow, then stood up, undoubtedly noticing the man who approached.

Good, Carrie thought, hoping the outlaw came to invite Chama on another robbery. The sooner the better.

Chama walked to the edge of the rise and waited for Whip, one of the twelve with whom he'd ridden out of the valley to rob the army. Chama supposed the returning gunslinger was coming to report on their success.

Whip, reed-thin but sinewy, saw him and raised a hand in greeting as he trudged up the forested incline.

Chama did the same. "Looks like you boys made good time," he said, though he didn't really care one way or the other.

Reaching Chama, Whip pursed his thin lips. "I did, anyway."

"Have a seat," Chama said out of bare politeness, nothing more. He pointed toward the logs.

Once they were settled, Whip gripped his bony thighs and looked at Chama, his gray eyes flint-hard and hollow within the shade of his low-crowned hat. Deep lines etched the sides of his mouth. "I just rode in a few minutes ago. I come by to tell you about the ambush."

"I figured as much," Chama droned, unable to muster the least enthusiasm in his voice. "How'd it go?"

"It was a massacre."

Chama should've been overjoyed, but felt only the barest spark of pleasure. Another thing Carrie had stolen from him. "How many bluecoats did you kill?"

More lines scrunched Whip's already worried brow. "No. You don't understand. *They* killed *us*. I'm the only one left. I was positioned way in the rear to signal the others when the soldiers came riding by. Anyway, one of them idiots, probably that yeller Mex, started shootin' before the troopers was even in the trap. Damn bluecoats beat a fast retreat out of range. Then, before our men could get out of the rocks and to their horses, the soldiers charged up the bluffs, surroundin' Potfeld and the rest. Must've been thirty or forty of 'em. They eventually picked everyone off. The shootin' kept up a good two hours. I almost went crazy just crouchin' down there, listenin'. I would've helped if it would've done any good. But there was just too many of 'em." He grabbed Chama's arm. "You do believe me, don't you?"

Chama looked down at the man's fingers digging into his shirt sleeve, then returned to the gaunt face. "Sure, Whip. It happens that way sometimes."

"The bastards didn't even bother to bury the men. They just rode off, leavin' them to the buzzards. After they was gone, I checked to see if anyone was still alive. But no chance. They all had eight, ten bullets in 'em."

"Yeah, guess you lucked out this time." Losing interest, Chama shifted his attention to the dying embers.

Whip heaved a sigh and stood up. "Well, guess I'd better get on back. It's been a long ride, and I'm real tuckered out."

Chama also came to his feet. "Appreciate you taking the time."

Whip hadn't been gone two minutes when Chama saw Carrie come out the door. She walked straight toward him with a stubborn look on her face, and Chama knew he'd have to deal with her now, too. He fortified himself with a deep breath and returned her inflexible stare.

She halted directly in front of him. "Did the man come to ask you to go on another robbery?"

"No."

Her lips parted slightly.

If Chama hadn't known better, he would've thought she was disappointed.

"I see," she continued after a moment. "Well, then, did he come with news of my father?"

"No."

Her eyes narrowed. Her face reddened. She looked ready to explode. "Did anything he say concern me?"

"Nope."

"Very well," she bit off. Wheeling around, she stalked back to the cabin.

With a relieved sigh, Chama sat down and picked up his wooden horse.

❦ 24 ❦

THE DOOR RATTLED with a sharp pounding, jarring Carrie from a deep sleep.

"Miss Jackson! Wake up!" The coarse, out-of-breath bellow sounded like Karl's.

Carrie sprang out of bed, ripped the bar from across the door, and flung it open. "Is it Esperanza's time?" she asked the lumbering hulk who literally hopped from one foot to the other, causing the glow from his lantern to bounce crazily into the darkness.

"Yes," he sputtered. "And she told me to hurry."

Carrie spotted Chama moving into the wildly dancing light. He clutched his friend's shoulder.

Karl gasped and swung around. If Chama hadn't dodged, the big man's hefty arm would've waylaid him.

"Hold on, Swede. It's me, Chama."

"How'd you get out here behind me?"

Ignoring Karl's question, he turned to Carrie. "Hurry up and get dressed. We don't want to keep our little mother waiting."

Accompanied by Karl's constant prodding, Carrie and the two men hurried through the wee hours of morning to Esperanza. When they arrived, Karl burst through the door with such force, Carrie feared for the hinges. Then he practically threw the lantern on the table beside another one as he passed on his way to the bed.

Esperanza, propped on pillows, put a finger to her lips and pointed to tiny Ingacita, asleep in her padded crate on the floor.

Karl bent over Esperanza and asked in a loud whisper, "Are you all right?"

"*Sí.*" She craned her neck past him. "*Dónde esta* Señora Jackson?"

Carrie pushed past the hovering man. "I'm right here."

Esperanza caught her hand. "Bless you. You come *pronto.*"

Carrie noticed Esperanza's mussed hair was damp with sweat. She turned to Karl. "I'll take good care of her. Don't worry. Now, go on, get out of here."

Karl looked down at Esperanza with hound-dog eyes. "I'll be right outside, sweetheart."

But when he stayed planted where he stood, Carrie picked up the crate with the sleeping tot and handed it to him, then pushed him toward the entrance where Chama waited.

As she started to shut the door after Karl, he stopped it with his hand and peeked in again. "If you need anything, anything at all, you just holler."

"I will," Carrie said, giving him another shove. "Now, go."

Carrie's midwifing experience had been limited to the milk cow she'd kept until last year. But as a child in Carolina, she'd often overheard her mother discussing birthings with her friends. It had been a favorite topic, especially whenever a new baby was born on one of the neighboring plantations; and unbeknown to her family, she and her brother had peeked through a knothole on three separate occasions to watch one of their Negresses giving birth.

"How far apart are your pains?" she asked, bringing a bench and one of the lanterns with her to the foot of the bed and placing them there.

"*Dos minutos?*" Esperanza ventured uncertainly. Her face then went blank, and she clutched the blankets on either side. Stiffening, she began to pant rapidly.

Carrie watched the muscles across Esperanza's bulging abdomen constrict and estimated the seizure lasted close to a minute before her friend's body relaxed and her breathing slowed. Pulling the sheet away, Carrie felt around on Esperanza's belly, then smiled reassuringly. "From what I can tell, everything's where it should be."

Esperanza managed to curl the corners of her mouth. "*Bueno.* He is *muy grande* like his papa."

"I'm going to check down below just to make sure." With Esperanza's help, she pushed the nightgown out of the way. Then, while examining within the birth canal, Esperanza's body gave a sudden lurch, and a panicky feeling gripped Carrie as the girl began to grunt and push. *Not yet,* she wailed silently. *I just got here.*

When the pain subsided, Carrie tried to sound calm as she said, "That pain started less than a minute since the last one."

Esperanza wiped droplets of sweat from above her lip, then spoke in a tight voice. "*Es la hora.* He come soon now."

Carrie whirled around to check the articles placed neatly on the table. She counted several towels, a stack of sheeting, a large water basin. Then, at the sight of a sharp knife, her heart lurched. Feeling wholly inadequate for the task, she shot a fleeting prayer heavenward, then turned back to Esperanza. "Do you have water heating?"

"*Sí,* I do that before I wake Karl."

"Well," Carrie said with a nervous laugh, "looks like you got him up just in time."

"Better you go see if the fire still burns."

No sooner had Carrie stepped out the door than Karl rushed up to hover over her. "Is something wrong?"

"No, everything's fine." Patting his arm, she looked past to see Chama give her a helpless shrug. "I just came out to see if the water's hot. I'm going to need a lot. Would you two see to it for me?"

"Are you sure she's all right?" Karl asked.

"Yes." She gave his arm an extra squeeze. "She's coming right along. But I'm going to need that water pretty soon, so would you please see to it?"

"You bet," Chama said as he stepped up, a big grin splashed across his face—the first she'd seen in weeks. He rested a hand on his friend's shoulder. "Won't we, Karl?"

"Thank you," Carrie said, directing a cool reply Chama's way. One exuberant smile would by no means make her forget his previous behavior. Turning her back on him, she returned inside to Esperanza, who was again caught in the throes of a pain. She ran to the bed. Upon examination, she identified the beginnings of the baby's head at the entrance to the birth canal. Relief swept through her, since she was fairly certain the baby was positioned exactly where it should be.

A half hour later, after a dozen more horrific delivery pains—pains that wrenched unearthly screams from Esperanza—the baby hadn't progressed one bit farther. And the tiny young woman's energy was fading fast.

Carrie's confidence sagged as fear for her friend began to grip her. The baby was apparently too large for Esperanza to deliver.

Then Carrie remembered talk about birthing chairs that took advantage of gravity and, also, about how Indian women often squatted to bear a child. She glanced around the room for something that Esperanza might sit upon unrestricted, since by now the girl was far too weak to stoop on her own. Carrie spotted nothing that looked remotely suitable. She figured she might be able to support Esperanza herself, but then she wouldn't be available to assist below.

She knelt beside Esperanza's bed and looked into glazed eyes. "I'm going outside for a minute. When I come back, it won't be much longer. I promise." Taking a fortifying breath, she walked through the door to find Karl still on the porch, pacing back and forth like a caged bear.

He rushed to her. "Esperanza! The baby!"

"Not yet." She looked past him and saw Chama standing by the fire, a stick in hand.

His expression conveyed almost as much anxiety as Karl's.

"Chama," she said, sounding as calm as possible, "would you please bring in the kettle of water? I'm going to be needing it soon."

"I'll do it," Karl offered. Leaping off the porch, he rushed to fetch it.

"No! Karl! Let Chama bring it. You're so jittery, you'd probably spill it all over the place. Besides," she added, watching Chama wrap a kerchief around the hot handle and start her way. "I need him to move something for me."

Chama's mouth parted, and he stopped midstep.

She sent him an urgent summons by knitting her brows and motioning with her head.

"You're sure?" Karl asked, blocking her return inside.

"I know it's hard just waiting out here. But it'll be over soon. Go sit down and get some rest. Pretty soon, now, you're going to have your hands full with a new baby in the house." She stepped around him, then made way for Chama and the cauldron of piping hot water.

Walking past her, Chama gave her the harried look of a trapped wolf.

She took smug pleasure in it as she shut the door, enclosing the uneasy male in a birthing room. She followed him to the sideboard. "Just put it down there. I don't need it yet."

Chama set it on the counter, then shot a worried glance from her to Esperanza. He took a backward step.

Carrie caught his hand. "You can't go. I need you."

Still staring wide-eyed at Esperanza, he wagged his head. "Birthings are women's business."

A smile tickled the corners of her mouth. He was virtually scared out of his wits. "Not this time. I need a pair of strong arms, and you're elected."

He tore his gaze from Esperanza. *"What for?"*

"She needs help having the baby."

His eyes sprang even wider. "You don't expect me to, to—"

A groan began to build in Esperanza, stealing Chama's attention.

"As soon as this contraction is past, I want you to help me get her up. Then you're to sit on the bench at the table and support her. I'm going to see if squatting will help. She's not able to push the baby down into the birth canal on her own."

"You mean she might . . ."

Carrie nodded almost imperceptibly, on the off chance Esperanza could hear past the pain.

Then, as if by magic, Chama's apprehension seemed to vanish. He straightened to the powerful commanding presence she'd witnessed the first time she'd laid eyes on him, that presence she'd always relied on. "Tell me what to do."

With Chama undergirding Esperanza, the baby's head surged into the canal during the next contraction.

Carrie cried out, "It's coming! It's coming!"

"*Sí*, I feel it!" Esperanza panted as the pain subsided.

Chama adjusted his grip beneath Esperanza's arms and exchanged a look of profound relief with Carrie. He then leaned close to Esperanza's ear. "You're doing just fine, *mi paloma linda*."

Closing her eyes, Esperanza pressed the side of her head against his hovering mouth and managed a weary smile.

It took Carrie a second or two to interpret the Spanish phrase, then realized Chama had called the haggard, sweat-streaked girl his lovely dove. Such dear words. They made another small breach in the angry fortress Carrie had built around herself.

By the time the baby arrived, dropping into Carrie's waiting hands, Chama was laughing and sweating right along with the two women. Then, once the afterbirth emerged and the baby's cord was cut, Chama scooped Esperanza up into his arms and carried the spent new mother to her bed.

While Carrie tended the newborn at the table, she couldn't help watching the effortless manner in which he lay Esperanza down as if she were the most fragile and precious treasure beneath the heavens, the way he drew the blanket over her, then kissed her brow with the utmost tenderness and affection. But nothing touched Carrie quite so much as when he turned back to her, warmth filling his eyes. And his smile softened his expression more than she'd ever thought possible. For that one miraculous moment all else faded from existence. There was nothing but him and her and the charged space between them.

Carrie's heart leapt over itself as he came to her.

The baby cried out and squirmed beneath Carrie's hands, diverting her attention.

"What is it?" Chama murmured barely above a whisper. "A boy or a girl?"

Carrie looked down to reaffirm what she'd already discovered. "A boy, just as Esperanza predicted."

He swung around. "Did you hear that, *mamacita*? You have a son."

"*Sí,*" she murmured on a contented but very weary sigh, one that brought Carrie totally back to the business at hand.

"Chama, go out and tell Karl about his new son while I get these two ready to greet him. I'll call you when we're ready."

"Sure," he said, beaming broadly. "Karl's gonna be the happiest man in the world." Passing by Carrie on his way out, he paused behind her and placed a hand on her shoulder. "You did fine. Real fine."

"So did you. I don't know what we'd have done without you."

He brushed his lips across her cheek, stealing her senses. But before she regained her presence of mind he'd stridden out the door.

Had he returned to his old self just as Esperanza had said he would?

Continuing to stare at the door he'd closed behind him, doubts began to squirrel through her. It was quite possible he'd simply been caught up in the miracle of birth.

She dropped a washrag in a pan of warm water and wrung it out, amazed at how easily swayed she could be by a few kind words and a peck on the cheek.

✤ 25 ✤

MERE SECONDS AFTER Chama walked outside, Karl burst through the door, wild-eyed and grinning from ear to ear. "Spranza!"

"Get out of here," Carrie ordered, shooing him away. "They're not presentable yet."

"I don't give a hoot about that. I just gotta see 'em." He banged past Carrie with big clomping footsteps and dropped down on the floor beside Esperanza. Then, with a gentleness she didn't think possible in the lumbering man, Karl gathered up his tiny "wife" and began stroking her hair and kissing her while he murmured softly.

Carrie turned from them, sensing her presence was an intrusion on their intimate moment. As she did, she found Chama standing in the open doorway, toting a wide-awake Ingacita.

With a hopeful smirk, he shrugged.

Carrie eyed him with her stiffest raised-brow disapproval.

He didn't budge.

When she saw it was useless, she surrendered with a huff. "All right, all right. But take warning, you're going to make yourself useful."

Without the slightest hesitation, he walked across the threshold.

As he did, Karl barreled to his feet. "Move out of the way, Carrie. I want to get a look at my *son,* now."

Carrie glanced from him to the baby, still slick from afterbirth. "He isn't cleaned up yet."

"Don't make me no never-mind. I come from a dairy farm up Minnesota way. I've helped birth more calves than you can shake a stick at."

Carrie threw up her hands. "Fine. Have it your own way. You men clean up the baby and get him dressed while I take care of Esperanza."

It touched and amused Carrie whenever she peeked at Karl clumsily yet tenderly wiping the baby clean—with Chama and little Ingacita at his side, both giving unwanted directions and assistance.

Esperanza watched, too, with the dearest smile, despite her droopy, sleep-deprived eyelids.

If Carrie had ever harbored a doubt that Esperanza could love the lumbering, hard-drinking Swede, she never would again.

Once Esperanza and her baby boy were settled and asleep, Carrie and the men fixed breakfast in the early light. Then, while sitting outside on the porch steps, the men excitedly rehashed the morning's drama between spoonfuls of mush.

Too tired to maintain her animosity, Carrie began feeling warmly contented as she listened to Chama's account of his part in the birth. He grinned often while speaking in an energetic voice.

It's over, she reaffirmed to herself. *He's finally back to his old self.*

Finished with his third cup of coffee, Chama stood up. "Guess I'd better get home to feed Hickory. Oh, and by the way, Karl, do you know of any good saddle horses in the valley—one someone would be willing to part with?"

"About a dozen Apaches rode in with a string a couple of nights ago. From what I hear, they're camped at the far end of the valley."

"Which band?"

Karl wagged his head. "Sorry, pal, they all look alike to me. And when they rode through they wasn't in a real talkative mood."

"I'll head on back there. See what they've got."

"Take your time. I'll be here all day."

When Chama turned and walked away without so much as a look her way, Carrie tried to assure herself it was just an oversight. After all, he was going out to take care of business, the first since the Barney Kelso incident. Looking for a new horse to replace his beloved Eagle Wings, at that. Yes, she told herself, everything was going to be fine again. She plucked Ingacita from off the step and gave the little one a cuddling hug—a hug she didn't want to admit she needed far more than the tot did.

Even red and wrinkled, Karl, Jr., was by far the most beautiful baby ever born, Carrie decided as she stood at the table, removing the infant's diaper. And his fuzzy black hair felt as soft as a downy new chick.

While carefully cleaning around the umbilical cord, Carrie heard the sound of approaching hooves. She immediately assumed it would be Chama and found herself sighing with relief. He'd been gone for hours—not even returning for the noon meal. She tossed the washcloth into a pan of water and quickly tucked in her blouse, then checked for any straying strands of hair.

He rode within view of the front window on a golden stallion that flaunted streams of creamy mane and tail. Admiring the animal, Carrie couldn't remember ever seeing a prettier palomino. Its flowing tail almost reached the ground.

Karl stepped out of the woods, carrying a water bucket, and intercepted his friend near the beehive oven.

Chama remained mounted as the two exchanged a few words. After a moment, he unhooked a large stuffed bag from off his saddle horn and handed it to Karl. Then, without so much as a glance toward the house, he wheeled the horse around and galloped away.

Astonished, Carrie placed the baby in its basket and ran for the door. Opening it, she crashed into Karl.

He caught one of her shoulders and stepped back.

"Why didn't he come in? Where's he going now?"

Karl released her and glanced away, shifting his stance. He looked mighty uncomfortable. "Shut the door. We don't want to wake Spranza."

She did as he requested, then followed him off the porch

before confronting him again. "Well?" she asked, prepared for the worst.

"Well," he repeated, looking as if a gun barrel were pointed at him. "It's like this . . ." Pausing, he cowardly diverted his gaze again. "Some of the boys was leavin' to go rob one of them big British spreads up north. Up near Cimarron. You know, them foreigners what's tryin' to take over all the ranchin' up that way."

"Are you trying to tell me that Chama just up and left without so much as a good-bye?"

He returned his attention to her, with all the sincerity of a preacher. "Oh, he wanted to. He really did. But Jeb Farmer and his boys was all ready and waitin' on him. And, well, he needs the money. I suppose you saw that fancy horse he come ridin' up on. Chama got him on the come. He has to fork over six repeaters when the gunrunners come through again."

"Guns," she spat. "Always those damned guns."

Karl fiddled with a button on his protruding belly for a second, then perked up. "Oh, I forgot. He's gonna be on a mission of mercy, too. He's takin' Potfeld's pregnant widow to some pueblo where her sister lives on his way up north. That's a real Christian thing for him to do, don't you think?"

Carrie rolled her eyes at the ludicrousness of his last statement. "I see. Being such a Good Samaritan, he even took some of his precious time to bring me my things. That bag you've got there does belong to me, doesn't it?"

Karl glanced down at it. "Uh—yeah. He said you was to stay here with us till he comes back."

Carrie ripped the string-drawn sack from Karl's hand. "You mean, *if* he doesn't get killed first, *or* if he doesn't decide to take his *good deed* business elsewhere." Hoisting up the bag, she swung away from him and started for the porch.

"Don't you worry yourself none about that," Karl called after her. "He'll be back. He said he would. And he ain't never let me down yet."

She swung around, venomous sarcasm dripping from her words. "Well, now, aren't you the lucky one."

* * *

"Don't you worry yourself none about that," Carrie muttered to herself, repeating Karl's pitiful defense of Chama as she stirred a pot of stew over the flames. Eighteen days. It had been eighteen days. And although every one of them had been filled with innumerable chores for the recuperating Esperanza and her family, the nights had held nothing but a plethora of angry words she would rain on Chama's head when he returned. If he ever did.

Through with foolish hope and dangerous escape plans, she would demand he see her safely to Santa Fe. Or, better yet, to Denver. And get her started by leaving her with some of that money he hoarded for those precious rifles of his.

Every night she'd played out the scene in her mind. And each night her resolve strengthened. She would make a life for herself as a housekeeper or waitress or even a laundress if nothing else was available. Never again would she allow herself to be kept by another man, to trust one. To care. Chama and her father had certainly taught her better than that. From now on she would be free. Her own person.

Of course, the forever optimistic Esperanza had been after her to be patient and have faith. But the young innocent was entirely too naive. Just because a person wanted something didn't make it happen, no matter how right and good it might seem.

The ground beneath Carrie's feet vibrated with the rumble of several approaching horses. She quickly covered the kettle with a lid and turned toward the sound. Taking a fortifying breath, she waited. Chama was due. He could be among them.

Karl, who'd given up drinking since the baby's birth—another of Esperanza's "little miracles"—banged out the door. Recovered at last from the "shakes" of withdrawal, he looked more alert today than she'd ever seen him. Even that considerable gut of his had trimmed down. He trotted down the steps on springy, confident feet.

Just then, three riders, their wide-brimmed sombreros pressed back in the breeze, emerged from between the opposite cabins and entered the little square. Chama was not among them.

Carrie felt herself sag with disappointment.

As they reined their mounts to a halt just short of her, one of the Mexicans, who surely must've been covered with half the desert between here and the border, leered down at Carrie as if she were his own personal watering hole.

Knowing the Swede was coming up behind her, she stilled the urge to flee.

"Somethin' I can do for you?" Karl said in a none-too-friendly manner.

One, a fresh-faced young Mexican, whipped the oversize hat from his head and looked at Karl with an eager expression. "Esperanza Flores, she is here?"

Karl's features hardened even more. "Who wants to know?"

"I am the *hermano*. The brother. *Por favor*, tell me, she is here? I have come for her."

"Her brother!" Carrie rushed to the side of the young man's piebald pony. "Get down. Come in. Esperanza will be thrilled to see you."

"She is in *la casa*?" he asked, his voice pitching high with anticipation.

Karl brushed past Carrie, looking every bit as hostile as before. "How'd you know she was here?"

"My cousin, he rides with Moreno's *bandoleros*. He hear she is with you."

"That's right, and don't you be forgettin' that. You're welcome to drop by for a spell, but she's not going anywhere without me."

Any remaining trace of a smile left the brother's face.

His two companions, older and much more heavily armed, also stiffened and began moving their gun hands dangerously close to their holsters.

Reacting on instinct, Carrie stepped deftly between Karl and the men. "That's right. Karl is taking Esperanza to visit her family himself, just as soon as his friend Chama returns to guide them down to Chihuahua. Isn't that so?" she finished, glancing pointedly at Karl.

The muscles working in his jaw gave evidence to the fact

he didn't appreciate her interference. But he relaxed his stance, somewhat. "Yeah, that's right. Esperanza wants to show the little ones off to her family. And since you come all this way, you might as well climb on down and be the first to meet 'em."

"*Bebés*, she have *bebés*?" Eyes almost identical to Esperanza's widened with amazement, then the young man turned to his companions and rattled something off in rapid-fire Spanish.

Both men politely tipped their hats toward Carrie. Negating the respectful gesture, the lusting *bandido* added one last intimate invitation by slowly, suggestively, rimming his mouth with his tongue just before the two dug oversize spurs into their horses' flanks and galloped off in the direction they'd come.

Esperanza's brother dismounted and tied his scrawny horse with the mottled black-and-white coat to a tree, then started up the steps after Karl, his own spurs clanging against the planks.

The idea that a girl as sweet as Esperazna had an outlaw for a brother galled Carrie. "Young man," she called, stopping him. "If you've turned into a *bandido*, your sister is going to be very disappointed in you."

"No, no, señora." He thrust forth upturned palms. "The cousin of *mi papa*, he is *bandido*. He fix it for me to come with them to look for Esperanza. *Mi familia,* we are looking for her *muy* long time. Here, there. There, here. Ever since the Apaches take her."

Karl swung back to the slight-built young man, and his expression gentled. "Have you really? Spranza will be mighty happy to know you never gave up on her. Mighty happy."

Irritating light shafted across Carrie's eyelids, intruding on her much-needed sleep. The baby had cried several times during the night, disturbing her almost as much as the hard floor beneath the thin pallet she'd been using for a bed the past three weeks did. At the faint sound of footsteps, she opened her eyes.

"*Ayeee! Perdone*," Esperanza said in a lively whisper, "I

just come in to see about the babies."

"Come in?" Confused, Carrie sat up and looked around. Karl and Esperanza's brother, Pablo, were missing. Only Ingacita and Karl, Jr., still remained in their beds in peaceful slumber. "Do you mean," she murmured in hushed tones as she rose to her feet, "that I slept through all of you getting up?"

"And having breakfast," Esperanza returned with a smug smile.

"My goodness. Even Karl?"

Esperanza's smirk broadened as she lifted one of her flaring brows. "*Sí*. Now he no drink the whiskey no more, he wake up with the sun." She moved past Carrie on tiptoe to check on her dear little cherubs. Satisfied, she turned back for the door. "Coffee, she is waiting."

"I'll be right out."

While donning her clothes, Carrie marveled at the change in everyone since Pablo had arrived a mere three days ago. Esperanza was up and about most of the time now, nearly as good as new, happy and laughing throughout the day. And, even more astounding, Karl whistled almost constantly as he prepared for their imminent departure.

Pablo, a very persuasive young fellow, had convinced them to leave for Old Mexico with him and his father's cousin just as soon as Chama returned to collect Carrie. Pablo argued quite successfully that Chama would not be eager to go on another long journey so soon.

Carrie had also told them not to bother waiting for Chama, she'd be more than glad to accompany them to Mexico, leave all this Comanchero business behind. But Karl wouldn't hear of it. A few days one way or the other wouldn't make that much difference, he'd said. "And besides," he'd added, "I couldn't do that to my friend after all he's done for me."

"Men!" Carrie spat as she jerked her blouse down over her head. They were loyal as old dogs to their buddies. But with their women—only when it suited them.

Once Carrie was dressed, she walked out the door to find neither Karl nor Pablo in sight. Esperanza, alone, sat on the big stump near a blazing campfire. Stepping to the edge of the porch, Carrie looked up to study the sky and noted that it was no more than an hour past dawn. She strode out to join Esperanza. "Where did the men go?"

"To buy packhorses or burros, if any are for sale."

"Oh, yes, for all your things. I'm so pleased for you. I just wish I were going with you."

"Maybe Chama, he bring you for a visit soon."

Carrie expelled an exasperated breath. "I told you, I'm through with him, with *all men*. It would just be a lot easier if I could go with you and not have to face him."

Esperanza's big dark eyes mirrored her sympathy. "I am *muy* sorry. But Karl, he say you are Chama's woman."

Carrie nodded wearily. "I know, I know." Leaning down, she snagged a cup off one of the brim stones. Then, taking a rag from her pocket, she grabbed the handle of the coffeepot and lifted it off the tripod. From out of the spout, the steam-wafted aroma hit her nostrils with full force.

She gasped as nausea instantly convulsed her stomach. On the verge of gagging, she quickly replaced the pot and shrank back from the offending odor.

"Qué paso?" Esperanza stood up and approached Carrie.

"No, please." Carrie waved off Esperanza and the steaming cup she held. "Something must be wrong with the coffee, it gags me just to smell it." She backstepped farther upwind and took several gulps of crisp morning air. "Oh, yes. Much better."

Esperanza looked down at the brew she held, then back up to Carrie. She suddenly burst forth with that tinkling titter of hers and bobbed her head back and forth. "Now I am well again. Is your turn."

"No, I really don't feel sick. It's just the smell."

"The coffee? No, is fine. Is you. Is your turn to have the baby."

"A baby! My God! I can't!" Carrie's heart wrenched to a stop along with her breathing. When it started again, it came in hard thuds as she tried to force her reeling mind to remember when her last monthly flow had been... "My, God," she repeated with horror as she realized she hadn't had one since she'd come to the valley. And just how long had she been here. Six weeks? Seven? She didn't know. Why in heaven's name hadn't she kept track?

Esperanza moved close and took Carrie by the arm, looking up at her with all the earnest sincerity only she seemed capable of. "*Es maravilloso! Muy bueno!* You see. Señor José, he be happy. You be happy. Maybe you believe now. Baby Jésus, he make everything fine again. *Muy bueno.*"

No amount of naive enthusiasm on Esperanza's part could lift Carrie from the desperation she felt. It would've been hard enough to make a living on her own, but how would she ever manage with a baby?

Unable to endure Esperanza's happy expression any longer, Carrie tore away from her friend and ran toward the thick woods that edged the back of the cabin. Escaping into its deep shadows, she slowed to a numb walk.

Wandering blindly along the path to the stream, the sound of hoofbeats scarcely penetrated her consciousness. She didn't turn until the animal was almost upon her.

Chama!

He sat high above on his palomino. His expression held not the barest flicker of emotion as he stared down at her from the back of the splendid stallion. "I'll be back for you in an hour. Have your things packed and ready to go."

~ 26 ~

WHEN CARRIE ROSE and dressed the following morning, alone, in her own empty cabin again, she did so with the hopeless apathy of a condemned soul.

Pregnant. By a man who hated her.

She couldn't stay with him. And she'd rather die than go back to her father. Yet how would she survive on her own? Once she began to show, no respectable person would give her a job. And later there'd be a baby to care for. What kind of a life could she possibly make for herself and a mixed-blood bastard? Poor little thing.

If only . . .

No. All was past saving. Even if Chama had never actually said the damning words, his feelings couldn't be clearer. He would always blame her for Kelso. Since his return yesterday, he'd been even colder toward her than before he'd left—if that were possible.

All the day before, his face had looked as if it would crack into a thousand pieces if he so much as attempted a bit of pleasant conversation or, heaven forbid, a smile. And none of his bad humor could be blamed on a failed robbery, either. She'd overheard him tell Karl that not only had the "job" gone swift and clean, it had been far more lucrative than he'd expected, since the ranch was headquarters for a group of English investors.

More money to buy those damned guns.

If only Karl and Esperanza had taken her with them. But they'd ridden out yesterday, soon after Chama had come to fetch her. And now she felt so alone, she knew the very walls of the cabin would echo her despair if she but spoke. What she wouldn't give, right now, to be back in that houseful of noisy friends.

Hearing Chama outside, dumping logs onto the fire, she hated the very idea of cooking him breakfast. But if she refused, she'd hate even more having him work around her while she fixed her own. Already disgruntled before she'd gotten her first glimpse of "Old Flint Eyes," she savagely cut several strips off a slab of salt pork and flung them haphazardly into the skillet before taking them outside.

To her relief, Chama was nowhere in sight. Probably feeding the horses, she thought after she noted the coffeepot over the flames. Recalling the previous morning's nausea, she made a point of staying upwind of the brew while she bridged the frying pan across three rocks strategically set among the live coals.

Within seconds, the meat began to simmer, and the fat started changing from dull white to a slithering cream. And the first drifts of its aroma came her way.

Her stomach began to churn. She took several steps backward and breathed deeply of the fresh mountain air. Deciding it would be wise to keep her distance as much as possible, she went back to the cabin and sliced some bread while waiting for the bacon to fry. After delaying as long as possible, she started back, plate in hand.

Taking note of the light breeze's direction, she made a wide circle of the campfire. But it was useless. The aroma of bacon and coffee now virtually filled the air. Her stomach rolled, hot bile started upward.

She dropped the tin plate on a stump and sprinted away until she'd escaped the offending odors. Stopping beside an oak, she took several gulps of air. Her nausea gradually subsided, somewhat.

But even from there she could hear the loud popping of the bacon. It was in dire need of turning. She would have to do it, one way or the other. Pinching her nostrils closed, she held her breath and dashed back to the fire and picked up the fork with her free hand, then frantically scraped loose the sticking strips.

Before she could get them all flipped, her lungs threatened to burst from lack of breath. She spun around and ran away as fast and far as she could before she was forced to inhale. After taking in sufficient air, she returned, nose held again, mouth closed tight, to finish turning the pork.

"What the hell is going on?" Chama bellowed from somewhere behind her.

Startled, she swung around. When she did, she released her nose and gasped. The pungent odors flooded in. An instant later, a surge of bitterness forced its way up from her throat. She slapped a hand over her mouth and ran for the stream, banging past Chama and wildly dodging trees on her way down the hill.

She didn't make it. A few yards shy of the water, she stopped and yanked her billowing skirt to the side just in the nick of time.

"You're sick!" she heard Chama cry from the top of the hill as she bent over, retching. He started down. "You should've told me. I can fix my own breakfast."

By the time the convulsions had subsided enough for her to retort with at least a measure of the rage she felt, his moccasins and white-panted legs were blocking the view in front of her. "I'm not sick! If it wasn't for you I wouldn't be throwing up at all. But don't you worry, as soon as I rinse off, you'll get your damned breakfast."

"No. You go lie down. I'll finish cooking and bring yours to you, if you're up to it."

"What? And have the master serving his slave?"

"Cut the nonsense. You're sick."

"*I am not.* Now get the hell out of my way." Carrie pushed past him and stalked on down to the stream to wash the acrid taste from her mouth. When she finished, she turned back to find Chama standing where she'd left him, still staring. She shot him a menacing glower when she passed and ignored the fact that he followed close behind. Then, as before, she gave the fire a wide berth until it was downwind. Then pinching her nostrils again, she rushed forward.

"You're crazy. Let me do it," he demanded gruffly from behind. He reached for the fork in her hand.

"No!" she snapped, jerking away, releasing her nose. "I said I'd do it." Catching her lamebrained error too late, she clutched her stomach. "Oh, no! Not again!" Spinning around, she sprinted several yards away.

"For heaven's sake, Carrie. Stop being so blasted mule-headed. What's so all-fired terrible about being sick? Everyone knows women are naturally inclined that way," he added in a calm, placating tone as he walked toward her.

"That's a lie!"

"Look, you did just spill your guts all over the side of the hill, didn't you?"

She had the strongest urge to rip that smug know-it-all expression off his face. Gritting her teeth, she stepped toward him. "For your information, when a woman is pregnant, she throws up. That doesn't make her sick."

"Pregnant?" He flinched as if she'd slapped him. And his voice, she noted with supreme pleasure, had lost all its confidence. His gaze lowered to the region of her belly. "You're going to have a baby?"

"I don't know why you're so surprised," she spat, disgusted by his awed expression. "We haven't exactly been strangers, you know."

His forehead crimped. "But, a baby."

"I wouldn't get so worked up about it, if I were you," she struck out, wanting with everything in her to hurt him as much as he had her. "It's just a poor little bastard. Fathered by another bastard. *A thieving, kidnapping Comanchero bastard.*"

His nostrils flared. Veins popped out at his neck. At his temples. And his eyes . . . Never in Carrie's life had she come face-to-face with such naked fury.

Too frightened to glance away, she watched for the inevitable blow as she retreated slowly backward.

Taking a jerky stride, he lunged forward, filling the space she'd made.

As he did, she spotted his knotted fists, the bulging shoulder and arm muscles stretching the soft cotton of his Mexican shirt. She'd pushed him much too far. He was going to kill her.

238 / Elaine Crawford

He lifted a white-knuckled fist, stopping it at the base of her jaw. It shook with rage, rattling her teeth. He drew it back again.

She squeezed her eyes shut.

And waited.

At the rustle of his clothing, she pinched her eyes even tighter.

A growl as ferocious as any wolf's roared out of him.

Something breezed past her cheek. Startled that she hadn't been touched, she popped open her eyes . . . To nothing.

She whirled around and found him stalking away, down the hill. She couldn't believe he was leaving. Neither could her body, which began to tremble more than an aspen in a strong wind.

The smell of burned bacon sent her stomach roiling again. She clamped her hand over her mouth and navigated on rocky legs the rest of the way to her bed.

Something nudged Carrie's shoulder, waking her. She lifted her lashes to find Chama looming over her, glaring, those same veins bulging at his temples. She edged away.

"Get up," he cracked. "Pack your things. We're leaving." He wheeled around and headed for the door. "And load us up enough food for a week."

Well, Carrie mused grimly. Her master hadn't sold her off while he was gone. And it looked as if he wasn't going to kill her—at least not for a few days. And, she thought, her spirits inching upward, he was taking her away from here. Could it be possible that he'd finally decided to quit torturing her? Did he actually intend to free her? Maybe at one of the pueblos along the river.

At the thought, the darkest melancholy shuttered out any joy she should have felt. She was having his baby. He should want her. But he didn't. A sob welled up, crowding her lungs. She swallowed it down, and fetching a canvas tote from beneath the counter board, she started stuffing it.

Chama came in as she finished packing and changed from his soft Mexican attire into his sturdier, store-bought clothes.

From his trunk he also drew out his turquoise necklace. Holding it before him, he caressed the stone for a few seconds before tying it around his neck.

He certainly set a lot of store in that rock, Carrie reflected, hoisting one of the bags onto her hip and walking outside. She dropped the sack on the ground beside Hickory and stole another glance at him. Maybe it was a gift from his Kiowan mother.

Or, she thought, prickling with renewed ire, *some sloe-eyed Apache maiden. And he just might wish he was with her right now. Wish she was carrying his child instead of me.*

Leaving the sack in a heap, Carrie snatched up Hickory's reins and mounted the long-legged bay. She'd done all she was going to do for the betraying snake today. He could load the blasted horses without her help.

A moment later when Chama walked outside, she pretended not to notice as he glanced down at the canvas tote she'd left in the dirt, then leveled a stiff-faced glare on her. But he said nothing as he latched it and the others onto the two horses. She continued to ignore him even when he tied her own bedding behind her saddle.

Once everything was secured, Chama swung onto his palomino and without a word started down the hill.

As she followed, a vague uneasiness nagged at her as they trotted across the meadow toward the trail leading out of the valley. They were leaving. For where or for what reason she had no idea. She only knew he was removing her from the one place in which she'd spent the happiest days of her life. Swinging around, she gazed back at the small cabin. No matter how miserable the last few weeks had been, nothing could ever erase the memory of that brief blissful time they'd shared, that splendorous glimpse of paradise. A paradise he'd destroyed. For that she'd hate him till her dying day.

All the long afternoon, Carrie followed Chama's dust. After they'd climbed out of the lush valley and picked their way through the deep, narrow canyon, he turned the palomino north—much to her surprise. Not south toward La Mesilla or west in the direction of Las Palomas, but north into an even higher mountain wilderness, that most savage part of Apacheria yet to be conquered. *He was taking her to the Indians.*

As the day wore on, Carrie grew steadily more fearful. *Apaches.* Even Chama, who never found fault with his "brothers," had mentioned the Apaches' cruelty toward Esperanza. Had Carrie's words precipitated so much malice that he would sell her to them out of vengeance?

Dusk was upon them when he led the way through an aspen grove to a stream that shot downward through tunneled-out rock into a pool fringed with tall grass. He dismounted and unhooked one of the totes. They were obviously staying the night.

On the slim chance he'd think better of selling her to Apaches if she proved to be a willing helpmate again, Carrie worked with him to set up camp in a small clearing sheltered by a giant boulder with a wide overhang. While performing each chore, she unwillingly anticipated where he could best use her. And he accepted her help without question. Yet, as always, the tense silence between them remained unbroken.

In a short time, Carrie found herself sitting across a blazing fire from Chama with a plateful of food and a cup of coffee that, unlike this morning, smelled delicious. Propping her back against her saddle, she drank deeply, letting the hot brew do its magic—uncoil muscles unaccustomed to long hours in the saddle.

Too soon she'd swallowed the last sip. Setting her plate of as yet untouched food on the ground beside her, she rose for a refill.

Chama, sopping up the last of his bean juice with a piece of bread, steadily watched her as she did. And as she returned to sit on her pallet, he continued to follow her every move, yet not a single flicker of emotion betrayed his thoughts.

Trying to ignore his eerie behavior, she lifted her cup to her lips.

"Aren't you going to eat your supper?" he asked as if not doing so would've been a crime.

"I'm not hungry just yet. Maybe later."

"No. You eat now. I don't care how much you hate the baby, I'm not going to let you starve it out."

Utterly shocked that he would think her capable of such a diabolical scheme, she stared at him openmouthed. Then, wondering if it might be true, she suffered a rush of guilt. Quickly she picked up her plate and shoveled a spoonful of beans into her mouth.

As she chewed, she mulled the inconceivable idea over in her mind and came to the absolute conclusion that she could never, ever consider such a thing. Yet he had thought she might. After all they'd once shared, how could he think that of her . . . ? But why not? He already blamed her for Kelso, his horse, and God only knew what else.

When she awakened the next morning, his last mistaken notion continued to eat at her. Her malicious outburst of the day before had, of course, precipitated it. Making matters worse, morning sickness assaulted her again, driving her to the far side of the pond while Chama prepared a meal for himself. Even if she did hate him, how could she have said such terrible things about their innocent little baby? Placing protective hands over her belly, she knew she'd have to set it straight with him.

Once she'd made the decision to tender an apology of sorts, she relaxed and sat down on a flat stone. Selecting some small smooth pebbles from those at her feet, she idly passed the time tossing them into the mirrorlike pond while Chama ate his breakfast. With each lob, she watched the waves ripple away from where the rock entered, followed their spread into ever-widening circles.

After a while, it came to her how much alike her baby was to the waves. Starting as a tiny dot, it, too, now grew and spread. She looked down and wondered how big of a ripple her little one was making at that very minute.

"Carrie. Come."

Lost in speculation, she hadn't noticed that Chama had finished eating and now stooped at the water's edge directly across from her, washing out his breakfast pans. She returned to camp on reluctant feet as she steeled herself for the apology she knew she must make. Considering he was such an arrogant rogue, she hoped her mouth wouldn't balk when she tried to form the words.

She stepped up behind him and, with her hands clasped tightly together, spoke to the back of his head. "Yesterday I said some things. Awful things . . . about the baby. I didn't mean them. I just want you to know I'll do my utmost to take care of myself and the little one"—then, unable to keep the animosity from coming through, she finished with—"no matter what you plan to do with me."

Chama reacted not one whit to her words. He didn't even pause in scrubbing a pan with river sand.

Knowing she was being deliberately shunned, *again*, Carrie glared at the working muscles of his back, and her anger built until she envisioned a dagger piercing him just below his left shoulder blade. To the hilt.

Never again would she lower herself to apologize to him. And it would be a cold day in hell before she ever voluntarily spoke to him. Whirling around, she sent her long braid flying as she stalked back to the campfire.

They traveled north until noon, when they halted on a grassy level shelf beside a swift riverlet that careened almost straight down the pine-scattered mountainside. It raced toward a small valley dotted with meadows far below.

Dismounting, Chama startled Carrie by breaking the hours of silence. "Do you feel up to fixing lunch?"

"I think so," she mumbled begrudgingly without looking in his direction. She headed for a thick stand of firs to take care of her needs, then find firewood.

In the time it took her to gather enough, Chama had unloaded everything from both horses and had Hickory stripped of all tack. The gelding stood picketed in some tall grass a few yards downhill. However, the palomino remained saddled.

Very suspicious.

Was Chama planning to dump her on the side of this mountain and simply ride away? She shot furtive glances in his direction all during their noon meal, of which she ate with as much gusto as her unsteady nerves and delicate stomach would allow.

Chama, however, had no such problems. After polishing off everything heaped on his plate, he rose and strode to his horse. He mounted and, looking somewhere off in space, deigned to speak again. "I'm going hunting." Making a clucking sound, he guided the horse down the steep mountainside toward the valley.

Even if he was lying and intended to abandon her, Carrie felt vastly relieved by the fact that she wouldn't have to ride behind that haughty back one more step today. And determined not to spoil this gift of free time, she made a pact with herself not to let any worries steal her pleasure in her solitude.

Once the campsite was in order, she took a blanket and climbed up higher. She spread it on a cushiony bed of pine needles beneath a spiraling tree and lay down to gaze at the light fluffy clouds floating by overhead.

The tantalizing aroma of barbecuing meat awakened Carrie. Viewing the camp below her, she saw that not only had Chama returned without her knowing it, the meat he now turned on a spit looked almost done. She clambered to her feet and tucked any loose strands of hair into her braid. Then, catching up the blanket, she hurried down the sharp incline.

"I'm sorry, I didn't realize you were back." Before the last words were uttered, she could've kicked herself. She'd just broken her vow of silence.

"It's all right," he said as if nothing were the least bit wrong. "You need your rest." His eyes locked with hers for a brief moment, then he abruptly whipped his attention back to the roast over the fire.

Ha! Carrie thought as she walked away feeling quite victorious. *The "noble savage" facade is slipping.* He spoke when it wasn't the least necessary. The corners of her mouth twitched with amusement. He'd probably have to take himself out behind a tree, now, and give himself a sound thrashing.

Later, as they rolled out their blankets across the fire from each other at bedtime, Chama broke the silence again. "I guess you're wondering where we're going."

My, my, another unsolicited remark. Carrie looked at him, but refused to give him the satisfaction of a response, no matter how anxious to know she might be.

"We're on our way to Socorro." Then speaking as matter-of-factly as if he were mentioning they were having beans for supper, he added, "Socorro's got a padre. We'll be married there."

~ 27 ~

*M*ARRIED. THE WORD repeated itself over and over inside Carrie's head. She sank down onto her blanket and placed her hands on her ears until the chant merged into a muddled roar. Of all the things she'd thought he might do to her, that was the one possibility that had never occurred to her.

Forcing air into lungs stiff from shock, Carrie watched Chama drop to his bedroll and casually take off his boots as if he hadn't just exploded a cannon ball in her face.

His audacity renewed her own ire. She straightened and looked him squarely in the eye. "Fine. Take me to Socorro. But there's no way I'll marry you."

"Yes, you will." The dancing firelight gave an added fierceness to his glowering challenge. "No child of mine will be branded a bastard."

No matter how dangerous he looked, she would not back down. "Better a bastard in a home where there's love than the legitimate heir to the throne of England if you're surrounded by nothing but hostility. I was raised in a house like that. I will not allow that to happen to my child."

They continued to glare at each other, neither wavering a flicker, and Carrie knew exactly what it felt like when two gunmen faced off.

Chama's gaze shifted away first, and he stretched out on his blanket.

She'd won! A rush of triumph made her almost light-headed.

Chama rolled away, turning his back on her. "There's nothing you can say that will change my mind. We *will* be getting married in Socorro."

* * *

Carrie lay wide awake, her thoughts in a fevered turmoil as she stared up at the stars. Her mind jumped from plan to plan until, at one point, she almost talked herself into trying to sneak away on Hickory. But reason stopped her, only to send her back into the whirlpool of her dilemma.

Finally, near midnight, she'd come to the only solution that might satisfy her abductor as well as herself. "Chama. Wake up."

On reflex, he reached for his holster. "What is it?"

"I will marry you . . . on one condition. You must promise that as soon as we're wed you'll put me on a stage to Santa Fe and give me enough money to keep me till after the baby's born."

"You woke me up with that nonsense?"

She wouldn't be put off. "Think about it. We'd both be getting what we wanted. No one could ever call your child a bastard, and the baby wouldn't have to grow up in a house where its parents hated each other."

"I don't hate you. Now, shut up and get some sleep. You need to be rested up for tomorrow's ride." He rolled away from her and pulled his cover up around his ears.

She continued to stare at him as the minutes ticked by, her frustration mounting until she couldn't stand it for another second. "You're a mean, despicable man, just like my father, and you can't make me marry you."

"Shit!" Chama lunged up and jerked on his boots, then, grabbing up his blankets, he charged off into a silhouetted stand of trees a number of yards below their camp.

Chama sat in the inky shadow of a spruce, leaning against the trunk. Wrapped in his woolen covers to ward off the alpine night, he reminded himself of some old grandfather, withered and cracked with age, keeping himself warm while he awaited his time to die, his grandchildren caring for his needs. A peaceful thought . . . but one he doubted he'd live long enough to enjoy.

Sighing, he looked past the softly glowing embers to the one whom he would have chosen to be the old woman at his side.

But all he saw was the one person in the world who could rob him of all clear and decisive thought. The only one capable of leading him into fear's darkest hell. His hand automatically went to the chunk of polished turquoise at his throat to find it missing, and he realized he'd removed it before going to bed. He rubbed his weary wind-burned eyes instead. Then, letting out a long breath, he rested his head against the tree bark again, his attention returning to her silhouetted form lying just beyond the fire.

She has taken my life from me, yet she sees nothing of what she's done. And now this woman who comes wrapped in the colors of the sky accuses me of hating her. Impossible. Yet she has very nearly destroyed me.

But he would make himself stop loving her so much, even if it meant never lying with her again for as long as he lived. He would put an end to this fear she brought to him, this fear that stole every drop of his power.

How much simpler his life had been before her. Then there had been nothing but his vow and the enemy. No quaking with fright. No worry that he would get killed and leave her defenseless. If death had come for him then, he would have greeted his fate as one greets the morning sun. The ancient ones would have welcomed him, treated him with the honor of one who came to them without shame.

The distant campfire flared with new flames, capturing Chama's attention, and he saw Carrie standing beside it, rearranging the half-burned logs with a stick. "Why won't she go to sleep?" he muttered. "But, no, she's got to light up the whole blamed sky, invite every predator within fifty miles."

After a minute or so passed, she even poured herself a cup of coffee.

"If she thinks staying up all night will keep us from riding on to Socorro tomorrow, she's sorely mistaken," he muttered. His son would have his rightful place. He wouldn't have to die first to be surrounded by his people. He would have a father in this world, this life, to care for him. One he could follow with honor. One who would teach him to hunt and fish, who'd tell him when it was his season to seek his vision, receive his name.

He, himself, had not had anyone to send him on his own search. Chama closed his eyes at the painful regret. He hated his white name, Joseph Campbell, given him at birth. He used it only when necessary, as he would when he wed Carrie in the church. *José,* the Spanish translation of Joseph, pleased him even less. His nickname, Chama, at least held some meaning for him. The only happy hours in all his years at the orphanage had been spent discovering the wonders of the wilderness along the banks of the Rio Chama.

His mind drifted as it had on so many other sleepless nights to what his name might have been had he ever lived with his mother's people. He'd always hoped his quest would have brought him to a proud name, one such as Standing Bear or Lone Wolf.

Yes, he thought with a resolute nod, *his* child would not be left nameless. When his son reached that certain season, he would be given his father's blessing and sent in search of that which belonged to him alone.

An unsettling thought intruded. Chama now had double the reason to stay alive. Twice the reason to be stalked by fear.

In the distance, Carrie rose to her feet. She must've unbraided her hair, for its wispy outline caught the fiery glow and streamed a golden aura all about her.

He forgot himself for a moment, drinking in her shimmering glory, this loveliest of creatures who cradled his child within her.

She parted a section from the others and began brushing it with long fluid strokes.

Brushing her hair? In the middle of the night? That tomfool act brought him out of his trance. The woman had no sense whatsoever . . . unless she was deliberately trying to drive him insane with desire. The temptress had to know the hunger his body felt for her, and had for these last desolate weeks. Why else would he have slept out on the hard ground when there was a soft bed inside?

He knew he should turn away, yet the fluidity of her movements enthralled him completely. Lured him into thinking with the eyes of his childhood . . . They beckoned him to the early days, days on the windswept prairie when his mother's hair, too, would take on a life of its own as it swirled about her. Even now he could hear the light tinkle of Spotted Fawn's laughter as she whipped a strand from her lashes with long, nimble fingers. He saw her full, soft lips tip into a smile so wide it crinkled the corners of her eyes. Like Carrie, she had been a beauty by any man's standard, red, brown, or white. And gentle as still water.

Chama's attention focused on Carrie again as he recalled she'd once argued that Spotted Fawn would have wanted him to stop avenging her, would want him to start a new life with a family of his own. Yet, how could he ever forget his mother? Even more so now than before. No day passed that Carrie didn't in some way remind him of her.

A yawn overtook Chama, and he became aware that he'd lost all thought of sleep. This woman whom he craved so desperately he could no longer trust himself to touch was stealing his sleep again. *And* with as much power as ever before.

He took hold of his blankets and rose, moving to the other side of the tree. Away from her bewitching lure.

As he resettled himself, he noticed a faint patch of light that seemed to float in the air a few feet above. For a fleeting instant, he thought his Woman From The Sky had transformed herself into a spirit to further pursue him. Then logic took the fore, and he chalked off the phenomenon to a mist of descending dew drops that were mirroring Carrie's huge fire.

But the light grew steadily stronger, brighter. And from it emerged the face of his long-dead mother.

Carrie became aware of someone's hand on her shoulder, nudging her. Was it morning already? She felt as if she'd just fallen asleep.

"Carrie," Chama called in almost a whisper.

Opening her eyes, she looked up at him as he knelt beside her. "Do we have to get up so early? It's still dark."

"No. I'm sorry . . . I just . . ." In the dim glow of the dying embers, his expression seemed one of uncertainty. "I . . ." His voice faltered again, then a moment later, he started to rise.

Disturbed by this hesitation in one who always appeared so sure of himself, Carrie stayed Chama with her hand. "What is it?"

"As soon as we're married, we'll be leaving the territory. You once said you wanted to go to California—we'll go there. I could start a horse ranch. The palomino would make a fine breeding stud."

Carrie sat up and searched his face. Was this some new torture he'd devised? Tease her with her deepest longing . . . after it was too late. "I'm not going anywhere with you. Not now, not after Kelso attacked me, and you decided I was no longer good enough for you."

"What are you talking about?" He grabbed her shoulders. The strain in his expression matched that of his fingers biting into her flesh. With what seemed a great effort he eased his grip and said in a hoarse rasp, "You're everything to me. The most important— That's been the problem. You're too important."

At his confession, she felt her resolve begin to crumble . . . until his last words sunk in. "I see." Her chin rose with her anger. "It's all right to care a little, but heaven forbid letting a mere woman become too important."

"It's just that caring for you so much is . . . very hard. I'm not used to having someone else to worry about."

"Well, neither am I. But that didn't make me treat you like the dirt beneath my feet." She wrenched loose and lay down. Rolling over, she turned her back to him. "Go away."

"I don't blame you for being upset. But you have to understand—something happened to me the day Kelso attacked you. When I sensed you were in danger, I got so scared, my heart began to pound with such force, I thought it would bust out of my chest. I got sick to my stomach. I couldn't think. I ran my horse so hard, I ruined him. I had to shoot him. I killed Kelso, too. I can barely remember doing it. But I buried him, so I must have. That's how crazy with fear I was. Fear for you."

Carrie turned to face him and saw the truth of his words in his gaze. "If you hadn't come back when you did, there's no telling what would've happened to me."

"I know. And that thought has ridden me relentlessly ever since."

"I see," she said, unable to stop the warm feeling that had started in her breast from rising until it manifested into a smile. She reached up and smoothed away the lines creasing Chama's brow. "You've been treating me like this because you're scared of being scared?"

His intense expression melted into a sheepish grin. "Yeah, something like that. But I've decided to buck up and take a chance. Be brave for you."

For me. She came up again, this time into his waiting arms. "That would be very brave indeed."

He hugged her to him, and she felt the drum of his heart against hers, beckoning. He whispered into her hair, "I always thought the men who chose to stay with their loved ones on the reservations were the cowards, the weak ones. What a fool I was!"

She reared back enough to see his face . . . his pleasuring lips. "A fool maybe, but my fool." Then she remembered his pledge to his mother's people and her joy dimmed. "But what about your vow?"

Glancing away, he hesitated, then locked his eyes onto hers in what appeared to be a challenge. "My mother came and spoke to me tonight."

It was all Carrie could do to keep her own gaze from wavering. But she couldn't—not when he was taking her into his soul.

She must have betrayed no shock because he continued. "Spotted Fawn said the time had come for me to think about the future of my people, instead of fighting the wind for a past that can never be again. She said I must teach my son to walk the proud path of a Kiowa brave, but that path must now cross into this new world of our conquerors. She said that perhaps I had forgotten that the tree that bends with the wind is the one that outlasts the storm. And will, once again, stand tall and free in the sun."

Vision or no, he was saying everything Carrie wanted to hear. "Your mother is a wise woman."

"Yes, Spotted Fawn is almost as wise as she is beautiful. Did I ever mention how very much you remind me of her?"

At his last words, tears clouded Carrie's vision.

"Spotted Fawn gave us her blessing. And something else. I've been given my name. My Kiowan name. I am now Rising Hawk." His voice held an almost reverent pride as his own eyes grew moist. "A fitting name for a new life, don't you think?"

"Yes. Very fitting." With both hands, she reached into his hair and drew his face, his lips, to hers.

The first touch sent a jolt to her heart, followed by more waves as he moved his mouth across hers, at first softly, tenderly, then with increasing fervor. His swift breaths, and his swifter hands careening across her body, caught her up in the torrent of his passion.

"My God, how I missed you," he rasped between breaths. "I'll never get enough of you. I'll love you forever."

"Oh, yes. Yes." He was hers. Finally, completely. Carrie yanked up his tucked shirt and ran her hands over the smooth hard planes she loved so much that she barely noticed that he'd done the same, pulled up her blouse, and that his thumbs now played across her breasts, turning them to hard nubs.

He bent to take one.

At a loud crack, Chama's head crashed into her shoulder, knocking Carrie onto her back.

He fell with her, sprawled across her. Still. Heavy as death.

28

"I GOT HIM! He's out!" the bushwhacker yelled as he ripped Chama off Carrie and slung him to the side.

Carrie reared up, reached for Chama.

Raising a boot, the man shoved her onto her back again, pinning her chest with his foot. He leaned over her and, from beneath bushy brows, leered at her with watery eyes. His mouth slid into a slack grin.

Bill Fry! Father's deputy! Her every fear caved in on her. She closed her eyes and turned her face away. All was lost. Gone.

Fingers clawed into her hair, snatched a handful, and yanked her savagely to her feet, then spun her around.

Through a pain-fired haze, she came face-to-face with her father and the stabbing gray eyes that never failed to pin her where she stood. His thin, cruel mouth was outlined by deep creases, his skeletal face framed by his flaring thatch of silver.

Still holding her hair fast, he slapped her. Hard. "You filthy slut. You never learn, do you?" He then swerved his glance to Fry and jerked a nod toward Chama. "Hog-tie that by-blow breed over there."

"You bet, boss."

Father shifted his attention back to her and his sparse lips stretched into a smirk. "He's got a lesson or two of his own to learn before I see him hang."

The evil face blocked Carrie's view of Chama. She twisted to the side to free herself, to save him, but her father tightened his hold on her hair.

"You're not going anywhere, whore. You're going to stay

right here and watch. Just like before. Remember?"

My God! He's going to castrate him! Frantically she reached up to pry her father's hands free.

Although she dug viciously at his fingers, his grip held unhampered. "Just how sharp is that knife of yours, Bill?"

"Not very," Fry said, unhooking a length of rope from Chama's saddle horn.

"Good. It'll take longer."

Carrie slammed her bare heel into her father's shin and at the same time clawed for his eyes.

Her father flung her away from him, but didn't let go of her hair—his tether. "Turned into quite a hellcat, have you? A real-live Comanchero." Whipping her back against his chest, he clamped an arm across her, capturing both of hers, then slung her up across his hip where her flailing feet could do little damage. "But then we know exactly how to take care of Comancheros. Don't we, Bill?"

"Yes, sir." Fry stepped close and leaned within inches of her face while draping the rope across a shoulder. He then pulled his knife and ran his finger across the curved, mean-looking blade as he wiggled his shaggy brows above a lusting grin—made more grotesque by the firelight.

"Should've been there," her father continued in a sadistic taunt. "With the army all in an uproar over Custer getting all his men massacred up north, didn't take much persuasion to get them to return the favor." With his free hand he snatched her hair again, yanking her face up to meet his. "But then, we had to make sure every last Comanchero was dead, didn't we? Couldn't have none of that low-life filth talking about my whoring daughter, now, could we?" His steely grip on her hair tightened.

Already numbed with fear, Carrie barely felt the pain.

Her father swung his attention to Fry. "Get the breed tied up and get his trousers down."

"Yes, sir." Fry stooped and rolled Chama's unconscious form belly down.

Her head trapped in her father's clutch, her body pinned across his sharp hipbone, Carrie strained to see if Chama was bleeding, if his breathing was labored, but could discern little in the long shadow Fry cast as he looped the rope around Chama's wrists.

"Whoo-ee! You shoulda seen it!" Fry said as he tied off Chama's hands and took the remainder of the rope down to his feet. "Them soldiers plumb went wild. Killed anything that moved. Then they set torch to the whole blamed camp. What a sight! By the time me an' your pa lit out after you *and your lover* . . ." His voice slid slowly, deliberately, over the last words before going on. " . . . they had one helluva bonfire going."

Esperanza. The babies. Carrie's already galloping heart lunged painfully before she remembered they'd left the valley the day before she and Chama had. A true miracle this time.

"Primed and ready," her father added as he shifted her weight on his hip. "That's what those soldiers were. The timing of Custer's fall couldn't have been better. I already had them all stirred up over my *poor innocent daughter* being kidnapped and suffering God only knows what. But then you and I know better, don't we? We know all about how willing you are to spread your legs, don't we? Believe me, I wasn't the least surprised to hear you and some half-breed buck had been cozied up all summer. And now *after* your little honeymoon, I hear the loving couple is eloping. Anyway, that's what that fat greasy storekeeper said—just before I cut his throat. Stopped one more tongue from wagging. No one, not that scummy trash, and especially not you, is going to ruin my last chance to rise above the mess you sniveling Langleys brought down on me. I *am* going to be appointed the next governor." He swung Carrie off his hip and stood her before him. *"This little incident—my valiant, if impossible, attempt to save my daughter from her death at the hands of rampant lawlessness—will be my battle cry.* How could they not appoint someone with such a tragic loss, such a calling to rid the territory of all the vermin? Yes, my dear. I suppose you're finally going to be good for something, after all."

"Boss," Fry called in a shrill whine, his hands stopping their odious task. "Don't forget what you promised me. You said if

I came with you, did whatever you say, that you'd give her to me for a week before . . . you know."

"Oh, you've got nothing to worry about, my boy. I wouldn't dream of ending our little time together too soon."

Tearing her eyes from her father's murderous sneer, Carrie saw that the unspeakably vile deputy began working with the rope again with renewed gusto. Soon Chama would be as helpless as a calf at branding time.

Her father's fingers bit harder into her arms, forcing her attention back to him. "I want to thank you for making such a *good* friend out of Bull Dolan's woman. The whore couldn't have been more eager to trade you in on her lover."

"Yeah, she sure was a stupid bitch," Fry added, looping the rope into a knot. "Nell really thought we'd just let 'em go after she got Dolan to lead us up into the secret valley."

Her father moved within inches of Carrie's face. *"A real stupid bitch."* He then jerked his merciless glower back to Fry. "Get some water and throw it on that scum-sucking pig down there. We wouldn't want him to miss our little party, now, would we?"

The blood rushed from Carrie's head. Her vision dimmed, and she felt herself begin to sag as Fry sprang to his feet and trotted over to fetch the canteen she'd left beside the campfire. She shook her head to clear it.

The deputy tipped it over Chama's face, and water spilled down.

Chama moaned and moved a little.

Ripping out of her father's grasp, Carrie lunged toward him.

Before she could reach him, her father caught her around the neck and slammed her back against him. Then he bent her down low, giving her a horrifyingly close view of Chama, all trussed up and helpless.

Chama opened his eyes and blinked, but he didn't seem to focus on anything.

Her father dealt him a savage kick to the ribs.

Coiling against it, Chama groaned, his glance shooting upward to her profane father. Then it focused on her.

The look in his eyes ripped at Carrie, tore her asunder. She would give her life, her soul, to be able to save him from her father's wrath. "I love you," she whispered, the only comfort she could offer.

"I—"

Her father slammed his boot into Chama again, stopping his answer.

Carrie wrenched forward, fruitlessly.

"Pull down the bastard's pants," her father commanded.

"You bet!" Fry reached for Chama's buttons with eager fingers as Carrie, choking against her father's rigid arm, watched with paralyzing horror.

In a reckless effort, Chama twisted back and forth, eluding the deputy's efforts.

Fry threw himself over Chama to pin his squirming body.

Chama bucked him off with such force, Fry tumbled into the hot coals of the campfire. He screamed and leapt to his feet, brushing frantically at a smoking sleeve.

"For Pete's sake, Bill," her father spat. "Can't you do anything right? Get it done."

"You shoulda let me get his pants down before I woke him." Fry pulled his knife. "Maybe a gouge or two in the gut'll settle the Injun down."

"Just don't kill him . . . *yet*," her father said as he leaned over Chama. Bending Carrie down with him, his bony arm digging into her neck, he ripped down the bodice of her peasant blouse to expose her breasts. "I saw how much you were pleasuring yourself with these."

Chama froze, his eyes filling with disbelief, his jaw muscles knotting. "Do what you want with me," he gritted out, "but let her go. She's your daughter, for God's sake."

Carrie snatched the bodice from her father's grasp and covered herself again as he shot a glance down at Fry, who was now working Chama's denim trousers off unhindered.

Her father looked back at Chama, his gray eyes an abomination as they caught the fire's glow. "That's more like it, breed. I wouldn't want to inflict too much suffering on my *darling daughter* before I give her to her intended. Isn't that right, Fry?"

His lackey gurgled with laughter and sprang to his feet, Chama's britches now pushed down to his bound ankles. "All ready, boss. Would you like to do the honors? Or do you want me to?"

"Here, take Carrie." Loosing his hold on her throat, he shoved her to Fry.

The deputy caught Carrie by an arm, his other hand diving into her blouse.

Carrie scarcely noticed as she dragged the skinny man with her toward Chama.

"Let her go!" His back bowed, Chama strained toward Fry. "Fight me for her like a man instead of some squealing mud-wallowing pig."

The fingers kneading her breast froze. "Let me cut off his balls. We'll see who's the squealing pig then."

Her father withdrew his knife from his belt scabbard. "Sorry, but I have a prior claim." He stooped down on his haunches.

"Please!" Carrie cried. "I'll do anything. Say anything. Please. Don't."

"Don't beg the bastard, Carrie," Chama railed.

Her gaze shifted helplessly to his as Fry began to fondle her again.

Her father swiveled to eye her, showing not the slightest flicker of concern that his deputy was molesting her. "What could you possibly ever do or say that would be worth a tinker's damn?" His upper lip curling with disgust, he returned to Chama and grabbed for his exposed manhood.

Carrie screamed as Chama bucked and rolled.

"Get him!" Fry cried and leapt after them, taking Carrie with him. He removed the hand buried in her blouse and reached down to help his boss.

The pearl handle of her father's revolver stuck out, shining in the firelight. Carrie dove for it, and pulled it free of the holster.

Her father wheeled, coming up from his stoop and lunging for her.

She jerked the trigger.

The bullet struck him, knocking him back. He dropped the

knife, staggered, then regained his footing, his hand going to his shoulder.

Fry reached for his own gun.

Carrie swung the barrel toward him and fired again.

He grabbed the middle of his chest. In awe, he looked from her to the blood spurting through his fingers, then crumpled to the ground.

She swung her aim back to her father. *Just in time.*

Eyes wild with menace, he charged toward her. At the sight of the revolver pointed at his head, he halted. Mouth open, he looked from her to his oozing wound. *"You shot me. Your own father."*

"Untie Chama," she cried. "Now! Or I'll shoot you again where you stand."

Veins bulged fiercely at her father's temples before disappearing into his thatch of silver hair as his lungs swelled in rage.

Even wounded and unarmed, he sent a chill of fear through Carrie. Her hand began to shake. She covered it with the other one. "Do as I say," she ordered, but the words came out sounding weak, unsure.

Chama called up to her through a haze that was beginning to blur her vision. "Get the knife, Carrie. Cut me loose. I'll handle your father." With his feet, he nudged it toward her as best he could.

Profound relief poured into Carrie at the ring of his confident voice; still, her legs were starting to shake as much as her hands. Watching her father closely, she edged haltingly toward Chama and the knife. She inhaled deeply, praying her knees wouldn't give way when she crouched down for the knife.

They did.

Her father dove for the gun.

Screaming, she fired as he piled into her, knocking her onto her back. The revolver flew out of her hand. She reached frantically for it.

So did her father. His fingers surrounded it first. One covered the trigger.

With all the fear-charged strength she possessed, she sprang across him, ripped at his hand with both of hers.

"You bitch! I'll . . . I'll . . ." His strength faded with his words. "I . . . " Gradually he grew still. Silent. His heartbeat against her chest faded to nothing. He was dead.

Unable to believe it, Carrie rolled away from him and sat up. Wiley Jackson, *dead*. Impossible. He was invincible. The devil himself. Yet he lay in the dirt, limp, his shoulder covered with blood, and a second gaping wound oozed red from his side. She, too, felt wet. A cold breeze plastered her blouse to her. Looking down, she saw herself soaked with his blood. In horror, she dropped the gun and picked up her skirt. Frantically she started wiping at herself.

"Carrie . . . Carrie!"

Someone called her. *Chama*. She swung around, searching, and found him still on the ground, still hog-tied.

"It'll be all right, sweetheart. Cut me loose."

Chama. The knife lay near his feet. She crawled to it, her quaking arms and legs barely taking her there. She needed Chama. She'd never needed to be held by him more in her life.

Within seconds he was freed and had his trousers pulled up. He then ripped the soiled blouse from her body and wrapped her in the shirt he took from his back. Then his arms encircled her, pulled her tight against the warmth of his bare skin. "It's over, all over." He began stroking her hair, kissing the top of her head. "Never again."

She sagged into his comforting strength and drew from it. Twining her arms around him, she held on until the quiver ravaging her body subsided and she could truly, completely believe his words. Then remembering the hit he'd taken on the head, and the kicks to his ribs, she eased back and looked up into his face. "What about you? Did they hurt you?"

He pulled her to her feet. "Oh, I've got a lump or two, but— I know this sounds crazy—I don't think I've ever felt better. You were magnificent. I'll never forget your courage in the face of your greatest fear—your father. If I ever doubted your love for this beat-up renegade, I never will again. You saved me. Both of us. Our baby."

As his words sank in, Carrie became aware that she really had, after all these years, stood her ground. And for the first time in memory she was now delivered from her father's strangling hold, from the fear, his hellish domination. Along with her father, she was free to bury the past and walk into the promise of a new life with her man and the tiny new being she nurtured within her. Dear, simple Esperanza had been right all along. Now everything could be *muy bueno. Maravilloso!* Her joy spilled into a smile.

In return, that boyish grin dimpled Chama's cheeks.

She touched a finger to one. "You're so right. I've never felt better either."

Reaching down, Chama snatched up a blanket near his foot, then swooped Carrie up into his arms and started away from the carnage ... downhill toward the stand of trees, their tips glowing soft coral in the first blush of morning light. "Wait here," he said, putting her down on a soft bed of pine needles, "while I take care of things."

By the time he returned to her, all the horror had been buried with the night as the rising sun brought them a glorious new day.

She looked up into Chama's face. "Where is my Rising Hawk flying away with me on this first dawning of our bright new future?"

His answering smile left his lips and moved up to fill his eyes with the warmest gaze. He dropped to his knees and hugged her close.

With his shirt merely draped over her shoulders, she immediately became aware of the press of his skin as her own womanly flesh molded to it ... the pleasuring power of oneness. She ran a hand up his chest and along the side of his throat.

He inhaled deeply, and his gaze roved her with heightening interest. "Rising Hawk," he said slowly as his mouth slipped into a lazy, lopsided grin, "will be taking Woman From The Sky to a new land of peace. A land warmed always by our love. Where the grass is always green, the water swift and cool. A place where our children can grow tall and straight and free. All this I will do forever more. But first," he said, brushing his lips across her temple, "I must listen to the talking hands and turquoise eyes of my Sky Woman. They are telling me that I can do none of these things until I've answered every enticing request, conquered every hungering desire of her bewitching body."

Dear Reader,

As a fairly new author, I would love to hear from you. Your comments would be most appreciated. You may send your note directly to me at: 66-365 W. 5th Street, Desert Hot Springs, CA 92240.

I'll do my best to answer each and every letter. A self-addressed stamped envelope would be appreciated.

        Many thanks,

Elaine Crawford

Diamond Wildflower Romance

A breathtaking new line of spectacular novels set in the untamed frontier of the American West. Every month, Diamond Wildflower brings you new adventures where passionate men and women dare to embrace their boldest dreams. Finally, romances that capture the very spirit and passion of the wild frontier.

__TEXAS JEWEL by Shannon Willow
  1-55773-923-4/$4.99
__REBELLIOUS BRIDE by Donna Fletcher
  1-55773-942-0/$4.99
__RENEGADE FLAME by Catherine Palmer
  1-55773-952-8/$4.99
__SHOTGUN BRIDE by Ann Carberry
  1-55773-959-5/$4.99
__WILD WINDS by Peggy Stoks
  1-55773-965-X/$4.99
__HOSTAGE HEART by Lisa Hendrix
  1-55773-974-9/$4.99
__FORBIDDEN FIRE by Bonnie K. Winn
  1-55773-979-X/$4.99
__WARRIOR'S TOUCH by Deborah James
  1-55773-988-9/$4.99
__RUNAWAY BRIDE by Ann Carberry
  0-7865-0002-6/$4.99
__TEXAS ANGEL by Linda Francis Lee
  0-7865-0007-7/$4.99 (May)

Payable in U.S. funds. No cash orders accepted. Postage & handling: $1.75 for one book, 75¢ for each additional. Maximum postage $5.50. Prices, postage and handling charges may change without notice. Visa, Amex, MasterCard call 1-800-788-6262, ext. 1, refer to ad # 406

Or, check above books Bill my: ☐ Visa ☐ MasterCard ☐ Amex _____
and send this order form to: (expires)
The Berkley Publishing Group Card#_____
390 Murray Hill Pkwy., Dept. B ($15 minimum)
East Rutherford, NJ 07073 Signature_____
Please allow 6 weeks for delivery. Or enclosed is my: ☐ check ☐ money order
Name_____ Book Total $_____
Address_____ Postage & Handling $_____
City_____ Applicable Sales Tax $_____
(NY, NJ, PA, CA, GST Can.)
State/ZIP_____ Total Amount Due $_____